The Marriage of Elizabeth

Novels by Ethel Carnie Holdsworth

Miss Nobody (1913)
Helen of Four Gates (1917)
The Taming of Nan (1919)
The Marriage of Elizabeth (1920)
The House that Jill Built (1920)
Down Poverty Street (1921)
The Great Experiment (1923)
General Belinda (1924)
Equality Island (1925)
This Slavery (1925)
The Quest of the Golden Garter (1927)
Barbara Dennison (1928)
Eagles' Crag (1932)

The Marriage of Elizabeth

Ethel Carnie Holdsworth

with an Introduction by
Gemma Holgate

Kennedy & Boyd,
an imprint of
Zeticula Ltd,
Unit 13,
44-46 Morningside Road,
Edinburgh,
EH10 4BF
Scotland.

http://www.kennedyandboyd.co.uk
admin@kennedyandboyd.co.uk

Frst published in 1928
This edition published 2025
Copyright © Estate of Ethel Carnie Holdsworth 2025
Introduction Copyright © Gemma Holgate 2025
Cover photograph © Helen Brown 2025

Paperback ISBN 978-1-84921-252-6

To my mother

Introduction

'In the little house, working often with very inadequate tools, the housewife finds her wageless labour accepted as a right, not as a gift of love.'[1]

These words of Ethel Carnie Holdsworth in an article of 1921 titled 'Is Housework Drudgery?' capture a central preoccupation of her works of the early 1920s, the most prolific period in her novel writing career. Yet the subject of women's domestic work, both waged and unwaged, was not that for which she had initially attracted attention as a writer. Employed in a Lancashire textile factory from age eleven to twenty-two, Carnie Holdsworth's entry into professional writing had been firmly tied to her industrial background, beginning with her debut collection of poetry, *Rhymes from the Factory* in 1907. By 1920, she had published numerous articles for the labour press, two further poetry collections and three novels, but was still largely defined by her history of factory work, her books marketed with the label, 'by an ex-mill girl'. An ardent socialist who attended Social Democratic Federation meetings with her father from childhood, she did write extensively on industrial conditions, most notably in her strike novel, *This Slavery,* of 1925, published through a small radical press called The Labour Publishing Company.[2] Most of her novels, however, were published with the mass-market publisher, Herbert Jenkins, which aimed at popular entertainment rather than politics. These novels, of which *The Marriage of Elizabeth* was the third, represent the everyday experiences of women in working-class communities, while fulfilling the narrative expectations of the popular romance.

In a socialist tradition that has, until at least the mid-twentieth century, tended to understand politics as that which relates directly to the conflict between labour and capital, a struggle mostly undertaken by a male-dominated trade union movement, it is not difficult to see why this side of Carnie Holdsworth's output was largely overlooked until the recent revival of interest that has brought her full and multifaceted body of work into view.[3] Aimed at a wide readership of women, these novels do, at times, critique the exploitation of both male and female workers by capital, but their greater focus is on women's experiences in the home, a subject which did not initially mark them out as distinctly political or radically socialist works.[4] Contemporary reviewers primarily praised Carnie Holdsworth's authenticity, as a writer whose 'understanding has not come by means of study, but has been bred in her', and who depicted 'the homely life of the people [...] as only one who has lived it can do it'.[5] But far from 'simply describing her own people', Carnie Holdsworth used her fiction to espouse a form of socialist feminist critique, albeit a critique that owes more to the ethical socialist tradition, with its moral idealism, than to historical materialism. In *The Marriage of Elizabeth,* the eponymous protagonist, the relationship she develops with her husband, and the influence she has on her community, serve to guide the reader towards a model of womanhood, of marriage, and of community befitting to a socialist future. Moreover, the novels break down what Nicola Wilson calls 'socialism's tenacious hold onto the ideological divisions of a public and private realm', both by highlighting the interconnected nature of the two and by recognising domestic work in its many forms as an essential form of *labour*.[6]

Departing from the conventional marriage-as-resolution structure of the romance plot, Carnie Holdsworth marries her protagonists in the sixth chapter of seventeen, under somewhat unusual circumstances. Nursing her dying neighbour, Elizabeth Peel promises to marry the young woman's widow, and to help him raise their baby daughter. Unbeknownst to Elizabeth, said widow, John Stone, makes the same commitment, and a reluctant proposal ensues, which is accepted. Realising John's aversion to the marriage, however, Elizabeth's pride is enflamed, and she fulfils her obligation only on the condition that she works as his housekeeper, for wages, rather than acting as husband and wife where no love exists. At the level of plot, the novel is driven by the developing relationship between Elizabeth and John, as their artificial marriage grows into a genuine love connection. Recommending the book to its readers, the *Blackburn Weekly Telegraph* described *The Marriage of Elizabeth as* 'a battle of pride and will between two persons of strong character, who persist in misunderstanding each other while their mutual affection is growing into a passion'.[7] The underlying purpose of the romance however, is didactic, for Carnie Holdsworth demonstrates the factors of real importance in a good marriage, primarily through the contrast of John's superficial passion for his late wife to the partnership of equals that he eventually realises with Elizabeth.

Elizabeth is representative of several of Carnie's heroines, and shares many traits with Belinda Higgins, who emerged contemporaneously in short story form, before featuring in her own novel of 1924, *General Belinda*.[8] Both are exceptionally active in their social worlds, continually leading the way in righting wrongs among their families and communities. Significantly, neither are beautiful, but come to be appreciated both platonically and romantically on the basis of their character. Indeed, Carnie Holdsworth's protagonists frequently exemplify a model of womanhood founded in strength and agency, rejecting the association of femininity with weakness and shallow, myopic concerns. A *Woman Worker* column of 1909 sets out this vision most clearly:

> The womanhood that Whitman and Carpenter worshipped is the womanhood of to-morrow, and not the mawkish one of the writers whose heroines weep their way through thirty long chapters. The women who can swim, run, join in the games as well as the labours of their men mates, understand poems and grow roses [...] In sickness the hand that plies the oar will be as gentle, the eye that calculates to an inch the length that the ball must be thrown will be as tenderly pitiful, and the voice that speaks out for the oppressed and wretched will be as fitted (or more so) to tell fairy tales in the dusk to her own children than that which kept silence save on the common events of the day – milk puddings, the weather, and Chrissy's new hat.[9]

Changing long established notions of appropriate feminine behaviour is, however, no simple task, as *The Marriage of Elizabeth* makes clear. John Stone's first marriage is built on a foundation of inequality – he loves Mary not merely in spite of, but because of, her inferiority to himself, and her reliance on his greater strength and intelligence. She is the 'looking-glass' that Virginia Woolf described almost a decade later, in that she reflects 'the figure of man at twice its natural size'.[10] In contrast, Elizabeth makes him feel 'a fool' through her 'masculine' capabilities and their difference is made yet plainer through Elizabeth's physical stature, described most often as 'large' (p. 57). With little attempt at subtlety, Carnie Holdsworth guides the reader to the conclusion reached by John Stone – the ideal wife is not the feminine damsel in need of her husband's protection, but the independent, tenacious woman whose strength inspires his own. Insubstantial affection for women's weakness, she demonstrates, cannot compare to the satisfaction found in a marriage of mutual respect, of which passion is but 'a very small facet' (p. 245).

While the novel advances a more androgynous mode of womanhood, it does not challenge gender relations when it comes to men and women's responsibilities in marriage, in that Elizabeth dutifully fulfils the role of housewife without complaint at its limitations. More than this, the home that she maintains is a picture of sentimental tradition, a place of 'utter peace, wherein the baby crooned happily, the little silver bells on the pink rattle jingled merrily, where the black shining kettle was always singing' – it is 'a sanctum' with Elizabeth at its centre (p. 87). Such a description adheres closely to what Swindells and Jardine have termed 'the topos of the 'comely' family home' in English socialist culture, a romanticisation which tends to make invisible the struggles of the women within it.[11] But if the novel embraces the vision of home as 'sanctum', it does not do so in ignorance of the labour, much of it 'drudgery', undertaken to create this experience for others (p. 39). The romance plot itself serves to make this explicit, in Elizabeth's demand for wages for performing the role of housekeeper where an authentic romantic connection does not exist. Carnie Holdsworth's concern, then, is not that women leave the home to work elsewhere, but that women receive a fair return on this arrangement and are accorded the respect they deserve.

Carnie Holdsworth's approach to women's work here is, I would suggest, remarkably nuanced, and anticipates some of the key developments of feminist thinking in the late twentieth century, notably in feminist care ethics and social reproduction feminism. As Silvia Federici notes, socialist feminists have gradually moved from 'refusal to valorisation of housework', recognising that its transformation and reconstruction can serve to model 'an alternative to capitalist relations'.[12] Feminist care ethicists, meanwhile, have argued for the recognition of care work as essential to all human life, asserting its value 'while simultaneously challenging the norms that currently govern it'.[13] For Carnie Holdsworth, a fair deal for women is not predicated on the absence of domestic work; a position which she expresses more explicitly in her domestic service novel, *General Belinda*. Objecting to the exploitation of servants, as well as that of housewives, Belinda does not desire liberation from domestic labour in itself. She wants simply to be 'treated as a human being', given freedom and respect to both carry out this essential work and to participate in the world beyond it.[14] Women, Carnie Holdsworth argues, do not want 'to burn the broom' but, like all people, for 'the work of their hands to be appreciated'.[15]

As a former mill worker with a professed hatred of factory labour, Carnie Holdsworth's feminist perspective was not the same as the middle- and upper-class women who had, and continued to, argue for the entrance of women into the workplace. A huge number of working-class women knew the industrial workplace well enough, and while a not insignificant number had struggled politically to improve their pay and conditions, the preference for housewifery, where financially feasible, was widespread. The calm of Elizabeth's home is a relief, indeed, for John Stone, returning from 'the quivering heat of the blasting furnace, the shuddering pulsed floor, and the clattering of the iron-ore' (p. 87). For working-class women, there are multiple reasons for preferring home-work, not least the fact that the woman who works is faced with a double burden, expected to fulfil her domestic role in the limited time remaining to her outside of waged work. But beyond this, and importantly in Carnie Holdsworth's case, the outcomes of the housewife's labour are tangibly beneficial to her family and her community – she is one step removed from the alienating work of producing profit for capital. In an early article on 'The Home of Life of Factory Workers', Carnie emphasised the workers' greater appreciation of the home as a space of comparative freedom and leisure, and one in which labour is at least undertaken for the workers' own benefit.[16] The home is, of course, inextricably connected to the workplace, and financially reliant on it, but it also offers an opportunity for relationships and labour that depart from capitalism's economic imperatives – that is, that seek to sustain and to care, rather than to extract and profit.

Thus, in Carnie Holdsworth's novels, women who work in the home have significant agency to change their communities for the better. In *The Marriage of Elizabeth*, it is Elizabeth who stirs a sense of anti-capitalist discontent in her husband, though this does not develop into class consciousness of a communal kind, but simply motivates him to move beyond his low-paid position. After years of unthinking labour at the foundry, John's love for Elizabeth rouses in him 'a deep unrest', a realisation that 'he had been a slave until now', which drives him to design a safety invention that can be sold to employers to reduce industrial accidents (p. 140). (It is made clear, of course, that the owners only adopt this invention on the basis of economy, though they pretend philanthropic motives.) John Stone is but one of many characters influenced by Elizabeth over the course of the novel. She supports her neighbour to stand up to her husband's domestic abuse, violence which has been normalised and tolerated by the community. Domestic violence was a longstanding theme in Carnie Holdsworth's poetry as well as her novels: a poem published in her 1914 collection, *Voices of Womanhood*, describes the negative consequences when women are encouraged to 'forbear', to 'suffer and forgive' in the face of abuse.[17] But the solution in the novel is, again, personal, in that Elizabeth herself enacts punishment on the abusive husband, leading to his reform.

In fact, all of the social problems exposed in the novel are resolved individually by Elizabeth, almost to the point of incredulity. She settles conflicts between family members; she nurses and consoles women in need while reprimanding their absent or abusive partners; she provides compensation and employment support to her tenants struggling after the death of their main household earner; she supports John both physically and financially following an injury at the foundry. There is seemingly no limit to what she can fix, and we may question whether these tidy resolutions preclude the full exposition of the systemic issues underlying the array of problems presented, which Carnie Holdsworth herself recognised as resulting from capitalist patriarchy, and not merely the misguided decisions of individuals. It is here that the influence of the ethical socialist tradition can be felt, in the conviction that the moral belief and action of the individual could be a source of broader social change. The figure of the sympathetic heroine, leading by moral example into a new socialist way of life, appeared in an earlier wave of socialist feminist novels at the turn of the century, including those of the Independent Labour Party's Katharine Bruce Glasier.[18] But unlike some of these earlier novels, Carnie Holdsworth makes clear that there must be no moralising from above: Elizabeth's work is effective because she understands and lives the life of her community, standing distinctly apart from 'those awful women who take tea and red flannel to poor folk' (p. 89). As Roger Smalley describes, Elizabeth serves a kind of 'teacher' to both the novel's characters and to the reader, demonstrating how positive social improvements can come about in the absence of wholesale governmental reform or revolutionary change.[19]

The conclusion of *The Marriage of Elizabeth* does not counter expectation but proceeds towards an apparently inevitable resolution. Unlike some of Carnie Holdsworth's novels, such as *The House that Jill Built* of the same year, that, at least obliquely, gesture to a socialist future in their closing pages, *The Marriage of Elizabeth* concludes on a more private note, as Elizabeth and John 'passed into the house that was now a home and closed the door gladly on the outer world' (p. 26). For all that romance serves as entertainment in Carnie Holdsworth's novels, she herself defended its importance in literature in its own right, for love is just as integral a part of human life as 'the bread-struggle'.[20] To marry for love, Carnie argued, to forge relationships through affective rather than economic considerations, is at present only a privilege, where it should be a right.[21] Pamela Fox reads the very desire for romance as radical for the working-class woman, in that it signified 'a utopian private arena in which one is valued for one's gendered "self" alone'.[22] Taken in the context of this novel as a whole, however, in which Elizabeth's interests very much extend beyond the confines of the nuclear family and towards the good of the wider community, the final lines seem more of an observance of romance's narrative conventions – the neat finality of the protagonist's 'happily ever after' – than a decisive turn from social concerns.

In her popular romance novels, Carnie Holdsworth is not in the business of painting pictures of misery, despite her vocal criticism of both class and gender oppression elsewhere in her work. Her heroines are not descendants of the late-nineteenth century 'New Woman' who forge their own path, to the detriment of their survival in a society hostile to their desires. Rather, they are ordinary working-class women who make the best of the hand they have been dealt, just as the author makes what political critiques she can within the bounds of the genre and form that gave her the popular platform from which to make them. In 1920, Carnie Holdsworth could write from a position of relative optimism: the Great War was over, the British Labour movement had grown into a major political force, and the feminist movement had at last achieved at least partial enfranchisement for women. By the mid-1920s, Roger Smalley suggests, 'her dream of a socialist utopia had evaporated', but she nonetheless continued her work as writer and activist for at least another decade.[23] The fuller picture of her work provided by this series is most welcome in this twenty-first-century moment, when the gains of feminism are coming more and more under threat from reactionary forces. The message, finally, of *The Marriage of Elizabeth*, and of much of Carnie's work in this period, is that marriage is not a simple solution for women and does not signal the end of struggle. But rather than reject marriage outright on the basis of the inequality and exploitation it has entailed, she suggests that a better way is possible, in which men and women share mutual respect, and domestic work is recognised and compensated as the essential form of labour it is.

Notes

1 Ethel Carnie Holdsworth, 'Is Housework Drudgery? The Protest of the Modern Mother', *Woman's Outlook*, January 1921, pp. 66–67 (p. 67).

2 Ruth Frow and Eddie Frow, 'Ethel Carnie: Writer, Feminist and Socialist', in *The Rise of Socialist Fiction 1880–1914*, ed. by H. Gustav Klaus (Harvester, 1987), pp. 251–66 (p. 251).

3 The renewed interest in Carnie's work owes much to Roger Smalley, whose research has been critical to expanding the biographical and bibliographical record, while Nicola Wilson has been instrumental in the republication of her novels. Roger Smalley, *Breaking the Bonds of Capitalism: The Political Vision of a Lancashire Mill Girl Ethel Carnie Holdsworth (1886-1962)* (North-West Regional Studies, Lancaster University, 2014).

4 As Lynne Hapgood argues, 'playing a significant part in the achievement of socialism meant being defined in the public arena as a worker or agitator and as male'. Lynne Hapgood, 'The Novel and Political Agency: Socialism and the Work of Margaret Harkness, Constance Howell and Clementina Black', *Literature and History*, 5.2 (1996), pp. 37–52 (p. 44).

5 'Ethel Carnie Holdsworth. A Notable Lancashire Woman Novelist', p. 294; 'Marriage of Elizabeth. New Novel by Ethel Holdsworth', *Blackburn Weekly Telegraph*, 26 June 1920, p. 7; 'Lancashire's Mill Lass Novelist', *World's Work*, May 1922, p. 3; 'Marriage of Elizabeth', *Blackburn Times*, 26 June 1920, p. 11.

6 Nicola Wilson, 'Politicising the Home in Ethel Carnie Holdsworth's This Slavery (1925) and Ellen Wilkinson's Clash (1929)', *Key Words: A Journal of Cultural Materialism*, 5 (2007), pp. 26–42 (p. 27).

7 'Marriage of Elizabeth. New Novel by Ethel Holdsworth', p. 7.

8 Ethel Carnie Holdsworth, 'Belinda: The Story of a Domestic Servant', *Wheatsheaf*, July 1920, pp. 101–2; Ethel Carnie Holdsworth, *General Belinda* [1924], ed. by Nicola Wilson (Kennedy and Boyd, 2019).

9 Ethel Carnie, 'Modern Womanhood', *The Woman Worker*, 4 August 1909, p. 100.

10 Virginia Woolf, *A Room of One's Own* (Hogarth Press, 1929), p. 53.

11 In *This Slavery*, Carnie Holdsworth paints a far less appealing picture of the poverty-stricken working-class home, as Nicola Wilson discusses. Julia Swindells and Lisa Jardine, *What's Left?: Women in Culture and the Labour Movement* (Routledge, 1989), p. 13; Wilson, 'Politicising the Home in Ethel Carnie Holdsworth's This Slavery (1925) and Ellen Wilkinson's Clash (1929)', p. 30.

12 Silvia Federici, *Revolution at Point Zero: Housework, Reproduction, and Feminist Struggle*, Second edition (PM Press, 2020), pp. xiii, xvi–xvii.

13 Fiona Robinson, 'Care Ethics, Political Theory, and the Future of Feminism', in *Care Ethics and Political Theory*, ed. by Daniel Engster and Maurice Hamington (Oxford University Press, 2015), pp. 293–311 (p. 308).

14 Carnie Holdsworth, *General Belinda*, pp. 155–56.

15 Carnie Holdsworth, 'Is Housework Drudgery? The Protest of the Modern Mother', p. 67.

16 Ethel Carnie, 'The Home Life of Factory Workers', *The Woman Worker*, 24 March 1909, p. 270.

17 Ethel Carnie Holdsworth, *Collected Poems: Rhymes from the Factory (with Additions), Songs of a Factory Girl, Voices of Womanhood* (Kennedy & Boyd, 2020), p. 199. See also, 'Shame', from the same collection, p. 164.

18 Katharine St John Conway, *Aimée Furniss, Scholar* (Clarion Press, 1896); Katharine Bruce Glasier, 'Marget, A Twentieth-Century Novel', Weekly Times and Echo, 21 September 1902 – 1 March 1903.

19 Roger Smalley, 'The Life and Work of Ethel Carnie Holdsworth, with Particular Reference to the Period 1907 to 1931' (University of Central Lancashire, 2006), p. 182.

20 This comment came in response to a critique of *This Slavery*'s romance plot in the labour press. Belinda Webb, 'Introduction', in *Miss Nobody*, by Ethel Carnie Holdsworth, ed. by Nicola Wilson (Kennedy and Boyd, 2013), pp. ix–xxix (p. xix); Ethel Carnie Holdsworth, *Sunday Worker*, 26 July 1925, qtd in H. Gustav Klaus, 'Silhouettes of Revolution: Some Neglected Novels of the Early 1920s', in *The Socialist Novel in Britain: Towards the Recovery of a Tradition*, ed. by H. Gustav Klaus (Harvester Press, 1982), pp. 89–109 (pp. 96–97).

21 Ethel Carnie, 'How Colour Is Introduced', *The Woman Worker*, 7 April 1909, p. 323.

22 Pamela Fox, 'The "Revolt of the Gentle": Romance and the Politics of Resistance in Working-Class Women's Writing', *NOVEL: A Forum on Fiction*, 27.2 (1994), pp. 140–60 (p. 142).

23 Roger Smalley, 'Introduction', in *General Belinda*, by Ethel Carnie Holdsworth, ed. by Nicola Wilson (Kennedy and Boyd, 2019), pp. ix–xix (p. xvii).

Contents

Chapter I

Elizabeth gives a promise

"An, 'Lizabeth, I said to her," stated Mrs. Peel, "there's more fish in the sea, Mrs. Frankmore, than has never bin asked out on it. It's early days to say what'll happen to our 'Lizabeth. We can live in hope if we die in despair. An' wi' that, I settled her off."

"Two lumps, mother?" queried Elizabeth.

Only in the large lines on which she was built did she resemble the woman rocking herself disconsolately by the side of the table under the window that looked out on a tiny back garden.

"Ay, two," said Mrs. Peel, indifferently.

Elizabeth dropped them into the willow-patterned cup.

She knew that her mother was very much "put out". Only then did she disregard the stealthy encroachments of her arch-enemy—fat.

"Don't worry, mother," said Elizabeth.

Mrs. Peel stirred her tea round, with that pleasure belonging to this after-dinner hour, with Jack just gone back to the factory.

She shot a glance at her daughter—the daughter she admired in the same way that she had admired her husband, long since dead. Then—she mustered courage.

"Why didn't ta take Tom Hardacre?" she asked.

Elizabeth blushed, whitened, and—just for a moment a spark appeared in her almost sleepy grey eyes.

"Mother," she said, sitting down, and the spark dying away, "never you tell anyone that Mr. Hardacre ever gave me the chance." There was silence in which Mrs. Peel's eye-lashes flickered, and the case-clock ticked weightily.

"Because he didn't," finished Elizabeth.

Whilst she alone knew how perilously near the edge of a proposal she had stopped him.

"An' to think," said the stout lady, sighing, "I'd had twins, an' our Jack, an' thee, when I weren't as old. But then—you never know what the Lord can do! Remember Sarah."

A blackbird burst into full song as he swung on the elm at the foot of John Stone's garden. Elizabeth lost the sense of her mother's voice, even as James Peel used to lose it, when he pondered his roses.

"Sarah who?" queried Elizabeth, dreamily.

Mrs. Peel knew so many people.

"Why—Sarah in the Bible, of course," said Mrs. Peel.

Elizabeth's eyes looked as they did when her Uncle Benjamin was telling a good joke. Then—her laughter rippled upon the sleepy air of the afternoon kitchen, where the smell of baking clung everywhere, from matted floor to snowy ceiling.

Her laughter certainly was younger than her twenty-eight years, and when it ceased there were delicious tears of mirth on her lashes.

This was the last straw to Mrs. Peel.

Her eyes became what her son Jack termed "water-works".

"It's me has to f-face it out," she sobbed. "They th-think there's summat wrong wi' thee, or summat."

Elizabeth's bearing changed.

To an outsider there would have been something comic, as well as tender, in the spectacle of this big, not unhandsome young woman mollifying her parent

2

for yet being at home. But neither Mrs. Peel nor Elizabeth were conscious of it.

They drank a peace-cup of tea together.

Elizabeth cleared the table of all save the row of shining, golden brown cobs of bread, then set her mother the buffet to rest her feet, as was usual in the afternoon.

"I think that oven'll be ready for the sweet-bread," urged Mrs. Peel, looking up from the contemplation of a huge hole in Jack's sock.

Like most middle-aged women who have abandoned the work of the household to a practical daughter, she still kept her hands on the reins. Elizabeth did not mind in the least. But she knew the oven was too hot.

"I've not put in the sultanas yet," said Elizabeth, to gain time and save arguing.

Mrs. Peel's consternation at the hole's dimensions made her forget her point.

Then she forgot even the hole and her grievance that Jack didn't settle down with his long-courted sweetheart, Letty, who would then struggle with the socks. For, having no real troubles, Mrs. Peel had the human failing of liking to believe that she had.

"'Lizabeth!" she said, "something's wrong at the Stone's!"

Elizabeth looked startled, as she listened.

"It's th' parrot screaming," she said, after a moment.

There was no sound from the next door house other than the slamming of a door.

Then Mrs. Peel spoke.

"That's Letty Fairbody's voice!" she asserted.

"Happen it's a miscarriage!"

"Mother!" said Elizabeth.

For there had been something almost callous, to her, with her tender interest in the young couple next door, in her mother's gossipy curiosity, untouched by feeling.

3

Mrs. Peel eyed her daughter with mild antagonism.

"Well, there are such things," she said.

She was preparing to sulk.

"There is something wrong," said Elizabeth, "that's the front door, and John's footstep."

"I couldn't hear it," said Mrs. Peel.

"He was running," said Elizabeth.

"'Lizabeth!" yelled her mother. "Look what tha'rt doing!"

Elizabeth looked down to find she was putting salt instead of sugar into the loaf. She managed to scoop off the salt.

"Or th' child's in a fit, an' she's run out o' th' seet on it again," guessed Mrs. Peel. "What poor critturs some men takes to theirsels!"

Elizabeth's face was white now.

She was thinking of that stiff little form, the twitching muscles, the baby head shaking galvanically—and John Stone ripping the clothes off the child, a crazy giant, whilst she got the bath ready, whilst Mary—.

Even at the time she had marvelled that that did not break a man's love in two.

For Doctor Conrad had been quite right, when he stated to his wife that Elizabeth Peel might have the innocence of a child, but she had also the brain of a man.

"I hope —," said Elizabeth.

Her voice trailed off.

Then, she gave a final determined stirring of the sweet-loaf mixture, spooned it into the tin, and put it into the oven, shutting it in very gently, as though she were putting Mary Stone in prison for running away from her child when it was in a fit.

"'Lizabeth, John Stone's beckoning thee," she heard her mother say.

She looked through the window.

Looking at her over the hedge dividing the two gardens was a tall workman, his fair hair blowing wildly about a distracted countenance.

So soon as he caught Elizabeth's eye, he waved at her tensely, and vanished.

"It is another fit," said Mrs. Peel.

Elizabeth was already leaving the house.

Her knees felt to tremble—her heart was shaken in its socket, for it was a tender, woman-heart. But she had not forgotten to take a dry towel to rub the baby down, this time.

She mastered the trembling before she had passed the last of John Stone's raspberry bushes. Through the window she recognised the back of Letty Fairbody's bonnet, wagging its wheatears violently, to the clink of teacups. When she passed into the small, untidy kitchen, she found it full of old women. Her glance went straight to the right ingle-nook.

Down in the cradle was a rosy, happy little Mary, the fat fingers of one hand holding a wrestling contest with those of the other, to an impartial glee gurgled forth in a baby voice.

"It's my firm opinion she were deein' when I piked her up from behint the door," said Letty Fairbody.

Elizabeth looked dazed, in the centre of the kitchen.

Her eyes fell on a blue apron of Mary Stone's hung over a chair-back. She was beginning to understand.

"Sit down, lass," said Letty Fairbody.

"Ay, sit down," echoed another. "It's as cheap sittin' as stannin'."

To which argument there was no answer.

Elizabeth sat, pondering on this unexpected thing. The clatter of tongues gave her the opportunity to piece together the fact that Letty Fairbody had come to John Stone's house with a message from his mother, Bella Stone—only to find that she could not open the door for something behind it—which turned out to be Mary Stone, in a heart seizure.

Elizabeth looked up to see John Stone at the foot of the stairs.

She arose in answer to that brief motion of his hand.

"Get them out," he said, in a low voice.

He referred to the old women.

Thus was Elizabeth given the unpleasant task of turning out women old enough to be her grandmothers. Wincing within, but calm without, she obeyed John Stone's command. Consternation, surprise, sympathy, turned into scorn—all passions expressed themselves in the backs of that little crowd of turned-out old dames, filing along between the raspberry canes.

"You can tell which way th' wind blows!" said Letty Fairbody, meaningly, as she shut the gate.

John Stone came downstairs on hearing the door close.

"They've gone, then," he asked.

"They meant well," replied Elizabeth.

John Stone did not answer that gentle reminder.

"Mary is goin'," he said. "Conrad gives her till midnight. Can you spare the time?"

Elizabeth nodded.

"She asked for you," he explained.

As the doctor came down, John Stone went up the stairs again.

"Oh, you here, Elizabeth," said Doctor Conrad, pleasantly surprised, as he peeped into the kitchen.

He sat down, chatting for five minutes. Then came out the old query as to whether she was keeping company yet. Elizabeth knew it had to come. For the first time it annoyed her. Baby Mary began to cry, tired of her self-organised wrestling match, so Elizabeth took her up.

"Getting your hand in, for all that," chaffed the doctor, as Elizabeth sat the child on her knee.

Then—he missed her usual smile.

"No offence, Elizabeth," he said.

Elizabeth smiled a full smile, then.

"Jokes do get threadbare in time, doctor," she said, "even the best."

"You staying this out?" queried the doctor.

Elizabeth nodded.

"If she gets rough send for a powder," he said. "Heart. May be a fight for breath. Poor little thing. And the young man. She asked for him so soon as she saw me. Well, Dick will have to do as well as he can. These things will happen."

Elizabeth fancied the doctor had made a mistake in John's name.

After he had gone, tapping the weather glass to a sound that somehow reminded Elizabeth of earth falling on a coffin, she took the baby to her mother, satisfied her enquiries—and left that person seeing another door of hope opening for Elizabeth.

Elizabeth had put the sweet loaf on the second shelf. Mrs. Peel said she would see to it.

For an hour afterwards, Elizabeth worked quietly in John Stone's untidy kitchen, not caring to intrude on the young couple. The murmur of their voices came down to her. Once Mary's tone sounded whimpering—like a weak child's. Then there was a long silence—followed by the creak of the stairs under John's feet.

"Mary has asked for you," he said, on entering.

The distressed look on his face was mingled with another—a curious look which Elizabeth felt vaguely, without understanding. It was one of dazed wonder—of stocktaking almost, as though he had never seen her before.

"Yes," said Elizabeth.

She went up to that room on whose little dressing-table was still the pincushion for the baby's pins. Elizabeth's present of eight months ago, when the little one was born.

The great four-poster bed had its clothes a little discomposed. Otherwise—there was no sign of anyone

7

in it. Bella Stone's great eiderdown appeared to be spread over nobody. Elizabeth sat down and waited. There was a slight movement after a time, then—

"Dick?" came in a whimpering query.

Elizabeth straightened the eiderdown, uncovering a tossed head of tawny hair, a countenance where death was written, and two eyes—yet alive, burningly alive.

"John is downstairs," said Elizabeth.

Mary moaned.

"Is—have you a brother Dick you want to see?" asked Elizabeth gently.

Mary shook her head wearily.

She appeared to calculate.

Then she said—

"Is the bedroom door shut?"

Elizabeth nodded.

"John can't hear?" queried Mary.

Elizabeth shook her head.

"Dick—is my sweetheart—my old sweetheart," said Mary. "I can't die without seeing Dick. I can't. He wouldn't settle down. An' we quarrelled. An'—I married John inside three weeks. An' it's killed me. It's killed me. But I want to see him— only once—this once—!"

She burst into weak crying—muted crying, conscious of John downstairs. John who might hear, John whom she had deceived, John of whom she was afraid on that account.

"You—you think badly of me?" she asked of Elizabeth.

"No—no," protested Elizabeth.

She had received a very painful shock.

Every day, for two years, she had seen this young woman be kissed daily by John Stone, at the gate, before going to work. A dream was shattered.

She took the cold little hand into her big warm one.

"Where does this Dick live?" she asked.

And Mary laid her head on Elizabeth's breast, and sobbed out the whole story.

"It's been here," she said,"a big weight—till it's broken my heart. Dick said I was all heart. All heart. And he ought to know."

"You can't see him," said Elizabeth, "because he couldn't get here, even if you knew where he was. Besides—Mr. Stone—."

"No! He couldn't come," said Mary, childishly yielding. "But I'd got to tell someone. I was afraid I'd have to shriek it at John, if I didn't tell you. Poor John."

"You will never tell John?" she asked, suddenly, fearfully.

Elizabeth promised.

"There are some letters," murmured Mary, "his letters. I dared to keep them. They are in my work-box on the mantelpiece. I kept them there, because no one would think I'd keep them there. The key — is in my—oh, I don't know. Bella Stone—she'll come rooting round. Don't let her get them, Elizabeth. Don't let her," she urged excitedly.

Elizabeth promised.

Her brain whirled a little. She might be promising more than she knew how to fulfil.

"Is there anything more?" she asked.

"Bury them with me," asked Mary. "An' don't let them bury me in my wedding ring. It's heavy, though it was the least ring in the shop. An' don't let them weight my eyes down with pennies,"

She whimpered her fears forth childishly, through her gasping, and the audible sound of her poor, almost worn-out heart.

Elizabeth promised once more.

Then came the thunderbolt.

"And, Elizabeth," said Mary, still holding Elizabeth's hand, "if John asks you to marry him, you will, won't you?"

Mary Stone was cunning as a cuckoo seeking a safe place for its young. After Dick—she loved her baby.

"He likes you," she urged, "I know he does. Do you like him?"

There was silence.

"Marry him, then," said Mary, with uncanny insight.

"But—Mr. Stone," faltered Elizabeth.

"Will turn to you," said Mary.

Elizabeth felt a momentary suspicion.

"If of his own free will, Mr. Stone asks me—I will marry him," she answered. "But—"

"John does not know I'm asking you," said Mary, hoping she would be forgiven. She had dodged the query as to whether she had asked John to marry Elizabeth.

And the innocence of Elizabeth's heart made her ashamed of believing a dying woman capable of intrigue.

Three hours later Mary Stone knew nothing. Sunset turned into dusk. The throstle sang wild spring joy. Venus shone bright as another moon. John and Elizabeth sat in the bedroom where Mary was "going out" not "rough" but very calmly. Once, as Elizabeth's hand touched her forehead, she smiled, lisping "Mamma!" to a mother dead these fifteen years, whilst Elizabeth's eyes brimmed tears.

The end came just as the foundry whistle sounded for the night shift.

"John'll want his supper," she said, suddenly sitting up, and fell back on Elizabeth's arm.

John Stone bent over from the other side of the bed.

Elizabeth never forgot his face. After a while he saw hers, with something in its expression that told him all was over.

"No," he said doggedly.

Elizabeth bent her head.

He staggered out of the empty room.

Mrs. Peel came in ten minutes later. She found John Stone sitting in his chair, staring at Mary's empty one, the armless little nursing-chair where she had rocked the baby, without ever singing.

Elizabeth came downstairs just in time to prevent her mother worrying the bereaved man.

"Gone!" said Mrs. Peel.

She had the commonplace belief that death was the greatest tragedy.

Elizabeth nodded, thinking of what Mary's soft little heart had suffered before the great peace came.

"Are the blinds down?" asked Mrs. Peel.

Elizabeth nodded.

"Letty Fairbody'll lay her out," said Mrs. Peel. "Has ta tied her chin up?"

"She's washed," said Elizabeth, simply.

Mrs. Peel stared.

Elizabeth took her mother upstairs. She had tied a white silk muffler of John's on Mary Stone's head, so that the pretty dimpled chin was held up. She stood with her finger-tips gently pressing the chill eyelids, that had feared pennies on them, from a childish memory of horror at such a sight.

Mrs. Peel burst into noisy weeping.

"Poor thing", she snuffled. "She was only like two matches nailed together." Then she said in a hushed whisper, "'Lizabeth—the sweet loaf is burnt!"

When they went downstairs John Stone had not changed his position.

"Our Jack'll come an' sleep wi' thee, John," said Mrs. Peel.

She took John's silence for consent.

Elizabeth looked up at the mantelpiece, on which stood the work-box.

She meant to tell John Stone Mary had wished her to have it. But she could not ask now.

She went out with her mother, and upstairs into bed, where little Mary put out a childish, gripping touch, touching her breast. Something woke within her. Her arms closed around John Stone's baby. It was curious that she thought of little Mary as John Stone s baby rather than as fruit of the dead woman.

Jack Peel found himself locked out when he tried John Stone's door.

All night, in a turmoil of this breaking up of her calm life, Elizabeth could not sleep. Stars died out and the sun rose. At four o'clock the throstle started to go mad for joy—throb, throb of rapture pouring into the dawn. Elizabeth heard it, with little Mary asleep on her breast. She heard it with a joy and a pain—a subtle perception that John Stone was hearing it in torture. For herself—into the void she had scarcely been conscious of, but which she now knew had been there, had stepped John Stone. She knew now that this sympathy of interest that had bound her to her neighbours, was through John Stone— that she had always liked him. More than, that she would not acknowledge to herself. Elizabeth Peel was proud.

Chapter II

The burying

Elizabeth found herself in a quandary during the next three days. She felt that she could not now go into John Stone's house. Her own pride forbade it, inexorably. Moreover, she had lost the least ray of her childlike innocence. She was a little afraid of what Little Hareton might think, as she had never been before.

It fell to Mrs. Peel to step into the breach, which she did, willingly enough.

Elizabeth heard details of the wilderness of the drawers Mary Stone had left, of how John Stone had ignored food and advice, and how Mrs. Peel had even had to see about the grave, the cards, and everything. Whilst her heart trembled lest the box on the mantelpiece should fall into other hands. At length, she went in, with her mother, determined to get the letters at this opportunity, for Mrs. Peel said Bella Stone was coming soon.

"Upstairs again!" sighed Mrs. Peel, flinging off her shawl, as they entered. What'll he do when they take her out o' th' house?"

John Stone came down, hearing Mrs. Peel's voice.

Unshaven, his face having lost its healthy colour, he presented what Mrs. Peel had well described as the look of a "warmed-up" corpse. His demoralised difficulty in keeping herself unshaken by it, even whilst the fact that Mary had cared little for this man, who was eating his own heart, gave her a sense of the sad ludicrousness of life.

She was conscious, all at once, that John Stone was a weakling, condemning him as one man might condemn another. He was letting the canker of grief undermine his manhood, as some allow drugs to poison them.

Mrs. Peel went upstairs to see Mary in her shroud, which little Miss Higson had fitted for her, saying she had shrouded Little Hareton for fifty years, and never a bonnier corpse, though she could have wished the flesh had not been so soft, as it generally meant another.

"Mary wanted only me to have her work-box, Mr Stone," said Elizabeth.

She saw him lift it down.

"There's a key—somewhere—" he mumbled. Elizabeth received the box, with a sigh of relief. Then she administered her reproof.

"You have the baby, John Stone," she said, simply. He gave her an irritant look.

Elizabeth made herself ignore the misery of the man. She was striking at the healthy manhood of him, not the grief-drugged one.

It was impossible to ignore Elizabeth's look.

"I'm not a woman," he gave back.

"The baby'll be one, some day," Elizabeth proceeded quietly. "It's doin' things when they don't seem to matter just as if they did matter, that counts. It's pumping water out o' the boat when you don't care if it goes down or not, that counts. If everybody committed suicide when some big grief put the sun out, perhaps half the world would be missing."

John Stone winced as well as started, when she wound up with the last sentence. Moreover, she had razzled him. She was the first woman who had "preached" at him.

"My life's my own," he stated off guard.

"Act as though it is, then," said Elizabeth.

Her pitiless logic started a fury in him.

"What do you know?" he began.

"You can see that tree," answered Elizabeth, pointing out of the window. "Well, I've seen that look like a stick, a dry stick, pretending to be alive, and the leaves—they weren't leaves, they were dust, coloured dust, an' I hated people's voices, an' the birds, an' the sky was something I crept under, an' th' dawns used to blind me, an' the back o' my eyes was hot sand, an' I couldn't even cry. An' all the time I looked after the house, just the same, an' did everything to clock-time, and smiled when it felt like my face'd crack. An I'm only a woman, John Stone."

Her neighbour was looking at her in an almost paralysed way. Quite suddenly, he had seen a naked human heart.

A shamed silence fell between them—the shame of one reproved, and one now ashamed of reproving.

"But it was a man?" asked Stone.

Colour tinged Elizabeth's cheek. It was the colour of shame, for having preached at John Stone.

He took it for some other acknowledgement, this painful blush, the overcast expression of her usually frank face.

She bent her head.

John Stone was the only human being to whom she had ever expressed any of the heartbreak she had felt when her father was brought home, dead. Killed on the instant in the old quarry.

"There is Doctor Conrad." she said, quiet again. "He has buried four sons, and the fifth is going the same way. He goes about as bright as a button. Nobody'd guess. And scores of folk in this village, and out in the world, thousands, millions, with one load or another. They wait till their time comes."

15

"You should have been a preacher," said John.

Elizabeth accepted the antagonism she had roused as her reward.

She smiled—her big smile.

"I should never beg questions," she said. She looked like a commander at that moment.

John could well believe it. He was thinking, irrelevantly, that since Elizabeth had evidently had a tragic love affair, which had ended in the man dying, there was no danger of her accepting him when he proposed to her, as he was bound to do, to keep his word to Mary.

"Promise me," said Elizabeth, impulsively, "you never will."

John eyed her. He knew well what she meant.

"Because," she said, "supposing you could wake up after, you'd very likely be sorry."

Which actually made him smile for the first time—since.

So—she could beg questions.

"Well," he said.

In that one word he gave his promise.

The shadow of that fear went from Elizabeth.

Mrs. Peel came downstairs, wiping her eyes, and found John Stone having a meal.

"Now why shouldn't it be?" she thought.

Aloud she only said, with that amazing lack of tact that had been transmitted to Elizabeth as childlike purity of thought,— "I thought I'd just look at her, John, afore she was screwed down. She's just beginning to turn colour, poor thing!"

As they left the cottage, Elizabeth could not forbear saying to her mother, "Mother, do you think Mary Stone is in Heaven?"

"Ay, sure, where else should she be, poor lammie?" said Mrs. Peel.

"Well," said Elizabeth, shortly, "by the way you cry, one might think something quite different."

"Eh, tha'rt thy father o'er again, sometimes!" said Mrs. Peel, who never said anything else when Elizabeth was like this, which was, however, very rare.

"'Lizabeth," said Mrs. Peel, soon afterwards, "John's mother has come."

And Elizabeth knew that her chance of putting the letters inside Mary's coffin was gone. In which she was quite correct, for when she went up to see Mary again, for the last time privately, Bella Stone stood in the room with her, doing the show-business, and Elizabeth went down with the love letters in her big under-pocket. They bumped against her knees at every step she took down, and she had a half-hysterical thought as to what would happen if they dropped out.

John Stone was trying to read. Elizabeth noted it with quick sympathy. Her reproof had not been lost.

"Happen tha wouldn't mind cornin' to hand 'em the wine an' biscuits afore we bury, 'Lizabeth?" asked Bella Stone.

John Stone lifted his head slightly. His mother was usually jealous of dividing honours.

"I'll come," said Elizabeth.

"An' to be here an' wait when we land back," said Mrs. Stone.

Elizabeth nodded assent to that also.

"She's like our Alison, John," vowed Mrs. Stone, when Elizabeth had gone.

Which was Bella Stone's highest mark of favour. Though for the life of him John could not see any resemblance between Elizabeth and his dead sister.

It was a walking burying. The church was only a stone's throw away, and Little Hareton was sufficiently "out of the world" to cling to old-fashioned customs.

Bob and Charlie Stone, with their respective wives, were the first to arrive. They were hard featured lads, with their mother's deep-set eyes and shrewd expression, and looked ill at ease in their black garments and high collars. The feeling was doubtless increased by the darkened house, the way in which everyone whispered, with the exception of Elizabeth, whose voice, as she bade them take a glass of wine and biscuit, was quiet and pleasant as always.

Mrs. Robert Stone had brought a harp of lilies with a broken string. Mrs. Charles, a cross of narcissus. Both went upstairs and came down crying, though neither of them had been in the habit of visiting the gentle little Mary.

Elizabeth caught that almost frenzied look on John Stone's face, such, as it had worn when he asked her to get the old dames out.

Of all the houseful of mourners who gathered in that house, only two felt real grief, real loss. John Stone, meeting Elizabeth's eye, as one after another came downstairs, realised that Elizabeth's was the other heart that mourned, for all her serenity. These two shed no tear.

The women's grief expressed itself in handkerchief work. The men looked more nervous and didn't know where to put their feet.

It was an English funeral.

Those who would have spoken naturally were rebuked by the atmosphere they found themselves in, yet withal, even the handkerchief-users were sincere. Perhaps regret that they had not known Mary better wrung a few of those tears from the womenfolk, or reading her tender age on the coffin lid.

But it was a great relief to all when the minister arrived.

Billy Higson, a hale old undertaker of seventy, in his character as a carrier, helped Charlie, Bob, and Uncle Ned Stone to get the coffin down into the parlour. More handkerchief work from the females.

Mr. Sykes made a short, characteristically English prayer, in which he pointed out that Christians sorrowed not as those without hope. On the whole it was a wholesome, rational little prayer, without much insight into human grief, and everybody approved it with the exception of the one whom it most concerned, and Elizabeth, who, in the close sympathy she had for John's grief, was perhaps hypercritical, though she did not fail to realise, good Churchwoman though she was, that to speak the right words, to give balm to a stricken heart is difficult in an official position.

The most awful moment in the whole business came.

"Well," said little Billie Higson, clearing his throat, "if anybody wants to look again—"

Several of the women looked again.

"Let our Emily touch her," said a stout woman, in that hushed falsetto, "then she'll not dream on her."

But Emily, a nervous girl, shrunk back. Elizabeth drew near and took her last farewell. The little hand, without the ring, lay across the peaceful breast It seemed, as Uncle Ned had said, "a sin and a shame to put her into t' groun'," so fair she was, with that elusive smile, and even the tinge of colour that yet mocked at decay.

John Stone stepped up and looked. Then he stepped back. They filed into the kitchen, whilst that saddest of all sounds came to them, the screwing down" of the lid.

Elizabeth watched the little procession file away out of sight. Then she left the parlour window for the kitchen, and, sitting down in a chair, shed a few quiet tears for the sake of that pang of John's as the lid went on, and from her big, warm sisterly affection for Mary Stone.

But when they returned, she was her cheerful self, and everything was ready to sit down to. The blinds were pulled up, and a more cheerful air prevailed generally, though that spirit of restraint still made enjoyment of the meal impossible. Perhaps it would have to be a unique sort of personality, which, having passed hence, would, leave such a minimum of restraint behind it that men would not feel ashamed to eat or even to smile, though at its funeral board.

"Someone at the door, 'Lizabeth," said Mrs. Peel, who, in a new white apron, was "cutting-up" in the scullery.

Elizabeth went. She opened it. A stranger smiled into her face.

"This is John Stone's, isn't it?" he asked.

Then he saw her black dress, heard the teaspoons that told of a gathering. As for Elizabeth, an awful presentiment was dawning on her. She guessed who this was.

"Is—the baby—?" stammered Dick Burnham.

There was fear on his face. By its agony Elizabeth knew that this was Mary's old sweetheart, come at last to his friend's house.

"It isn't the baby, Mr. Burnham, nor Mr. Stone," said Elizabeth. Dick was too agitated to notice that she knew his name.

Elizabeth was trying to blame him. It is hard to blame a man who looks crazily at you, all the colour emptied out of his face.

"Mary?" queried the young man.

"Put your bag in the parlour," advised Elizabeth, "and I'll bring you a glass of wine."

Which she did. She was afraid that Dick Burnham's appearance, the effect of the shock, would make him give himself away.

The cosmopolitan pulled himself together. He did it well. Never had Elizabeth seen anything so fine as his entry into that kitchen, his gripping of John's hand, his quiet talk of his journey, his quietly expressed regret at John's loss.

"Doesn't look quite as fresh as when he left these parts," commented Uncle Ned. Whilst Elizabeth marvelled that any man who had looked as Dick Burnham looked on hearing the news, could think of passing the salt to his neighbour at table.

Soon the house was emptied of its guests. Bella Stone went home with Bob and Charlie and their wives, who all lived at Hill Top Farm since Mr. Stone's decease the summer previous. Elizabeth and her mother washed all up and were about to depart.

"Oh," said John Stone, suddenly, "who was responsible for Mary being buried without her ring?"

"I was," said Elizabeth. She had kept that promise.

John Stone looked at her and hesitated.

"It's all right," he said, "I only wondered."

But with swift intuition she knew his thought. He believed her a parsimonious person who would not bury a "valuable" with the dead.

"It is in that box," said Elizabeth, casually.

There was a short silence. Then John asked—

"Could you keep the child a day or two, until I look around me?"

Mrs. Peel burst into protestations about the child being no trouble. But John was looking at Elizabeth. She nodded.

They went out, leaving the two men alone in the firelight, and Elizabeth felt that if John Stone had not been half-mad with his own grief, he would have noticed the haunted look in his old friend's eyes.

Next day Jack Peel said he had seen "the fancy chap" on Little Hareton platform, off back to London.

"I wonder," said Mrs. Peel, "what he'll do now."

She referred to John Stone. Jack Peel was brushing his hair, ready to go out courting.

"He'll drink hissel' to death, it's my opinion," he said, "like his grandfather did. Anyhow, he's made a start, an' when Stone does aught, he does it reight."

Mrs. Peel could drag no more out of him. Jack was a curious mixture of silent father and garrulous mother.

Elizabeth passed an unquiet, quiet evening. She heard John Stone go out, locking the door behind him. Despite her common sense, she could not forget that with Dick Burnham there had been thirteen at table. Whilst, from its cage, the parrot John had bought two years ago occasionally broke the silence by screaming "M-Ma-ary, Mary," as it had done during the funeral tea, to the discomfiture of the guests. Its harsh call sounded through the thin, jerry built walls to the house where Elizabeth sat—making a new little bonnet for John Stone's baby.

"I knew," said Mrs. Peel, "he'd feel it worse when they'd ta'en her out o' th' house."

Elizabeth did not answer.

"'Lizabeth," said her mother, slowly, "I've found out where tha's missed thy way. Tha's too little to say for thisel'! Now——"

It was about John Stone, of course. The same sentiments had been given out linked up with other widowers' names, Elizabeth sat quietly stitching, and smiling. She had, during this past week of upheaval, found life to hold subtler shades of tragedy and lights of comedy than ever she had guessed.

She stitched ribbons she had worn in her brief girlhood neatly on little Mary's bonnet.

"I hope," she said, without apparent relevance, "that they'll give me an Irishman's funeral when I die. Did you notice Uncle Ned Stone taking a pickled onion as if he were robbing the dead?"

"'Lizabeth!" said Mrs. Peel.

Then she burst out laughing also.

Chapter III

"Cuck-oo!"

"'Lizabeth!" exclaimed Mrs. Peel, handing her daughter the evening paper, "look there."

Elizabeth laid down her tatting-shuttle, and scanned the following:

"Wanted, a working housekeeper by foundryman with one child. Apply between seven and eight in the evening. Stone, Little Hareton,"

Mrs. Peel tried to read Elizabeth's face. It showed only mere neighbourly interest.

"So we'll lose the child," added Mrs. Peel. At that she saw another expression flicker for a moment over Elizabeth's face. Then her daughter took up her shuttle, going on with the collar she was making as a wedding present for Jack's sweetheart, though no one knew when the great event would take place.

They heard their neighbour go out after the clock struck eight, the time limit for the applying of housekeepers. Mrs. Peel went to the front door and watched him, hidden by the lilac bush.

"He's gone to the pub," she announced, triumphantly. "Now, if any housekeeper did come, he'd be fit to choose one, wouldn't he? Anyhow, he'll get let in. A chap as could pike a wife as couldn't wash clothes no better'n she did, winnot ha' much scent for a housekeeper."

Elizabeth went on tatting.

Little Mary cried twice from upstairs. Elizabeth being firm with little Mary was a great joke. When the child cried the third time, Elizabeth brought her down, laid the tatting aside, and rocked her to a slumberous tune that made the eyelids flutter down over the blue eyes that were like John's,

It was thus that John Stone saw them in his coming there from the inn. He heard Elizabeth's singing cease suddenly. It reminded him that he never had heard Mary sing to the little one.

John Stone was very miserable. The thought of the kindness the Peels had shown was a constant reproach to him. He knew that he was not doing "that as he should," as Bella Stone would put it. The fact that Elizabeth was becoming to him an outward symbol of his own inner conscience, did not make him like her any better, rather adding to that antagonism to her which had commenced to grow so soon as Mary had wrenched that foolish promise from him.

He had not intended to call in on the Peels this night. The white door glimmering as he fumbled at his own gate had fascinated him, in some way. As he stood, swaying a little, a nasty spirit of pride sprung up in him, sudden as a typhoon.

"Sit down, an' have a cup o' coffee, John," said Mrs. Peel.

"I'm come to take the child off your hands," he said.

He really made himself believe that this was the reason he had called. Mrs. Peel looked at the clock. Elizabeth did not speak.

He observed in the curiously detached way of that self of his he could not drown in "The Bluecap's" beer, the tatting laid down, the brightness of that kitchen, which made his own, in contrast, like a grave. There were muffins, each with a browned ring inset where they had touched the oven, ranged on the white-covered dresser, where the two gay vases had lilac sprays sending out sweetness.

"I'm come to take the child home," he reiterated. Still Elizabeth did not speak.

24

"Has't got a housekeeper, John?" asked Mrs. Peel.

He had. He had engaged her without even seeing her. She was Billy Hatchitt's cousin, "out of a place." He had been playing dominoes with Billy Hatchitt in "The Bluecap" and the advertisement had been mentioned.

He just nodded to Mrs. Peel's inquiry. His gaze was on Elizabeth, as he repeated that he had come to take the child home.

Her face turned his way.

"She's undressed," remarked Elizabeth.

Her big serenity of look had never been more noticeable.

"She'll dress," he said.

There was a moment's silence, then the clock struck ten.

"Is there a fire in thy house?" queried Elizabeth.

He had let the fire go out.

"She's where she's stoppin', then," said Elizabeth, calmly.

Mrs. Peel gave her a look which Elizabeth utterly ignored, just as James Peel had used to ignore it when he did not wish to see it.

Mrs. Peel beheld with keen disappointment that her daughter was "crossing" John Stone.

"Have a bit o' sense, John," she said, in a mollifying tone.

"It's mine, isn't it?" asked he, stubbornly, still looking at Elizabeth.

A little spark woke in her grey eyes,

"That was just what Joe Crowther said when he kicked his dog," she smiled. "We've had the child so long, John, we'll not be hurt by keeping her until tomorrow."

A spark woke in John Stone, now. Still with that feeling in the back of his mind, engendered there by Elizabeth having taken the wedding ring from Mary's dead hand, he wilfully twisted her speech into a statement of his indebtedness to them.

He disliked Elizabeth Peel at this moment, with an intensity that surprised himself.

"I am taking the child home," he said, with authority. "And I'll pay you for the trouble she's been."

He sat down. The intention to sit there until the child was dressed was intimated in his manner.

"Nay, John, we want no brass," began Mrs. Peel.

She looked at him in a hurt way, but he noticed that her voice lacked vigor. Then she looked at Elizabeth.

Following her gaze, John Stone saw that he had moved Elizabeth out of that sereneness of look that he had used to admire in a neighbourly way, but which now seemed like a sermon to him.

She wrapped the child round and round in the great blanket. "Make the clothes into a parcel, mother," she said.

She had turned pale. It was human anger. It was north country pride against north country pride, and of these two proud hearts, Elizabeth's was the prouder. John Stone, without provocation, it seemed to her, had come to insult them.

He watched her with a slow, malicious satisfaction that he had pierced the masculine rationalism of her. But he got no single word even when Elizabeth handed little Mary to her mother, and Mrs. Peel put the flannel bundle into his arms, saying anxiously, "Be careful wi' her, John, that's a good lad."

Whilst he knew he was not a good lad, and that calling him one wouldn't hypnotise him into being one, and that Elizabeth knew he was not one.

"Tak' him a cannel, 'Lizabeth," said her mother.

"If he lets that child fa'—"

Elizabeth wavered.

John swaggered down the dim passage with his property, but before he reached the vestibule,

Elizabeth had the taper, and, shielding it with her hand, lit the way down the snowy step upon the cobbled path. The scent of the lilac came to them, and Venus shone through the boughs.

"If tha' brings a penny piece for our nussin' th' child, John Stone," said Elizabeth, "I'll put it down a drain-hole."

By the flickering taper light he saw her face. It impressed him, as did the sound of the pure, broad tongue, vibrant with feeling, thus spoken by Elizabeth.

The air suddenly gave him the feeling of intoxication, that had died down somewhat, whilst watching Elizabeth make the baby ready. He mumbled some thing sarcastic about the "Penny Savings' Bank .

Just then the wind blew out the taper's light.

Elizabeth dimly saw him stagger up over his own step, anxiously heard him pass along the cobbled path. He fumbled for the key. There was no key; he had lost it.

For half-an-hour he searched, Elizabeth had taken the baby back home out of the cold. He was almost sober, and a little ashamed, when he found the key where he had put it, under a lad's love bush in his garden.

Elizabeth was warming little Mary's toes when he re-entered the Peels' cottage. He checked a half-impulse to say that the child might stay, and took her.

An hour later, Elizabeth Peel went into the coal-nook for coals, so that Jack would have a good fire on his return from his tramp to Dimpleton, where Letty lived.

The window of John Stone's house was dark, but she could hear him rocking and singing, and the "la-la-la" of the child's plaintive, tired cry in that fireless kitchen. There was, no fire. The white blind would have showed the tiniest flicker of firelight. She made quite sure. Elizabeth stood, shawl in hand, her lips compressed. She was registering a vow.

27

Little Mary's previous convulsions had been caused by colds, which had the effect of sending up her temperature at once.

Elizabeth could not sleep that night until she had heard their neighbour climb his stairs and knew the child was safe. Its cot, she knew, was close behind her own bed-head, only the wall was between. She also knew by the watch on the small table that John Stone had had the child in that cold kitchen two hours.

Next morning, Mary Jane Hatchitt arrived on the scene. John was at his work, having lost two hours waiting for her arrival, and forced to leave the baby and the key with Elizabeth.

"He told Billy," said Mary Jane, "if he wasn't in I could come here for the key."

She had missed her train.

A young woman with high colour, a cast in her eye, and of a mildly patient aspect, Mary Jane was barely out of her teens. Elizabeth gave her a cup of tea after her journey, introduced her to little Mary, and showed her round John's house.

"I like bairns," she said of the child, which was very true.

But Mary Jane never got used to the idea of the parrot, and always jumped nervously when it burst out into its screeching of "Mair-y," and its harsh ridiculous noise, that was termed for courtesy, "laughter."

As for John Stone, it seemed to that wretched young man that his home became new "lodgings." Mary Jane in curling pins; Mary Jane resting a dingy elbow on the table whilst she waited for him to come to his supper; Mary Jane surprised that he did not like cheese and onions; Mary Jane indignantly tearful on his suggesting to her that if she put a fence round the salt pot the cooking would be improved; Mary

Jane clumsily counting her wages to see that it was quite right, and apologising for doing so by saying she had been brought up to believe "right was right, both sides." His head was full of pictures of her. Mary Jane smashing pots and saying it was good for trade, as though a foundryman could support such wholesale philanthropy towards the pottery industry, would have made him smile if he had not been so impoverished, and if he had not seen life through misery's focus.

It was three days after Mary Jane's taking hold of the domestic reins that little Mary's cold, which had shown itself on that morning after John had her in the fire-less kitchen, developed towards that danger point which Elizabeth had feared. Mary Jane informed Elizabeth that little Mary twitched a bit in her sleep, like.

This was in the morning after John had gone to his work. Elizabeth went in and gave the child a hot bath, wrapping her in blankets. But the cold was not to be thrown off.

The Peels were sitting at dinner when John Stone leaped the hedge and came to the back-door.

"The child's in a fit," said Elizabeth, taking the words out of his mouth.

He nodded. He was white to the lips.

"You gave her that fit," said the woman at the door. Even as she spoke she snatched a towel and gave a command for hot water to her mother.

"I—gave her it!" ejaculated John.

In almost telegrammatic economy of words, Elizabeth traced the child's condition to its source. He had the dual feeling of being utterly humbled and yet highly indignant against her spartan callousness in accusing him at such a moment. This, had he only known it, was the carrying out of Elizabeth's inward vow as she had seen that darkened kitchen and heard the poor baby crying its tired cry.

John saw a superbly calm Elizabeth enter on the tragic little scene. Mary Jane's hands were shaking, utterly incapable of untying the child's clothes. He was conscious of a mixture of gratitude and resentment.

But as Jack came in with a pail of hot water, which he emptied into the tepid bath-water, and John saw Elizabeth get hold of the stiff body, a little resentment vanished.

"We shall have to put her in, clothes and all," said Elizabeth. "We shall never get them off, she is too stiff."

John Stone obeyed that calm voice. Between them they forced the child into the water. In a clock minute, that seemed an eternity, the body softened, the twitchings ceased, there was a baby cry.

"She's out!" said Elizabeth.

There was a great rubbing of the child, and wrapping in a blanket. Elizabeth sent Mary Jane off to fetch Doctor Conrad.

The foundry hooter blew as Elizabeth sat gently rocking the child, which huddled close to her, its face still deathly, but showing no more those terrible galvanisms.

"If she had another—" said John Stone, hesitantly.

"I'll stay the afternoon," said Elizabeth.

As he bent down over the child before going to his work, he saw a great tear on the baby's cheek. It was quite the biggest tear he had ever seen. He realised that it had dropped from Elizabeth's eye in her joy that the baby was "come out" of the fit.

He went away with the awkward feeling he would have had had he surprised another man showing the weakness of tears. With Elizabeth he was never conscious of being in the presence of a skirt.

When he returned from his work, Mary Jane was full of the news that the baby had been about to have another fit, but that Miss Peel had thrown it off, and of what Doctor Conrad had said, which John heard with a hurt guilt, for what Conrad had said was the same as Elizabeth had said coming down between his raspberry canes, in her austerity, and with the long towel.

This little episode was barely closed when Mary Jane began to prey upon John's mind. He felt uncomfortable, as he ate, with her hovering about like a third-class waitress, pressing upon him what he did not want. When she kissed the baby, he wished she would not, though he did wish she would wash the baby's ears.

The end came when he heard of her being out in a dress of Mary's.

Accusing him of casting an orphan upon the wide world, and prophesying that it would "come home" to him, Mary Jane made her exit. Even whilst he was considering the proposition of putting the child out to nurse and doing his own housework, Mrs. Biers providentially drifted to his door. He took her on with a desperate recklessness caused in his anxiety to avoid dumping the baby on Elizabeth again.

Mrs. Biers' name, and a pebble brooch curiously suggestive of a granite tombstone, were the only mournful things about her. She had a leaning to the occult, said John's face was so familiar to her that she must have known him in some prior existence. She was not a bad housekeeper, but her curiosity to dip into the future resulted in a lessening of interest in the present.

She allowed the dough to run over on the hearth whilst seeking second-sight people with the great question as to whether she would outlive Mr. B—, and came back, triumphant, to tell John she was told she would, and that she was to marry a man about his complexion. John felt more uncomfortable even than when putting the dough into the tins. When

Mrs. Biers read his tea-cup at supper time, and said that he was going to marry again, to a woman of her complexion, he began to feel that even Mary Jane would have been preferable to a grass widow.

What would have happened can only be conjectured. Mrs. Biers had already had a spring cart come, bringing to John's house some of her own household goods, out of nowhere. Her eiderdown was on his bed, her fire-screen in his room, and she had begun to meet him on his way from work with the child in her arms to his no small annoyance.

Then out of nowhere came Mr. Biers, a masterful thick-set man with a sarcastic tongue, who took back Mrs. Biers and her "things" on the spring cart, back into nowhere—a weeping Mrs. Biers who still, unshaken in faith, asserted to John that this was a punishment for some forgotten sin in a prior existence, which gave John to think furiously on what a multitude of sins he must have committed in past lives.

It was Doctor Conrad's wife who suggested to him that he take a little servant girl of her own training, which he did. Little more than a child, Elsie Chapman was a treasure, but with the cessation of the irritant feelings Mary Jane and Biers had caused, his old agony rose uppermost again.

Ill luck had it that Elsie's mother fell ill. She returned to her native country. She did not come back, Elsie's father writing and stating that they could not spare her at home, and would John send the flannel petticoat she had left behind, and thank for them the young woman next door who had taught her to make pies and pastries. Whereupon John began to realise several things.

Abandoning the housekeeper proposition as beyond him, John Stone wrote a letter to his mother. It was a signal of distress. Bella Stone's answer enraged him even whilst it made him conscious of an internal struggle going on between the units at Hilltop Farm since his father died. That letter told him plainly that, far from being able to help anyone else, she was having a terrible struggle to maintain her own. Charlie and Ted were trying to buy her out of the farm lease, which she had shared with them. The lads' wives wanted to push the old woman on one side.

That way being closed, John Stone was ignominiously compelled to seek the Peels once more.

The simple manner in which Elizabeth received the child back again, the easiness of mind with which he could leave her there without uncanny fears that had haunted him whilst she was in the charge of either Mary Jane or Biers, was almost the only domestic comfort he had in this chaotic time.

Sleeplessness had become the companion of his grief. He would snatch a half-hour between lights only to be awakened by the throstle's song, each note a mockery. Amidst it all, the thought that from beginning to end of their married life he had made Mary happy, was the one consoling joy.

His hands awkwardly performed the household cleaning after the swooning heat of the foundry. He had quite original methods, and sometimes argued to himself on the waste of energy femininity put into its work. John Stone, having cleaned the steel-topped fender, put it down only when he was locking up the house, and took it up again, covering it with brown paper, only when he was in. He stripped the place of all hangings and cushions, until, Mrs. Peel feelingly remarked, it looked like a "padding-can".

Meals were taken on an old newspaper to save a cloth, but more often were not taken at all. Whilst even as he told himself that all this saved labour, the dark, bare look of the house further shook his jagged nerves.

There were moments when the temptation to have done with it all, came over him again, but concurrent with it was always the recollection of Elizabeth's remarks on such, the clear look of her, the spartan harshness of her, which said "if men will die when a big grief comes, all the world will take its life at one time or another."

Sometimes in his weakest moments he cried like a little child, for the pity of that chair empty before him. Sometimes after his sojourns in "The Bluecap," the parrot screeching "Mair-y!" appeared as a fiend in pink and grey feathers. He had to beat down an insane desire to choke it.

Through all the gamut of the tragedy of human loss, he went, until he came to that place where no tears fall, where exhaustion comes, physical, moral and mental. Worn out, he slept o' nights now, though he always woke with that puzzled wonder at the weight at his heart, soon realising it as his familiar friend. Sanity came back, looking stoic-like upon the ravages in himself and his home. With it came the necessity of reckoning things up, a realisation that he could not go on like this much longer, and the remembrance of his promise to Mary, that he would ask Elizabeth Peel to marry him. He did not want to marry anyone. In all the history of his family, no Stone had ever re-married, neither had there been in it any jilter or adulterer.

For John, re-marriage was a treachery to those two years he had lived with Mary, but the necessity to keep his compact with the dying grew larger and larger in his eyes after the dull settling down to accept grief as his companion.

He had scarcely any fears that Elizabeth would accept him, but he had to ask her as a preliminary towards putting his house in order. Afterwards he had some hazy idea of asking Mrs. Conrad to get someone to look after the child for him, and of going out west to struggle in some rough corner of the earth where the fight for life would be so keen as to drag him out of this morbidity that had settled on him.

His passage from a half-mad anguish to save acceptance of a broken life, by the calendar had taken six weeks. The exhausted cessation of struggle in the victim was the point of its greatest grief.

Blue Magdalens were beginning to come up in the little front garden. Elizabeth Peel spent her afternoons sitting out in the fields full of wind-flowers, some of which she gathered to the sound of the cuckoo's calling. John Stone s baby would be sleeping on a rug under the shade of a hedge. As she sat she was tatting away at Letty's collar, whilst she unconsciously fell to counting the shouts of the cuckoo. According to northern superstition each call meant a year of single blessedness for the listener.

This cuckoo had called twenty-three times. She smiled at the end of the counting, and a young lamb straying near her feet, she mimicked it so nicely it came even nearer, whilst she dropped on her knees. Its mother was cropping at the end of the field. The lamb seized on Elizabeth's thumb and sucked it vigorously in happy self-delusion.

She watched it with that softening of the large, almost Juno-like countenance that made her almost beautiful, then as it skidded away to the voice of its dam, she picked up John Stone's baby and wended her way back towards Little Hareton, treading cautiously to dodge the thickly-sprinkled windflowers, all nodding and a-blowing in dim lavender pink beauty.

Out of the midst of evening that was coming in a golden glow, a sense of unfulfilment was in her heart. She thought dreamily that next to a baby a lamb was the most humanly helpless thing. Never had the close of a day so full of "well-doing" left her so dissatisfied.

She passed a pair of lovers as she followed the baby-wide path between two clover fields, modest country lovers linking fingers and walking in a dream.

"I wonder," she said to herself that night, looking in her mirror If I had set myself, now—"

Her face smiled rational scorn at her own fancy.

She knew that in the make-up she had, was an utter lack of those qualities that "set themselves" to catch the hearts of men. She was at once too child-like, too masculine, too strong of heart and bone. The cuckoo had called twenty-three times. She believed that if John Stone did "turn to her" out of his grief it would certainly be no sooner than that.

Chapter IV

John keeps a promise

Every Wednesday evening at seven o'clock to the minute, Mrs. Peel, in a huge nursing apron, walked importantly into John Stone's house, shouting at the baby as she walked.

This ceremony was to prevent the baby forgetting her father, for John saw very little of the child nowadays, and once or twice her lip had wobbled on her looking up into his face,

John could always tell just when they started out from the next doorstep. Mrs. Peel asking the baby where she was going to now, assuring her that she was "a reight little grand un," or exclaiming "bless thy bonnie e'en, they're as breet as two beads," or asking Letty Fairbody if she ever saw such legs, made a sort of chorus preceding the grand march up the passage to the jingle of the rattle with the silver bells and pink ribbons. Then, when she got inside, Mrs. Peel would sit for five minutes, baby in lap, detailing all the wonderful things little Mary had done, occasionally breaking out into such alarming remarks as that she could eat it, with a pinch o' saut, or declaring that she would kill anyone who offered to hurt it, just as though anyone did.

Her departing remark was invariably "either our 'Lizabeth or me'll fetch her back, John," but John noticed, with some relief, that Elizabeth never did fetch the baby back. He began to fear less and less that Elizabeth Peel might accept him when he proposed to her, as he was bound to do to keep his promise to Mary.

It was early in June, on an evening when he sat brooding in his kitchen, a map of the world spread out significantly on his table, that he heard Mrs. Peel set out, as usual. Her shouting at the child suddenly ceased, John guessed that she was gossiping. He detected a tone or two of Letty Fairbody's voice in its shrill, "You never say!" "Well if ever!" He noticed that Mrs. Peel looked a little embarrassed, and that her eyes shone excitedly as she came in. She did not stay either, as was her usual way, but she quoted her old litany that either 'Lizabeth or her'd look in and take the baby back.

When she had gone, John sat down in Mary's chair rocking the baby. Little Mary stared up at him in great wonderment, finally venturing to smile. Then he fell back on the thoughts Mrs. Peel had interrupted. Through them he heard the "gur-gur" of contentment, the jingle of the little bells. In his mind he was leaving the baby comfortably with someone, whilst he roamed the world, to drug himself with an eternal kaleidoscope of fresh scenes and faces.

The baby ventured another smile, slightly more confidential. The "gur-gur" grew more delirious. Quite suddenly the baby laughed, little hands beating time to the ecstatic emotions, every pulse of the soft body aquiver, little feet in the blue socks dancing, so that John could scarcely hold her. Even whilst John was drawing a parallel between this ecstasy and that of young lambs jumping in the gloaming fields, that wonder happened which always seems a miracle.

"Dad-dad-dad!" gurgled little Mary.

John sat quite still. His child had spoken to him. It was like a call, a claim. She took on a new significance.

"Dad-dad!" he repeated to her, trying to get her to do it again. But she was now interrogating her blue socks and trying to bite off the topmost silver bell on the rattle, by turns. John Stone sat, still moved by this new thrill. Even Mary had never moved him more than at the moment when this creature of his own blood called to him.

The door opening, still found him engrossed, shaken, struggling between this new claim he had felt and that map of the wide world with its anodynes.

It was not until Elizabeth Peel stood on the threshold of his kitchen that he realised it was she and not her mother. Even in the uncertain light her face struck him as tired, pale and a little less cheerful than usual.

He had already discovered that whilst Mrs. Peel did the "show-work" with the child, it was upon Elizabeth that the drudgery fell. Moreover, he had heard at the foundry that Elizabeth had been sitting up o' nights this week with Melia Young, a poor girl who was dying of heart-break and shame at her betrayal.

"Take a chair, Elizabeth," invited John.

She sat down like a big tired-out child. To-night he was not conscious of the usual impression of large dignity she usually carried about with her, neither was he conscious of her almost unfeminine vigour.

"How is Miss Young?" asked John.

Even as he spoke he perceived that it was a delicate question for a man to broach, but Elizabeth never made him conscious of her femininity. After having seen her go up a ladder to clean the rain-trough out, cementing a wall, and whitewashing, it was hard to realise she was akin to Mary.

Elizabeth stirred in her chair at his query.

"She died at six o'clock." said Elizabeth.

In the ghostliness of the gray kitchen, he felt rather than saw a massive frown knit her brows, and he remembered to have heard that James Peel, her father, whilst an astonishingly mild man, had been dreaded by mean people. He poked up the fire. By its light, he saw that Elizabeth had a besmudged countenance, her eyes were red and swollen. Elizabeth had been crying—crying over that little wretched, sordid tragedy, like a big, soft-hearted child. Now she had passed out of that stage, and was in a spiritual sort of rage against that weak lover of Melia's.

"A sad affair," said John.

Her puckered brow, frowning eyes, the cold, masculine judgment of her—he felt it, even as she sat before him, physically tired out, and the baby, awakening, stretched out its arms and cried to come to her.

The half-terror he had always felt of the big woman, came back to him. She said no word on the scene she had recently left, but her attitude bespoke her mind. It would be the meeting of a feminine Hercules and a pigmy, if ever she came across Joe Briggs, and she would have no mercy.

"I mustn't stay. Mother's got cramp," she said quietly. It was at once a statement and an apology for coming in.

"There's no hurry, is there, Elizabeth?" quoth John, who saw her mind.

Like a man in a dream he was watching the baby, its finger curling round Elizabeth's big one, its eyes blinking' up at her face; hearing its croon of content as it lay in the large lap of the blue and white checked apron.

They spoke of the weather, of the bolt that had fallen on the policeman's cottage at Niffleigh, two miles away, of how his raspberry canes were coming on, of how the green fly was bad this season, and the wonder of the blossom this year, which probably meant a hard winter, according to Little Hareton belief.

Then they drifted on to roses, for Elizabeth had a middle plot that would not have disgraced a prize grower. James Peel had been great on roses, and as Elizabeth had to help him, she had learnt much. Like her father she never sold them, though sometimes giving them.

Conversation dragged. The tock-tock of the clock became heavy and embarrassing. Elizabeth was rising to go. It was then that John Stone heard himself say, "Don't go yet, Elizabeth. Sit down. I want—"

He had decided to get that promise to Mary off his chest. This seemed the most fitting opportunity. Anyhow it might be weeks before another presented itself. He was eager to get the shadow of this Damocles' sword from over his head. It was only a shadow, he felt that, and whilst talking with Elizabeth it had seemed so flimsy a fear that he decided to get rid of it once and for all. He had a hazy notion of enlisting Elizabeth's services in getting a place for the baby, whilst he got away from Little Hareton and the foundry. For it had become a matter of self-knowledge to John that but for his having Mary dependent upon him, he would not have stayed at the foundry so long. All this was in his mind as he looked across at Elizabeth, Elizabeth with wide, innocent eyes and a waiting expression.

"I've been wondering what to do, Elizabeth," he began, cautiously feeling his way.

Elizabeth's gray eyes looked across at him. She was just a big child again. The baby was gurgling at her, trying to catch her looks.

"I'm in a bit of a hole," said John, whilst a slightly ironic self laughed silently.

Elizabeth's gray eyes were disconcerting. He had the awkward feeling that he was about to drop a bolt upon her.

"Yes?" said Elizabeth.

The baby was becoming frantic that its appeals for notice went unheeded. Just before it broke into a cry, she smiled down at it. John paused a moment.

41

"Will you marry me?" he asked.

Elizabeth looked at him. She had made an unscientific movement that disturbed little Mary, who cried. But he had seen a look of infinite surprise cross her face. She had made a movement that told she would have liked to retreat further into the shadows.

"Will you?" inquired John, tensely, when the baby was quietened.

Elizabeth looked at him like a woman in a dream. Whilst, nerve-shaken as she was, he was drawing an absurd comparison between her and Mary. She was rather like a big Newfoundland dog, whilst Mary had been a pomeranian. Then he was fascinated by her big hands. One of them was fondling the baby's absurdly wee one, the other was almost childish, plucking at her apron. Her eyes were looking away from him, now. He could not see them. But she had blushed, blushed as he could not have believed Elizabeth could blush.

Finally she looked at him.

"Yes, or no, Elizabeth?" said John.

He was sweating. He was as soul-shaken as when he had waited for Mary's "Yes." But this time he was waiting for "No." When the baby cried again, he wanted to shake his child. Couldn't it be quiet until this awful business was settled.

Even as Elizabeth's lips opened, John began to speak. So strong had his fear grown again, a thing of substance and not of shadow, that he had to point out to Elizabeth a little of the exact position. That much he felt he could do without going back on his promise to Mary not to tell that she had asked him.

"I haven't any love to offer you, Elizabeth," he said, watching her narrowly. "You know what Mary was to me."

Elizabeth bent her head.

"In a way," said John, "people have no right to marry unless there is that strong bond, and it's just that the housekeepers have worried me so. They're so costly, too. Mary Jane—the pots she went through, and the waste of Mrs. Biers. You see, Elizabeth, I'm just asking you because you'd be cheaper to me."

He was looking at her with an intensity of anxiety of which he was certainly not quite conscious. Elizabeth's now pale face looked into one as pale. She thought he was very conscientious, that was all. She was rocking to and fro with the child, though it was not restless.

From the definite Elizabeth Peel came a curiously indefinite answer.

"I—don't—know—John," she said. "I'll—think it over—a week."

She'd think it over! John felt sick.

"I'd like to know, now, Elizabeth, if you could possibly," he said, dully.

Elizabeth had realised her own compact with Mary. If John turned to her, she would say "Yes". She was bound. Besides—to help John Stone, to save him from the sort of discomfort he was suffering, she realised, would be a vocation to please her. Whilst John was thinking that he would not have believed, had anyone told him, that Elizabeth would marry a man who had told her plainly he wanted her for domestic convenience, and because, like yellow labour, she was cheap.

Elizabeth had risen from her chair, now. The child's head was fallen against her shoulder, asleep from the rocking motion. The big shadow of her with the child in her arms, was on wall and ceiling, just where Mary's little shadow had used to fall, the little shadow that would come no more.

"I should esteem it a favour if you could decide now, Elizabeth," said John Stone.

He could not face the idea of being on the rack a week.

"Tock-tock," said the clock. A cinder fell. The hooter went for the night shift at the foundry. Elizabeth stood in the centre of the kitchen.

When she spoke, her voice was very clear and calm, as was her look.

"Yes, John."

The man in the chair stared at her in a bewildered way for a moment. The door closing behind her and the child roused him. He dashed out of the little house like a madman, after having sat in a stupor for half-an-hour, conscious of nothing but of Elizabeth Peel, big, shadowy, and child in aims, standing in the middle of his kitchen, saying "Yes, John.' He walked at the rate of six miles an hour, right on to Niffleigh and Dimpleton. He did not see any of it, though he was dimly conscious that there were stars and trees and water all mixed up together. People were singing in one little cottage at Niffleigh. Never had he heard such awful singing, it seemed. He wanted to knock at the lighted window and insult them about it. He walked himself into a sweat. He took at an impossible speed. He went over walls, as the crow flies. He walked until he reached his own village in a state of exhaustion.

Almost all lights were out, save those at the inn.

John entered "The Bluecap."

"Whisky," was his terse answer to the landlord's look.

Even there the merry company did not blot out that photograph of Elizabeth saying "Yes, John." He bore it out again with him into the wide night. For he was walking again. This time he did not travel either so fast or so far. His legs were a-jelly. There was not far to travel. He was going to lie down and die on Mary's grave.

He fell once or twice on the way.

The moon was drunk whenever it peeped at him though a tangle of trees. The suppressed grief of his mind oozed up from his heart, no longer soberly proud. His face was wet as he went along.

Mary was dead and he was going to lie down on her grave and die too, whilst somehow he knew all the time that it could not be done.

He found the wicket-gate in the churchyard closed. The white, tall tombstones rising high in the moonshine were doubly drunk, as he saw them through tears and whisky.

He was trying to find Mary's grave with the rosebush at head and foot. It was curious. Every grave looked like Mary's. He counted up to six and started over again, but at last he found it, and laid down by it, calling through the soil to her, and at last he fell asleep. Something, a rat perhaps, woke him by running over him. The moon was still drunk, but not quite so bad. He stumbled out through the wicket-gate back to the world of living, carrying with him, under this maudlin self, a sober self, the self that stubbornly refused to be made quite blind, and this self carried away a sense of corruption from that silent place, and of having a weight of earth piled over his living heart.

Little Hareton was fast asleep! Only in the house where Melia Young was laid with a dead babe on her right arm (a babe whose face was not much larger than an apple) a light was twinkling, lit by Elizabeth, with a pagan comforting to the dead that was strange in a good Churchwoman.

The big gray moths were circling near that lighted window. Their shadows magnified, were on the white road over which John's feet went stumbling. The maudlin self was dying down now, the sober one was rising up, more wretched every moment.

He looked up at the open windows of the Peel's house. White curtains fluttered ghost-like. Mignonette sent its sweetness at him over their railings.

Pushing back his own gate he stumbled over the cobbles, but he could not find the keyhole. Everything was against him, even the keyhole. If it had really

45

mattered, of course, he told himself, he could have found it, but it was such a trifling thing.

He laid himself down on the garden, his hat over his face ; soon he was in an almost piggish soundness of slumber. For he had walked fifteen miles since Elizabeth Peel had said "Yes," had drunk eight noggins of whisky, and realised that it would soon be time to go to work.

Elizabeth Peel woke two hours later, when the moon was setting, and that dim blueness stealing into the air which made the light in Melia Young's room look sickly.

She could hear someone talking, in a familiar, yet unfamiliar tone. She got out of bed softly, and looked out on the two gardens. In John Stone's she saw a prostrate figure, its head resting on its arm. Even as she looked, she guessed somewhat of what had happened; his voice came to her, speaking disjointed words that transfigured her out of an anxious-eyed angel into an indignant one.

"Marry Elizabeth Peel," quoth John. "I—well, I did promise, Mary—but I didn't think—hic—I didn't think she'd have me. She said—hic—'Yes, John.'"

Horror stricken, Elizabeth listened.

Suppose anyone overheard.

That was certainly her main thought even whilst her brain strove with the other details, the intrigue of the dying Mary, who had got John to promise even as herself, the misunderstanding of John Stone, who, from his tone, had evidently thought she supposed she was going to take Mary's place.

One thing was certain. The man could not be left there, to talk under windows that might open at any moment.

Jack Peel stared as he opened his door to Elizabeth's tapping to see her standing there in her dressing gown.

46

"John Stone's sleeping out on his garden,' she began.

Jack swore and was about to close the door. He was not in a dressing gown and was cold. He had guessed burglars at the least.

"Put your breeches on, Jack, and get him into his house," said Elizabeth, putting her slipper in before the door could close. She had bathed Jack when he was four and she was eleven. He was still a little boy to her.

Jack stared at the tone. He forgot his bare knees, but he was absurdly conscious that Elizabeth's slipper was a big slipper. She had once slapped him with one of their father's, in a very old-fashioned way, for fighting a lad less than himself.

Elizabeth's expression was stern as one of those angels blowing their trumpets at the Last Judgment, in a picture they had in the parlour.

"And he's talking about me" she said.

Jack looked as if he was going to burst out into swearing. Elizabeth went. As Jack descended the stairs, she followed.

"Don't hit him," she commanded.

The white pride of her face with its dusky hair about it, the darkness of her indignant eyes, met his own furious look.

"He asked me, last night, to marry him," she explained. "He's repenting it, on the garden path, for all the world to hear."

Jack Peel's neck muscles twitched. His hands clenched, too. Elizabeth followed him down the passage.

"If you fight. Jack," she said, "it will get me talked about. Think on it. Not a finger on him, and not a word of this to anyone."

He looked at her, honest brute-anger in his eyes.

Elizabeth was a rare woman. No one could live along with her without finding it out, though she hid it very well, and he was her brother.

"All right, Tizzie," he said.

She knew he had promised. It was his old baby name for his big sister.

Elizabeth sat down in her father's chair in the kitchen with its blind yet down, listening to the bird twitterings. All the strength had gone out of her. She trembled at the least sound whilst she stared at the clock in the corner, with its dial ornamented with suns, moons and astronomical signs. It had ticked away a very useful, happy, contented twenty- eight years, despite her mother's five year old lamentations that no man asked her to marry him. She had been born with wide interests and had never felt "yearnings."

Yet, all this time it had been ticking her life off, bringing her to this moment. She was eight and twenty. She had waited until she was eight and twenty to accept a man's offer that she be his housekeeper in the only way she could be, because she was not seventy and wrinkled, and then he had insulted, mistaken her.

She heard Jack getting John Stone through his doorway, protesting all the time.

It seemed quite an eternity before her brother came in. He was hot and cross-looking.

"Were any of the windows open, Jack?" Elizabeth asked.

"Not one," he answered.

Elizabeth's stiff figure grew limp.

"Shall I get some water?" asked Jack.

She smiled. "I haven't fainted," she said, with working-class contempt.

They heard the clock tick a few times.

"I think I should have died if anyone had overheard him," said Elizabeth, shuddering at a past horror.

"He told me," said Jack, "that he was going to be one of the family."

Elizabeth's face was sphinx-like. She got up out of her father's chair, walked wearily to the foot of the stairs. She was so tired, so very tired, as though she had been "cleaning through" ever since she was born, without stopping. She had gone through all her powers of emotion in this last twenty minutes, she didn't feel any now, only a consciousnesss of heart tiredness. She crept into bed and slept, a sleep of utter exhaustion from the weariness of emotions she was not used to.

She had quite forgotten to warn Jack not to say a word of it to their mother. When she came downstairs, Jack was gone to work. Mrs. Peel was up.

"Tha ne'er heard me call," she said.

She was very light and cheerful this morning. Had she been less preoccupied, Elizabeth would have noticed this. As it was, she was only conscious of an inward smart as though she had been burned. But she knew quite well that she would not marry John Stone now, no, not even to keep her promise to the dead.

Mrs. Peel went out and did all the errands, whilst Elizabeth bathed the baby. She was a long time gone. When she returned she had flashed the news all round the village, for Jack had "split," and pulled himself up too late. He had only told his mother that John had asked Elizabeth to marry him, not that he had gone in to carry him off the garden path, lest all Little Hareton should hear his self pity that he was to marry Elizabeth. Horror-stricken at what he had done, Jack had made his mother promise not to tell Elizabeth that he had told her. Mrs. Peel had laid the same injunction on everyone she had told.

Unconscious of the net that was closing around her, Elizabeth, with a candle and complete letter-writer, sat late that night in her bedroom. The letter-writer was opened at page 24, the chapter was headed, "How to Refuse an Offer of Marriage." Whilst as she wrote, she could hear the glug-glug of milk out of the bottle into little Mary's mouth. She had fetched that milk all the way from Doctor Conrad's that afternoon, for the Doctor had just purchased two fine Jersey cows, whose milk was, as the Doctor said, "superb."

The Doctor had trotted out his old joke that someone was standing in his own light. Elizabeth had smiled, but for a moment, she had felt as though that smile would crack her face, just as she did after her father was dead. Now that it was all over, she realised how deep was the pang that the new vocation she had been looking forward to was closed. She could have done so well for John Stone. But, as she wrote the letter, she had never been so determined in her life. And she had het father's will. Quiet, gentle —on some points he would have his own way. Elizabeth had never been so like him as she wrote that formal letter, and then hid it in a little trinket-box on her dressing table, a trinket box whose contents were recipes for making old wines, salads, country pies, and cakes. She snuffed the candle, with more peace falling on her mind than had possessed it since Mary Stone had upset its contents by asking her to marry John. After all she had been born for an old maid. It had never worried her, she had known it when she was quite young. Uncle Benjamin had said she would be one, when she sat on a little buffet in that old house near the graveyard, making him a Sunday watch-chain out of black beads. Aunt Sarah had bidden her to leave off sweeping the hearthstone so often, as that was a sign of single destiny, too, and she had always been left to take the last piece of bread on the plate, so there was nothing new in the idea.

She crept down into bed beside John Stone's baby, and made herself sleep.

Melia Young was being shrouded to-morrow, and Elizabeth had promised to go and see all things arranged for the funeral. There was no "burying-brass" to lay Melia and the apple faced babe away. Miss Higson, however, had undertaken to see she was buried like a Christian on the sole strength of Elizabeth's promise that the sum would be paid.

Miss Higson had thought of some sort of public contribution. Elizabeth had not. She was burying Melia Young, No hat was going round for that dead mother with the babe on her right arm. But it was a case of dodging Mrs. Peel. For there was something in Letty Fairbody's saying of Mrs. Peel, that she would not part with the steam of her own breath if she could help it.

Elizabeth fell asleep, to dream that she was plucking roses to put in Melia's coffin, and that as she plucked them, they each turned into little babies, with faces no larger than a good sized apple, perfectly round and all asleep.

If Elizabeth Peel's rare dreams had been dissected as an index to her mind and heart, it is possible that they would have vied for sheer beauty and whiteness with any maiden's of sixteen. But her dreams were few, sleeping and waking, which is said to be the sign of an unegotistical personality.

Chapter V

"Pride mun abide"

John Stone did not see Elizabeth for two days.

"She's busy buryin' Melia,' Mrs. Peel explained, when she took the baby in each night.

There was a familiarity in Mrs. Peel's manner which made John suspect that Elizabeth had told her of his proposal. But Mrs. Peel said nothing. She was realising that she had said quite enough. Indeed, Mrs. Peel was now living in monstrous terror of the news finding its way back to Elizabeth. Elizabeth, to her mother's dread, had not yet breathed a word on the subject. Elizabeth was in one of her most silent moods—kindly and useful as ever—but, like her father on such occasions, not to be approached on personal topics. Elizabeth was distressed, too, because there was some trouble about Melia Young being able to have a grave in the consecrated section, Mr. Sykes urging that she had left the Church an unbeliever. In the end Elizabeth won Mr. Sykes over. She had not been able to bear the thought of Melia laid in that cheap, unconsecrated corner. It was a weakness bred in her by her creeds, but it had this splendour that to Elizabeth it seemed like adding another indignity to all the poor girl had suffered.(Mr. Sykes always nodded at Elizabeth almost deferentially, ever afterwards).

This done, Elizabeth could do no more beyond inviting the few relations the girl possessed. She also watched, very anxiously, the rose-bush in their back garden. She was bent on having those roses lie on the cheap coffin, ever since her dream, in which they had all turned into baby-faces quietly asleep.

There had been eighteen opening buds on that night of Elizabeth's dream. When Melia was coffined, they were the size of half-crowns, and showed pink at their hearts.

It was whilst looking through the kitchen window, that Elizabeth saw John Stone looking over the dividing hedge. Apparently he also, was looking at the roses. Elizabeth withdrew rapidly from the window. She wondered what he had thought of the letter she had put under his door, then she resolutely put all thought of John Stone out of her head.

It was at noon, just two hours before the "burying", that Elizabeth arrived home from town, bringing her "black" by hand. She crossed over to the kitchen window, looking towards the rose-bush. Mrs. Peel was pulling the cradle-string in the corner.

"Where are the roses?"

Mrs. Peel looked guiltily at her daughter, as Elizabeth spoke.

She faltered explanations.

"You—sold them!" gasped Elizabeth.

That bush had been given to Elizabeth when she was seven, by Uncle Benjamin. It had borne hundred weights of roses. Never one had been sold to Elizabeth's knowledge.

"I don't see why roses shouldn't be sold, 'Lizabeth," said Mrs. Peel weakly.

Elizabeth did not argue. Neither had James Peel ever argued with Mrs. Peel.

"If ever you sell another rose from that tree, mother," said Elizabeth, "I walk out of this house, an' never walk into it again."

Then she stood, frowning down at the matting.

"'Lizabeth!" called Mrs. Peel, a moment later, "where arta goin'?"

For a moment she believed that Elizabeth was leaving home.

"I'm goin' to give Annice Fairbody her money back," replied Elizabeth, and closed the door.

Mrs. Peel pulled the cradle string. Never again would she dare to dodge Elizabeth about selling roses. It was a great blow. Whilst the haunting fear that she would get into trouble about spreading the news of John's proposal deepened. She had hoped that Elizabeth herself would publish the news before now, but Elizabeth had not yet told her own mother. It was upsetting all Mrs. Peel's calculations. Whilst the great anxiety as to whether Elizabeth had or had not accepted what Mrs. Peel believed to be her last chance, was another trouble.

"Did ta give her the money back?" asked Mrs. Peel feebly, as Elizabeth came in again. Elizabeth nodded.

"Where's—where's t' roses, then?" asked her mother.

Elizabeth had answered the question by a look. She had refused to have the roses back. Mrs. Peel sighed at the strange fact that this was her own daughter.

Elizabeth said nothing of having wished to place those roses on Melia's coffin, but she went out into the garden, took the half dozen yet left, making it up into a bunch with other flowers.

She had gone off to the little house where Melia lay, when Jack Peel came to dinner from the factory, and Mrs. Peel made another attempt to get him to say whether or not Elizabeth was having John Stone. But Jack took refuge in saying that he did not know. Jack could be taciturn too, when on guard.

Coming home from the foundry that evening, John Stone was waylaid by the niece of Letty Fairbody (who was also her namesake).

"So you are going to get married again, Mr. Stone," said the disappointed fair one.

John stared.

"It is rather soon," said she, thoughtfully, "but circumstances alter cases."

John flushed at the tone. It revived a thought that had momentarily passed through his head once, when pondering his promise to Mary, a thought that had he been choice-free, he would have sooner married Miss Fairbody,

"I should like to know," he said, after more conversation, "how you got your information."

"Why—from whom could it come, but the bride elect?" asked Letty, wonder-eyed.

John Stone went on his way, conscious of a sharp disappointment in Elizabeth Peel. He had not thought that she would blazon the news all about so soon. It struck him that she was making sure of him.

"Well, John!"

The greeting, to which he merely nodded many times, as he went towards his house, conveyed to him in its tone that all Little Hareton knew.

It was to be.

In very irony of spirit he "dressed up" after tea, and walked down to the vicarage, watching Mr. Sykes write down particulars in a little parlour, where lilies made him think of those on Mary's coffin, and of Mr. Sykes' prayers that men sorrowed not "as those without hope." He had a dull sense that Sykes was seeing in him a symbol of the short-livedness of human grief and affection.

"She is one of the finest women in this county or the next," said Mr. Sykes warmly.

As he had been writing down their names, to call out on Sunday, he had really been thinking that it was the best thing any man in Stone's position could do.

John went out, hearing Sykes' praise of Elizabeth, dully conscious that he had signed his own doom.

Walking towards his own house, he determined that the next thing to be done was to go to Mrs. Peel, and ask for her consent. He was to ask for Elizabeth's hand, just as if she had not got him in the hollow of it, and was not making him feel like a dancing puppet. She had fastened him down properly. She had told the whole village.

"Eh, come in, John lad" invited Mrs. Peel, as she opened the door.

He could feel the mother-in-law atmosphere about her. It sickened him. She looked on him as gratefully as though he were a philanthropist. He felt more sick.

She set him a chair in the spotless kitchen, and as he saw her kneading the cushion for him, the first sense of the ridiculousness of it made him want to laugh.

Baby Mary was lying on a crawling rug made from loom-flannel. It was bordered with cats and dogs in red and blue appliqué. Little Mary herself looked like a little blue frog in her crawling suit. The fireplace was filled with passion-dock flowers, ragged robin, red clover and sprays of fern.

John knew that in all this was Elizabeth's touch. He sat with his cap between his knees, pondering the paradox of a woman at once so womanly and so vulgar.

"Goo-gurl-ee," gurgled little Mary.

He could not forbear a smile at the child's self-praise, whilst he guessed also that Elizabeth had said this to the little one.

"Bless thy silver bubbles," exclaimed Mrs. Peel, snatching the child up.

John was astonished to find that Mrs. Peel had actually a streak of poetry in her nature, since she could classify the dribble of tooth-water from a child's mouth as "silver bubbles."

"Here, tak her, Jack," said Jack's mother. She dumped the bairn on her son's knee. Jack Peel looked more like a clumsy bear than ever.

"'Lizabeth!" called Mrs. Peel, from the foot of the stairs. She only just stopped herself from saying "John's here."

"Down in a minute," called Elizabeth.

"Them's ribbands off 'Lizabeth's frocks," said Mrs. Peel, to no one in particular. "But she soon came past her ribband days." She held up a little muslin frock for John's inspection, and he observed Elizabeth's silver thimble and her neat workbasket on the table.

"Very nice," he said, feeling he was expected to say something. He felt like a fool.

Elizabeth and Elizabeth's work always did make him feel like a fool. With Mary he had always felt twice the man. A minute passed. He looked at Mrs. Peel, who had taken the baby from Jack, asking him indignantly how he expected to go on if he couldn't hold a child different to that. Jack escaped into the scullery to wash himself, ready for a Dimpleton excursion to see Letty.

The moon'll be comin' up soon, for him," smiled Mrs. Peel, knowingly.

John smiled awkwardly. His future mother-in-law took an almost childish delight in lovers, weddings, and babies.

John suddenly blurted out his errand. Whereupon, in her great relief that she could now confirm the rumours she had set afloat, Mrs. Peel burst into tears.

"I don't know what I'll do without her," she said, which John felt sarcastically was a very true remark.

It was at this interesting stage that Elizabeth came rustling downstairs. He scarcely knew her. She had on a stiff bottle green silk dress, a gold chain gleamed round her neck. She bent her head slightly to say that she saw him.

"Goo-gurl-ee!" gurgled the baby, making more silver bubbles, and almost dancing out of Mrs. Peel's arms, whilst Mrs. Peel wiped her eyes, and murmured something of Elizabeth being going to a jumble sale to help off the church debt.

Elizabeth was plainly surprised to see her mother wiping her eyes. For a vulgar woman who jumped at a man, and trumpeted her own engagement, she had a peculiar fineness of presence.

"I have been telling your mother that you have done me the honour of accepting me as your future husband." said John.

He spoke in a stiff, embarrassed way.

Elizabeth turned red and white. The red was momentary, the white stayed. Her look was a mingling of brazen innocence and had in it something indignant.

"Could we have a word in private?" he asked.

"Tak' him into th' parlor, 'Lizabeth," said Mrs. Peel, with eager haste. John wanted to laugh again. There was a funny side to this bad dream.

Elizabeth "took him".

When they got inside she carefully closed the door. Did she think he might flee, if she did not, thought John. Yes, he was sure now that there was a funny side to it.

"Sit down," she told him.

He seated himself.

Elizabeth sat down on the opposite side of the room.

"When can we be married?" asked John, brusquely. Now that it was to be, he wanted to get it over.

Elizabeth's dress rustled. She rose from her chair, as though her mental attitude could not be borne seated.

The sun's setting light was on her face, with its magnificent scorn. Her eyes had darkened. Her great brows knit themselves in a way almost too grand in a mere woman.

"Never," she said.

Her voice was very calm. It was also unutterably "distant."

John stared at her, an incredulous smile dawning on his face, then his jaws grew squarer.

"Never!" he remarked. "What! When the tale of it is all over the village, and of your telling too. You've got to marry me now. I'll be no woman's fool."

His voice was low and even on account of Mrs. Peel.

She gave him a look which he could not understand. There was incredulity on her face now. Then she appeared to think, and gave a little start.

"I have told no one," she said, "excepting Jack. I overheard you repenting your proposal, when you were drunk, on the path, and was afraid all Little Hareton would hear, so I got him to get you inside. At my time of life it's rather a come-down to have people think you've been asked and then thrown back."

There was an embarrassing silence. Then she added, "Jack promised not to say anything. I suppose mother got it out of him."

They stared across at one another. John could not find a word to say. If there had been a gulf between them before, it was an impossible one now.

"Drunk"—"repenting"—"I got Jack to get you inside—" The phrases burnt themselves on his brain. She had given him a great shock. He felt meaner than a worm in her presence.

She seemed to read into the debasement he was experiencing.

"I sent you a letter," she said, and now her voice sounded tired. "Didn't you get it?"

John shook his head. Her stateliness was crushing.

"You've got to marry me, now, he said, almost brutally. "The village rings about us."

"Let them talk," said Elizabeth. But the colour wavered up again in her face. He saw a tear on her eyelash, and knew it for pride.

"Besides," he added, "I've put the banns up."

She looked at him like a trapped thing.

Mrs. Peel tapped at the door.

"Come to your suppers, you two," said she, mother-in-law daubed thickly on once more.

Elizabeth waited until Mrs. Peel was out of earshot, then she said, very slowly, "I don't want talking about —any more than you—John Stone. I'll keep your house for you, and look after Mary's baby. That was all I ever meant to do when I said "yes.""

"But supposing you ever meet anyone you—care—for," said John.

He was acutely conscious of the turn of the tables. The magnanimity of her crushed him. He was the trapped one, now. Hers was the favour. He admired her more and more, whilst he liked her less and less. This kind of generosity; he thought, was a masculine attribute. Hence, whilst he did not abandon his intention to make her marry him, his stumbling half-apology for doing so.

Elizabeth smiled. She shook her head definitely. Then, as she caught his gaze on her face, she blushed.

"There is no chance of that," she said, in a subdued tone, and the remembrance of the time when she had shown him a great past sorrow, in his kitchen, came back to him.

He noticed that she did not look at him. Her stateliness was shed from her. An anxiously tremulous look passed over her countenance. Then she turned the door-knob. He followed her out.

"Tha'll miss the jumble sale, Elizabeth," said Mrs. Peel, "but there's a day to-morn."

After supper Elizabeth put little Mary to bed. When she came down John was sitting in her father's chair. Mrs. Peel was patching Jack's shirt sleeves.

"Let's have a walk out," said John.

He waited whilst Elizabeth put her hat and wrapper on.

The moon was rising for Jack Peel. That young man had been too impatient to wait for supper.

John and Elizabeth walked through the little village. Children were called in this past hour. A few women were sweeping their flags, lest it rain in the night and leave "muck" behind. A new set of bell ringers were practising a peal in the old church tower. Half the round of the moon showed over a grey hill.

As they approached Letty Fairbody's door, John took Elizabeth's hand and pulled it into its conventional place. It lay there, quite unhappily. He noticed that she made an excuse to put her wrapper straight to get it away from him.

They walked through the fields, half-way to Niffleigh and back. The meadows were glorious. They paused once to watch a young foal with its mother. John felt that he ought to help Elizabeth over the stiles, but could not, somehow. She got over quite well without him, but once her dress caught a loose side stone in the loose wall, and John made a move towards her assistance.

"Thanks," she said, gravely.

All about them was the gloaming. Sometimes a bat flitted close to their heads. Whilst John realised as they walked on and on, that he had not put the question he had come out to put. They passed a pair of lovers once, in the tender gloom of a lane, where dog-rose and guelder-rose were in full bloom. Whisperings followed them. Going up the brow that led down on the other side to their village, John saw that Elizabeth faltered.

"Let us rest," he advised.

He realised that this must have been a hard day for her, that even a cast-iron woman might have bent under it.

They sat down by the wayside. Even in the dusk her face looked pale and tired, some of its big calm disturbed.

"I'm—sorry I—got drunk—and talked on the path," he said, lamely.

She smiled, then, turning her face full upon him, "Don't worry," she said.

"But—I am," said John, earnestly.

The tremulous anxiety he had noted in the parlour passed over her face again. There was a short silence. Elizabeth felt that John Stone expected some answer to his troubled confession.

"If it hurt me at all," she told him, "it was a hurt that soon passed away." With which she rose to her feet.

They plodded their way up the hill. It was as they descended, in sight of the village with its twinkling home lights, that John put his question.

"When are you coming to keep house for me, Elizabeth?" he asked.

"At your convenience," answered Elizabeth, calmly.

"When the banns are out, then," he said. She bent her head.

"I could clean it through for you, then, before the feast," she said, meditatively. She was alluding to his house.

"I hadn't thought of that," said John.

They bumped down, quite suddenly, on their village.

"You needn't work too hard," he said. "After all I can't pay you high wages."

He spoke with pre-meditation. Elizabeth was so magnanimous, he had had a half-fear that she would refuse wages. But she did not, which relieved him greatly.

"Eh! Isn't it time respectable folk were in bed?" said Letty Fairbody's voice, making them start.

John tucked Elizabeth's hand within his arm again, as he saw Letty. He did it because he had heard that the old gossip had said she had seen Elizabeth meant to hook him, before the other was cold.

"Just getting back," said John.

"Th' kettle's at the boil," said the old woman. "Won't you come in?"

To Elizabeth's surprise John; assented. But Letty's kettle was far from being at the boil. They had been in ten minutes when it began to sing, and Letty had had to poke sticks under it, whilst in between the poking of the sticks her sharp eyes had been watching them.

"So tha'rt tryin' again, John," she remarked at supper-table.

John nodded. He admired the unblushing calmness of Elizabeth.

"Well, they say th' second wife sits on the reight knee, 'Lizabeth," said Letty, "I hope it'll prove true, that's a'."

Elizabeth smiled and raised her cup of tea, quite steadily.

"I don't see why we shouldn't get on," she remarked, cheerfully.

"Well, you've one bairn to start wi', that's more'n most," said Letty with a smile.

"How has the jumble sale gone on?" said Elizabeth, evasively.

The conversation on the jumble sale did not last long, for Letty would switch back on the subject of themselves.

"It'll put hope into some o' th' left ones, 'Lizabeth gettin' off," said Letty. "I remember thy mother sayin', 'Lizabeth, that tha could go on hoapin'. An' one as is in her grave were warm an' wick, then."

John pushed his chair from the table. He cast a glance at Elizabeth's face, impassive, but a little worn looking.

"We won't keep you up, Letty," he said.

But she followed them to the door. It was ten minutes before they got away from her doorstep, and her voice still called out little sentences as they disappeared into the dusk.

John had so acted that Letty could not have the impression that the "love" was all on Elizabeth's side. He was going to explain partly why he had taken Elizabeth in to eat a second supper, but a woman came rushing towards them through the dusk.

"'Lizabeth!" she gasped. For the cottage light had fallen full upon Elizabeth. The woman was in her night attire, her hair streamed about her.

John Stone took off his coat, gave it to Elizabeth, and went on ahead.

This was the third time within a month that Joe Crowther had turned his wife out like this.

Elizabeth and Joe's wife passed on, Elizabeth shielding the woman as well as she could from the gaze of door-standers. John watched them pass, from the shadow of his own door. He heard Mrs. Peel open hers, and say "Where's John?" and then, explanations from Elizabeth, then indignation from Mrs. Peel, and Joe Crowther's wife passed in to tell her tale of woe.

John Stone felt sleepless—with his old ache for sleep that would not come on him again this night. But when all the village was dark, and asleep, he saw the light in the Peels' parlour. He saw shadows of Elizabeth and of the couch being turned into a bed, and the drooping outline of Crowther's wife.

"What would you do, 'Lizabeth, if you were me?" wailed Mrs. Crowther.

She was a poor creature, and Elizabeth flinging a sheet, appeared a goddess beside her. John could not help but watch them and listen.

"I should pray," came Elizabeth's quiet answer.

"I've prayed," sobbed Mrs. Crowther, "Every night on my bare, bended knees. I've prayed for all these years."

Elizabeth's figure-shadow emerged from the flappings of the sheet-shadow. John realised that she had a glorious silhouette.

"I should go on praying," said Elizabeth, "but when he came home, an' ill-used me, I'd let him get to sleep, an' stitch him up in the sheet, an' beat him well."

"Would you, 'Lizabeth?" moaned Mrs. Crowther.

Elizabeth's shadow gravely nodded its head.

"I couldn't," said Mrs. Crowther.

"If ever you want help—" said Elizabeth, meaningly.

Then silence fell. John withdrew into his own house. He was further oppressed by the great qualities of Elizabeth Peel, but they were qualities that had never appealed to him in a woman.

How quiet and dead his home looked as he lit the gas. A mouse scampered off the table as he made the light. He sat down and stared at Mary's empty chair. He thought of the little shadow her figure used to make on the wall. Mary had been something to "care for."

He sat brooding on the blow that had taken her from him. Then he realised that it would be better for him when Elizabeth came. Never would he need to come creeping into a dead house like a wandering ghost.

Elizabeth would look up as he. came in, at least, with house-keeperly welcome, and there would be the baby, the baby who had appealed to him when he was pondering leaving her.

He went to bed to dream that Elizabeth was stitching him in a sheet in the Long Fields, whilst all Little Hareton stood by, laughing, and he tried to get out by cutting it with his big toe-nail, which woke him up. On the opposite side of the wall he heard Elizabeth singing, very softly, to little Mary, trying to coax her to go to sleep. Little Mary did not want to sleep, either. Sometimes Elizabeth spoke in a very firm way to the baby, whereupon Mary cried "Goo-gurl- ee-e!" not in the least deceived. At last, though, the crooning died away, the baby noises ceased. Dawn was coming up.

The mad throstle got as excited as if it was his first dawn.

That morning John Stone called in to drink a cup of tea with Jack before going to the foundry.

Elizabeth, yet sleepy-looking, cut the two men slabs of her currant loaf, and put sugar in their tea.

Every morning afterwards he called. Jack and he always left the house together. Always Elizabeth gave them that warning to close the door gently, so as not to wake the baby, and John saw her making her mother a cup of tea.

Little Hareton said, on hearing the banns called out, that it had always known what would happen. Living wives taunted their husbands on the fickleness of man. Old women said they wouldn't have believed a Stone wouldn't have given his first time to get cold, before he took a second. Bella Stone wrote, somewhat to that effect. John was a good son, he gave no back-word, but he felt the irony of it keenly.

He saw himself as he appeared in the eyes of others, faithless in appearance, but in the depths of his heart he knew that his love for the little wife whom he had tried to shelter from the least pain, had never been so strong or so pure as now—when Elizabeth Peel was coming to share his solitude. He had realised that in taking Elizabeth Peel "to wife," at least legally, he had set up a buffer between himself and any other woman. It was a vow of celibacy he was swearing in that old church, where he had married Mary, with Elizabeth Peel holding him to it.

There was no thought in his heart that in years to come they might drift together. They had walked out twice in each week, for three weeks, and always her hand lay stiffly on his arm. Whilst as he sometimes observed her face, when it was meditative, he could see that over-gravity which told she was thinking of that old disappointment.

When he spoke at such times she would start, and look at him half-fearfully. He knew that whatever happened, she would never change, so that in that respect they were equals. It was something in common at least, he told himself.

On the evening before the wedding morn he went to see Mary's grave. Already the weeds were growing there. He plucked them away and set pansies there, white pansies, casting out sweetness. To-morrow he should pass along that path to the church-door. He stood looking down on the grave. Just about four feet of clay divided him from Mary. As he thought of it, the same sense of corruption that had shaken him sober, when the rat ran away in the moonshine, shook him again when he was sober. Involuntarily he moved a step away. Then he went back, a troubled look on his face.

Should a man have that sense of corruption when thinking of his beloved dead? He did not know. He put the thought aside hurriedly.

He tried to think of Mary as he had seen her in the house, but all in vain. Always, it seemed to him now, a corpse lay between him and Mary, the living Mary, since he had looked on that still countenance.

He thought of old Nathan Stone, who had been a widower twenty-five years and always spoke of his Alice as though she still lived, and apparently never remembered her as a corpse. But he set it down as a difference in temperament, and to a lessening of faith.

That night he sat late with the little ring in his hand, the ring that had been the least in the shop, yet was for ever slipping off Mary's finger. Its pathetic smallness brought a lump to his throat. That which he had bought for Elizabeth was twice as large. He recalled Elizabeth's expression yet, as he had asked measure her finger. She had measured her own finger, and handed him the measurement.

Chapter VI

The wedding

On a bright Saturday afternoon the white winding road leading up to Little Hareton Church was speckled by people all going in one direction. They were going to see Elizabeth Peel married, and as they went, those over thirty observed to each other, half in jest, half in earnest, "We munnot give up yet. Who'd ha' thought she'd get off!"

Whilst all about the cawing of the rooks mixed in with the unquiet, human voices.

Joe Crowther's wife, white and thin, was with Letty Fairbody and a little fat woman who kept the oldest fashioned shop in Little Hareton. This old woman, though Elizabeth did not know it, had been the chief instrument in getting her off the shelf. Sarah Briggs was as good as the bell-man for spreading gossip any day. It was she to whom Mrs. Peel had blabbed.

Letty and she were talking of John Stone.

"He's been up last neet an' put fresh flowers on th' grave," remarked Granny. "Pansies too. A sad waste. Flowers to the dead, an' thorns to the wick—that's how we do in this world. I'm not allus scrubbin' th' grave-stones round my mon's head, but he were kept clean whilst he were wick, an' never got a bed-sore though he were bed-fast two years.—Ay. 'Tis a fearful waste o' hard-earned brass, John stickin' them flowers on top of a corpse that can't appreciate 'em."

Liza Crowther, the amateur boxer's wife, sighed.

She couldn't imagine Joe bringing her flowers, either alive or dead.

They walked on until they came to the Peel vault, that ponderous, awe-inspiring thing crowned with a pinnacle of grey granite. It had been reared when the Peels had more money than sense.

Granny Sharp had been a great friend of Elizabeth's grandmother buried under it these ten years.

"If Betty could get up from under here," said Granny, "she'd be proud this day. She left 'Lizabeth them four houses, an' a bit of brass besides. Ay, she'd ha' been proud. But th' Lord knows best— maybe!" Though her voice was dubious.

Then she broke off.

"They're here!" she said, excitedly.

There was a rush from the rest of the crowd.

Mothers picked up their babies, flappers stopped talking and giggling—those reading old names on old graves left the dead to watch this bit of throbbing human life.

Jack Peel and his sweetheart, Letty, stepped out of the cab, Letty clad in blue silk, very red and perspiring of face.

"It'll be thee next, Letty," said somebody, with the genial familiarity engendered by village life.

"She's in black!" gasped an old woman who had been peeping inside the cab.

A little windy murmur of the news went through the crowd.

"Mind these eggs!" called somebody.

For there was such a rush round the cab the bride-to-be scarce had room to set her foot.

Elizabeth Peel stepped out.

Calm of face, with her hair in her usual five-year behind-the-times fashion, there was not the least sign of emotion.

"Married in black you'll wish yourself back," one woman whispered to another. It was in so loud a whisper that bride and bridegroom heard it. Looking down nervously, John Stone saw a little smile flit over Elizabeth's face. He had a vague feeling of irritation that she had clad herself in black, though his common-sense told him that she had done so out of respect for Mary.

He took her by the arm.

They climbed the worn, cracked steps. He noticed the things growing in the cracks of the pathway, just as he had done when he married Mary. But whereas he had carried with him a palpitating memory of that former scene, he saw it this second time with no other emotion than a feeling of irritation against all this staring, this morbid, foolish, curious human interest.

"A rare bonnie lass," said an old man, quaveringly. "As bonnie as thee, Joan, fifty years sin'."

The old woman who looked as if she was helping to prop the old man up, laughed in the loud, pleased way of the deaf, showing a pair of toothless jaws.

The crowd laughed, too, alive to the incident. It laughed in a softened, pleased way that lit up its face.

Whilst John hurried Elizabeth on.

Fifty years!

He trembled at the thought of living so long, felt one of those fresh spasms of agony that had touched him over the young dead, those desires to lie down and let the world go by. But they had reached the porch door, now. He noticed that Elizabeth's hand hung somewhat slackly, and hitched it up mechanically. A faint scent of roses floated to him. He knew whence it came. His foot almost touched Mary's resting place.

"Mary, the beloved wife of John Stone—"

The little words sung themselves over in his heart, his brain. How she had trembled when she had passed through this porch as Elizabeth was passing now. He glanced at Elizabeth. A lamp-post could have looked no more unmoved.

70

The sunlight of the outer world became a thing that was broken up through the tender blues, deep rose, orange, and purples of stained windows. The opening and shutting of pew-doors, an old woman coughing feebly, and the voice of the minister putting the momentous question—and soon, very soon, it was all over.

Whilst Elizabeth's big calm voice saying that she took him, John Stone as her husband, became another item to contrast with Mary's saying of the words. The minister had to say to Mary, very gently, "Speak a little louder, please." Elizabeth Peel spoke as if she was buying at market.

°Sign here—"

There was the old, bewildering repetition.

Only yesterday, so it seemed, he and Mary had gone into the vestry, with the same squeaky door, and Mary had signed in that book, her hand shaking, and making a blot and looking awfully scared at having made it—and full of tears. Elizabeth signed as legibly as to a grocery receipt. Her big, clear handwriting almost walked off the page. Of all the world of women he should never have chosen Elizabeth, he told himself for the hundredth time.

Out again, down the path, past Mary's grave, catching sight of the Peel obelisk through the trees, whilst the disquieting thought as to where Elizabeth would sleep when she died, would worry him.

"Much happiness, Mrs. Stone," said a pleasant voice.

It was Tim Hardacre.

Then there was a laugh.

Tim had kissed the bride—with such hearty goodwill that it brought forth that knowing laughter.

"Well, I wouldn't let another chap kiss my wife," said one of the crowd chaffingly, to John.

He glowered.

Tim held out his hand for the shilling earned by the one quick enough to kiss a bride before the bridegroom.

"I didn't think tha' could do aught like that, Tim," said a comely lass, looking as if she would not much mind if he repeated the offence, changing the victim.

"Live and learn," said Tim.

"Live and learn," said a part of John's brain, which seemed to be forming habits of repeating trivial things like an automatic machine.

"Tha'rt lucky!" said Tim, nodding sagely.

"Let's get out of this," muttered John, looking at Elizabeth. He found that she had blushed and set it down to Tim Hardacre's kiss. Whilst he was perplexed by a random thought. Elizabeth could blush like a girl. What would happen if she met some man who cared for her, and for whom she cared? He stole a look at her. She was pale again now. He put aside the thought that Elizabeth Peel would, under any circumstances, drag a man's name through the dust, eyeing her with grudging admiration.

"Dried up, mother?" asked Jack Peel, as they re-entered the house, to go through the farce of the bridal tea.

For Mrs. Peel had realised all at once that her daughter was going out of her old home, and every time she had been on the verge of breaking down again Jack had said, "Water-works on again, mother."

She gave him a playful push now.

Then she said to John Stone, "She's bin a good lass to me, John. If she's as good a wife to thee, tha'll ha' no cause to grummel. The Lord do to thee, John, as tha' does by her."

Then they sat down, and ate pink jellies, and white blancmanges, and seed cake, and currant cake, and red ham, and one thing after another—as if this also was a most important part they had to go through, and someone teased the bride for not eating much, and said she was so full of love good stuff could go a-begging, but that, after all, it was quite natural.

The comedy-tragedy was over at length.

Mrs. Peel would insist on giving Elizabeth all her little possessions, the presents of friends and people, mostly old people, many of them dead. A celery glass, a clock that would not go, a pot with a child with blue eyes and red cheeks painted on one side and on the other "A present for a good girl," a housewife, work-box, and a pair of blue and gilt ornaments won by James Peel for hitting the bull's eye at the fair.

"Here, John, take hold," said Mrs. Peel.

She gave him the clock and the good-girl cup.

They went out—to the house they had now to live in.

"Come in," said John, managing to unlock the door.

Turning unexpectedly he found a sudden gleam of humour in Elizabeth's eye. It was funny. It was—. He put the thing in strange masculine form. But that she should laugh at it. Humour, according to John, was also a masculine attitude. Mary had always had to have a joke explained to her.

He rattled the key into the lock.

They passed in, set the things they carried on the table, stirred up the fire, and Elizabeth went out to bring in the baby from a neighbour's.

"I believe she knows you," said John, watching the baby being undressed.

The words sounded fearfully bare to him,

"H'm," said Elizabeth. She had a safety pin in her mouth.

He watched her bathe the baby, feed her, the fire light flickering over the two, the big, calm woman and the tiny baby. Whilst he felt that he ought to say something, that the silence could be cut with a knife and fork, save for little Mary's "la-la-la," at intervals.

When all was finished, Elizabeth held out the child at arm's length, for him to kiss.

His brain repeated that "Live and learn," of Tim's, with its irritating automatic movement.

He brushed the child with his mouth, watched the woman's tall shadow pass from the fire-lit wall.

What on earth should they talk about when she came down?

Elizabeth soon cleared the problem for him when she came down, very softly.

"If you'll light the gas, Mr. Stone, we'll talk things over," she said, in a business-like way.

In that kitchen where he had talked things over with Mary, it seemed only yesterday night, after their wedding—they talked things over. The things they talked about were wages, hours, and what John liked to eat, what he did not like to eat. Whilst the contrasting picture, tender, fire-lit, with Mary on his knee, made this one more prosaic.

"In ordinary fairness I want to do my best," said Elizabeth, "since you cannot discharge me." She smiled.

John felt annoyed again at her sense of humour.

But meeting her eye—his own smiled.

"What do you think you're worth, 'Lizabeth?" he asked, despairingly.

"I don't think you'll be far out of it at seven shillings a week," said Elizabeth. "And I always want market days free, so you'll have to pour your tea out yourself those days."

"Seven shillings seems so little—" said John. It did. He had a sense of being under a debt. Elizabeth's handling of the baby was such a contrast to the hireling he had employed.

So the price was fixed.

But John Stone had not the remotest idea that for seven shillings he had also got a woman's heart thrown into the bargain.

Next morning, as he heard her come from the room that had been Mary's and his, he noted the steady foot-sound. Elizabeth Peel fall in love! No. He had got a treasure of a housekeeper.

"Breakfast is ready—John," she called at the foot of the stairs.

Last night it had been "Mr. Stone". He knew that she was being diplomatic. One's neighbours might hear heart-beats through these thin walls, if they listened long enough.

But she had spoken his name as soullessly as if she had said "Dripping."

"Any letters, Elizabeth?" he asked, when he got down. Whilst he was conscious that she had done something to the house that made it look pounds better.

There were three letters.

His mother had banged her leg on the tidy, and the skin threatened to break. He broke into a mental sweat at the idea of anything worse setting in. If Bella Stone came to be cared for there—! Well, it would not be easy to hide things from Bella Stone— in a house of two up, and two down!—Of course there was the attic.!

A programme for a pastoral play in Shirley Woods.

Elizabeth answered his query as to whether they should go in the negative, until he reminded her that they would have to go out sometimes together. Then—he bit his lip at her acquiescence.

"There's a letter!" he cried,, after reading the third.

He tossed it towards her with a freedom unusual towards a housekeeper. She: took it in a manner that reminded him of their respective dignities, very careful not to touch fingers as she handed it back to him.

Dick Burnham, cosmopolitan, artist, Dick, ever dabbling in new phases and experiences of life, had invited himself to their home.

"Shall I ask him to come, then?" asked John.

Two grey eyes reminded him that such a question was unnecessary in his own house, when he paid for her services at the rate of seven shillings.

He wrote Dick to come as soon as he could. It was only after he dropped it into the pillar-box that he remembered the two-roomed "up". But Dick was not his mother. If Dick guessed, he would say nothing. He even thought he might tell Dick. Dick would laugh.

He came back from posting the letter.

"It's gone," he said. "He'll drop on us at any time. I shall sleep down here on the sofa. Back for dinner at twelve, 'Lizabeth."

"Yes—John," she said.

On the mat he murmured to himself;: "Yes—Dripping."

He had great difficulty not to burst into laughter. Funny? It was howling! Whilst, though he did not realise it—he had not thought of Mary this morning.

***

John Stone was later than usual. The last hooter had gone. Little. Mary was abed; Elizabeth was very tired. It had been a day of fierce heat, There had been rumours that the foundry men would not work. Elizabeth had resented the fact of John Stone having to be in that hellish place on such a day.

She had been very busy. But she was always busy, dreading only those moments when she sat with empty folded hands, realising that her heart folded itself emptily, too.

From the pinnacle on which she had placed John Stone, many things had brought him down to the real world of men. The sight of her god, shaving, making faces at himself in the glass, had made her want to laugh. He hated the smell of onions. He liked sugar. He was hard, blind, tactless.

She hustled a photograph album out of sight as she heard the creak of the gate—the album where he looked out at her, a little boy with a mop of curls and—the same solemn determined eyes.

It seemed to her that he spent a long time scraping his feet on the mat. When his feet finally left it, his steps sounded uneven and lagging. Was he ill?

He came forward as if wishing to evade her eyes, her presence.

When Elizabeth poured out his tea for him she discovered the reason for John's wish to edge as far from her as possible without breaking himself in two. John had been drinking. Was he going to go the way of that other Stone whose name was a byword in the village? If he did, would not the village lay it to her blame?

Even whilst she thought this, and determined that it was more than she would put up with, John looked at her as if he had perceived her discovery of his having been in the inn. There was a challenge in his eyes. She was almost expectant of the words that left his lips.

"Well, what about it?"

As he looked at her, mischief in his eyes, she realised that he was asking her what she had to do with any thing he did, that she was only housekeeper.

She smoothed out a crease of the tablecloth.

Her eyes met his without flinching.

"If I call you 'John' because you are supposed to be my husband," she said quietly, "you won't drink—because I am supposed to be your wife. I won't be set down as a woman so remiss that her man takes to drink."

The foolish little light was in his eyes.

"It is the truth," he said, "that I didn't drink before Mary died."

"I shan't stand it," said 'Lizabeth.

77

She brought Dick Burnham's letter and set it by his plate.

He opened and read it.

"Dick's coming," he said, in relieved tones. "Sent word at the last minute, too. These unconventional folk are a bit selfish. But then Dick's worth it. About your way of saying 'John', 'Lizabeth. Practise it. It falls short of what it ought to be said like, by a week-old wife. Put a little warmth in it. It's awkward but necessary, that we both make an effort to look more like it. You might try leaning your hand on my shoulder at times —see, like this—now, that won't do. You'd give the show away if you drew away like that. Now, put it there. Not so stiff!"

He had taken hold of the hand with the brand-new wedding-ring on it, and placed it on his shoulder. There was no suspicion of mirth showing on his face. "You should smile," he told her.

Elizabeth smiled—somewhat wanly.

"Because Dick has sharp eyes," he said. "Anyhow, we've to-morrow to rehearse."

Elizabeth took her hand from his shoulder.

"Give Dick the best view," he said. And the attic— that would do for his easel and paints and brushes. There's a cupboard in it—with things Mary brought from home. Perhaps you could make it look decent. Have you been up in the attic?"

She shook her head. She had not yet had time to put straight that room of the green door, though she had closed the door once, because the wind blew it to and fro.

"I'll look up after tea," she said.

"Mary was always frightened when she thought Dick was coming," said John. "And he always changed his mind and never came. She didn't like what I said of him, somehow. He frightened her with his free ways, I reckon. She'd met him twice somewhere, before we were married."

"I shall do my best to make him enjoy his visit," said Elizabeth in her most housekeeperly style. Upon which John drew into his shell again.

When tea was over, he set her first seven shillings piled up on the table-corner. Elizabeth placed beside him a list of the week's purchases.

Both declared themselves satisfied.

"Don't wait up for me if I'm late," said John.

He went down the passage, hands in pockets.

Elizabeth studied his back, and found it unreadable. The door closed.

Whilst the fear of knowing whether he had gone to the inn warred with the housekeeper's calm—the calm of the hireling who makes the meals, brushes a man's clothes, but neither carries his purse nor inquires into his whereabouts.

Disillusion followed disillusion. Must she now see him sink lower than the beasts of the fields? That was the thought that filled her with dull horror, as she peeped inside little Mary's cot. A dimpled arm a dimpled leg, were thrown over the coverlet. Elizabeth covered them up again, and with broom in hand went upstairs to that attic room that was to be the artist's studio, from what John Stone had told her.

Three hours of hard work transformed the bleak room into one of primitive beauty. Whilst as Elizabeth worked, she knew that Dick Burnham was coming because he could not keep away. Like a man who had committed a crime, he was drawn irresistibly to the spot.

The task finished, she went down and into her mother's house. Mrs. Peel had preferred to keep the baby for a couple of hours.

Elizabeth bathed the dancing, dimpled Mary in the fire glow. If she had needed any compensation for the somewhat undignified position she held in this house, she found it in the child.

She did quite ridiculous things as she dried John Stone's baby, kissed the pink feet, pretended to bite the tiny toes, to the gurgling delight of the infant, who said "gain" times innumerable, without getting weary. Then Elizabeth sat feeding her, to the hungry cry that made the big woman smile, whilst she uttered soft reproof against impatience, that could not wait until the spoon came out of the basin.

It was only when the little one was tucked in bed, and Elizabeth stood a moment, candle in hand, taking in the picture of a child asleep, that she realised that she was very tired.

Sitting in John's chair—never yet had she sat in Mary's—with her feet in John's battered slippers, she fell sleep.

How long she had slept she could not tell. She was awakened, in a dark kitchen, by the violent flinging back of the front door.

"Anybody live here?" yelled a voice, loud enough to have awakened the dead.

"S—hush!" warned Elizabeth.

Half-dazed, she made a light. They came in.

"Sit thee down," went on the loud voice, speaking to some other person. "Sit thee down, man. Tha'rt as welcome at hoam as th'art anywhere else. He! he! We're allus at home when we're wanted. What art whinin' about, lad? It's a rare fine world. What ails it? Tha'rt at hoam, aren't ta? Cheer up, man, cheer up. Here's thy missus comin' to gie thee a kiss. Ay. An' a rare fine lass she is, too."

Elizabeth stood in the doorway looking at the speaker, Joe Crowther, wife-beater, boxer, and jack-of-all-trades.

Between them they got John on the sofa. Joe sat down.

"Get out o' that chair," Elizabeth commanded the pugilist. He was sitting in Mary Stone's chair that was only used for little Mary's day-time slumbers.

He sniggered aggressively. But finally, as she did not move her eye from him, he got up, saying apologetically, "He'd ha' got locked up but for me, missus."

"Thanks," said Elizabeth, with irony. "Won't your wife be uneasy about you?"

"It's the easiest time of her life when I'm out," confided Joe, with a grin.

"You ought to be ashamed of yourself," said Elizabeth.

Hundreds of folk had said the same time and time to Joe, from navvies to missionaries. But none of them had said it quite like Elizabeth. Joe Crowther coughed a little, then said, "I'm goin', missus. I wasn't allus what I am to-day. At his age—not so bad."

He spoke a maudlin greeting to John Stone, who murmured something about "old pal" and went out.

Elizabeth remembered that her mother might be bringing back borrowed loaf tins. She heard the gate creak. In panic at the situation that might ensue, Elizabeth turned out the light, poked up the fire, and covered John with a shawl.

"Eh—what a day it's bin agen!" said Mrs. Peel, canting in.

"Don't make a noise," said Elizabeth, in a whisper. "John's asleep. He's tired out."

Mrs. Peel flopped into a chair by the dresser end.

"Eh, I'm glad," she said. "Somebody'd been tellin' our Jack 'at he were drunk. It's queer how tales do get out. But I'm glad that's a mistake."

Then she said, "Isn't it hot enough without havin' that shawl on him?"

Elizabeth parried this as well as she could.

"I'm awful tir't, too," observed Mrs. Peel. "I think I'll be goin'." But she made no effort to depart.

But at last Mrs. Peel went—leaving her daughter almost sweating with the strain, for John had moved once or twice, and she had feared the truth would out.

To be looked on as a woman whose husband got drunk within a week of marrying her! Elizabeth Peel was seven-eighths pride.

When she re-entered the kitchen, after locking the door behind her mother, John scrambled into a sitting position on the couch.

He met Elizabeth's calm eyes.

"I'm not drunk," he informed her several times. "I can move my little finger."

She was glad he did not shout. Her mother and Jack were on the other side of that wall.

"Mary's dead, isn't she, Elizabeth?" he asked, after a pause. "Mary's dead, I say, isn't she?"

His voice rose so that Elizabeth was constrained to say "Yes, Mary is dead," to stop him from shouting.

John went on in maudlin fashion for ten minutes—then a savage mood took him.

"Elizabeth," he said, "I'm as good as thee."

She made no answer.

Her silence seemed to irritate him beyond endurance. He walked unsteadily towards her.

"Elizabeth," he told her. "I dare—kiss thee."

There was no other meaning conveyed in his way of saying the words than the bare assertion that he was brave enough.

"Sit down, Mr. Stone," said Elizabeth.

She was darning a sock and looking over the top of it—her lips firm, one on the other—her expression mildly indignant.

"In my own house," said John, with a dignity that became laughable, since his legs could not support it. "I shall si' down—I shall si' down, when I like."

After his prior attack she was glad to be reminded of her hireling position.

Even as she heaved a sigh of relief he came nearer to her.

"Get out of my light, John," she said.

But her face had whitened.

"Ay," he said, with bitter emphasis, "I did get in thy light, didn't I, Elizabeth?" He had read a symbolism into her statement that she could not see through him.

Then he said, "How if I won't?"

She looked like the splendidly pale creature who had told him she would never marry him—in that spotless parlour.

"I dare—kiss—thee!" he said.

She bent aside to get the light on the hole she was darning, ignoring him, but with her brows knitted.

"An' I will," he said, suddenly, and seized her arm roughly.

At the glance of her eye, under that frowning magnificence of brow, his grasp slackened.

"I could ha' done, 'Lizabeth," he told her, lamely.

She laid her work down on the table, made his supper, but not her own. It was as though she said she would not sit at table with him, as he was. He watched her take her candle, gather up the things needed for little Mary.

"Night, Elizabeth," he said, drowsily.

He rose from the chair into which he had sat whilst she made his meal.

"No ill will," he said, consolingly. "No ill will."

Then he repeated, "Good night, Elizabeth."

"Good night, John," answered Elizabeth.

The calm of her large countenance was broken up for a swift moment.

Before he had realised it—almost before the passionate impulse had sprung up like a typhoon—she had struck him full across the face with her flat hand.

Then he stood staring at her, sobered.

She also stood—transfixed with terror at this new self of hers, trembling with horror at having struck—her man.

She vanished with the candle, leaving him staring after her. Her breath was coming in quick sobs. The Amazon was gone. Only the woman remained—frightened at her own daring. What would her mother think, if she knew? What would Little Hareton think? What would Mary Stone have thought?

She felt bruised—breaking—under this ironic net of circumstances in which she was caught. She was losing her bearings, drifting away from the hard and fast rules of Little Hareton.

The soft breathing of the child came to her. She lay awake quite a long time, until John's stumbling steps came past the door. Then easier of mind, she watched the stars shining through the upper half of the window.

Through the open window came the scent of the flowers from the garden, where she had buried those letters from Dick Burnham, in the pretence of setting roots.

She was wondering how it was that some women had the power to win the hearts and souls of men, whilst others—

She had seen John Stone "cleaning out" at dusk, almost guiltily, for Mary, at the risk of being dubbed a "Molly".

The problem was beyond her. But, at least, she told herself, she would never stop to try. The barrier of pride had grown stronger in a night.

Elizabeth was the most feminine of women, despite her size and her clear brain. She believed in the natural history law, of the male doing the wooing. She had perceived John's illusion, on that night in the little parlour, in which he had believed she had been glad to net him.

If ever he won her over it would be a rough trail she would lead him, over that pride of hers, and a very different trail from that he had followed when he won the passive Mary who had taken him because Dick Burnham would not "settle down".

John got up early, because he felt very bad.

Elizabeth heard him. He sounded very bad. But she did not get up.

Just before the foundry whistle blew, she heard a voice say, "A cup of tea, Mrs. Stone."

Then the cup rattled as it was set on the bedroom step.

"Thanks," said Elizabeth.

He tramped down.

When he had gone, she crept out of bed, opened the door, and took in the tea. She took it in with the sarcastic thought that slapping a man's face did him good.

Then she imagined the gentle Mary slapping a man's face.

She drank the tea, which was smoked and too sweet. There was a biscuit in the saucer. She ate that, and crept down into bed with the baby. She pulled the little hand across her face, and closed her eyes at the touch of it.

Then she fell asleep.

The milk-man woke her.

As she set the can on the table, she saw a scrap of paper with something written upon it.

She read it. It merely said, "It shall not happen again, Elizabeth,"

Elizabeth crumpled the apology up and tossed it into the fire. Then she set to work to clean the house, in which she was not mistress.

It was Friday morning.

As she swept the flags, Joe Crowther went past, a pigeon-basket in his hand. He nodded, smiled, but the smile tapered off as he met Elizabeth's look.

"Stone'll be henpecked if he doesn't mind," was his thought. "Catch mine doing it on me." Whilst as he swaggered on to Dimpleton, he did not know that as Elizabeth watched his back, she was scheming how to strike a blow for that long-suffering, spaniel-hearted mate of his.

Joe had been left to God twenty years. Elizabeth was going to take a hand. She might not be able to manage her own husband—and didn't intend to try, but Crowther's wife, with the "going-home" look on her face, had now Elizabeth behind her.

When Elizabeth really set herself, she didn't talk about a thing, she did it.

Chapter VII

Mrs. Stone seeks "House and harbour"

The little house Elizabeth tended was in constant expectation of Dick Burnham's visit for three days. Which is only to say, that if a spotliness can be added to spotliness, it happened to John Stone's domicile. What amazed John was the amount of work Elizabeth could get through, with a minimum of noise. He always came into his house from the foundry, feeling that he had stepped into utter peace, wherein the baby crooned happily, the little silver bells on the pink rattle jingled merrily, where the black shining kettle was always singing, and Elizabeth moved around, a large calm presence.

After the quivering heat of the blasting furnace, the shuddering pulsed floor, and the clattering of the iron-ore, it was like coming into a sanctum.

He stuck so far to his paper promise "not to do it again," as not to go to the inn for three evenings, but he was somewhat piqued to notice that Elizabeth in nowise unbended on this account.

"It's like Dick," he said, on the Saturday afternoon when he came in from the garden, to find a telegram saying Dick was not coming after all. "He could never settle a thing till the last minute, and often not at all."

Elizabeth thought of the big thing Dick had not been able to settle. She felt that she understood Dick's wavering mind, now. He wanted to come to the place where Mary had died, he wanted also to stay away, because it was painful to come.

John went back to his planting of early chrysanthemums. He had enjoyed setting the bushes, but as he had pressed the soil around the root for a moment he had a shuddering fancy that he had his hands in grave loam. It was the old feeling, the earth as a graveyard, which had visited him frequently since Mary's sudden exit, but as he lifted his head he saw Elizabeth at the window, baby in arms. They were going to Niffleigh Market.

"Dad—dad—dad!" he heard the child gurgle. Then Elizabeth seized the pudgy, wobbling little hand, and waved it at John to show they were off. No other woman could have done such a graciously intimate thing with such a sense of detaching herself utterly from the baby's father.

It was her eyes, John told himself. Not that he wanted Elizabeth to like him, but at least, for a Christian woman, she cast off an atmosphere that made a mere human man feel that he fell woefully short.

John dug fiercely into the ground. He was sure her mind was anti-Christian, though Elizabeth had been baptised in the same font as himself, in the same little old echoing church at Dimpleton. She was not moulded gently enough for a real Christian.

Whilst he thus ruminated, Elizabeth was wheeling the perambulator through the sunny, sleepy streets, where the swallows and martins were circling low.

As she walked she talked to the child. She almost wheeled the thing into Dr. Conrad.

"Room for another one in there, Elizabeth!" he could not forbear jerking his head towards the perambulator.

Elizabeth understood his genial joke, but she stiffened.

"Dear me!" thought the Doctor.

This was the second time that Elizabeth had seemed to him in danger of losing her sense of humour, but when he turned round, she also was looking round, and smiling in her old way.

Passing Joe Crowther's ramshackle house, where children's faces shewed dingily through the grimy panes, Elizabeth smiled at the ghost of a woman staring drearily out on the matted wilderness that had once been a garden.

It gave her an idea. On her way back she would call on Mrs. Crowther. Joe never came in until the inn turned out.

The sun was going down when Elizabeth wheeled the baby's carriage along the path up to the dingy doorstep.

Mrs. Crowther opened the door about two inches, murmuring an apology for the state the house was in.

Elizabeth took the baby out of the pram and walked in.

Children! There were children everywhere, grimy, half-clothed, staring at her with big eyes. Mrs. Crowther looked apology for everything.

Elizabeth sat down.

Elizabeth in her "best", the white-muslined baby on her lap, wondered if she looked like one of those awful women who take tea and red flannel to poor folk. She hoped fervently that she did not.

Mrs. Crowther was still mumbling apologies for the house.

"You should see my place on a washing day," said Elizabeth, and smiled, shaking her head, to shew that Mrs. Crowther could not possibly guess the horror of untidiness it was.

The barrier went, which says a lot for Elizabeth. She had beaten down in a minute and a half things that expert social workers cannot beat down in a generation. But she wished, oh, how she wished that there was a square yard of clean floor to seat little

Mary on, just whilst she made those hungry-eyed children tea.

"There were lovely eggs at market," said Elizabeth. "Look!"

She opened her string-bag, revealing duck eggs, pale green and gloriously large-sized.

"I'm hungry, too," said Elizabeth, sighing wearily. "Boil them, boil them all, Mrs. Crowther."

Which little fake acted very well.

Four little boys, mounted on stools, soon had their mouths quite yellow with egg, and Elizabeth valiantly tried not to mind the dirty table.

After they were gone to bed, which, said their mother, "they got in as they got out on it," meaning the beds were not made, Mrs. Crowther unfolded to Elizabeth, told her of the passage from a clean house to this sort of going on.

"A few shillin's now an' then, that's all I get," said Ish. "Even soap costs somethin' and when you've nothin', where's it to come from? What'd ya do if you'd one like that? Yours is a good 'un."

Elizabeth smiled, ignoring the last bit.

"If I told ya, ya wouldn't do it," she said, grave again.

"I get desperate sometimes," said the amateur boxer's wife. Then "Tell me," she beseeched.

Elizabeth eyed her.

"I should start at the bottom rung," she said, with emphasis, and eyed the dirty floor. "I should get a good scrubbing-brush, steal it, if I couldn't buy it, I think," with a laugh, "and get a decent standing place in the world." She held up her hand to check interruption. There was a frank, open-hearted look on her face that took the sting out of the words.

"I should get that ground there made into a garden, grow things to eat, and cook them for the children. I shouldn't bother with him at all."

Mrs. Crowther burst out here.

"I'm so glad," she said, "you didn't tell me to try an' win him." She had evidently had some of that sort of advice.

Elizabeth smiled.

"I shouldn't think of that," she said, with dignity too high for scorn.

It was true. Then she observed—

"But give the children a clear start, don't let a man—break your heart." Then she said softly, "There's yourself, you know, too."

Mrs. Crowther began to sob.

"I—never could care for myself," she whimpered. That was true.

It was the stick that had beaten her, Elizabeth told herself, yet even whilst she felt herself thankful that the gods had built her on prouder lines, she felt that here was something that made the one nobleness in this poor, chaotic life.

"And—don't let him beat you," said Elizabeth, gently. "You should never pass over insults like those."

A fire shone in her usually quiet eyes.

Mrs. Crowther went on sobbing.

"I've wanted to hit back," she avowed, "often, but he's cowled me so I've got past it. I know if I could give him one good hiding it might be the making on him. But I can't."

Whereupon Elizabeth gave her promise to come, when next Joe came home a drunken tiger, and if he hurt her, to render justice.

Then indeed, Joe's wife gave a quavering laugh.

After Elizabeth had gone, she essayed to wash the floor, but so weak from malnutrition was she, the room spun before she was half-way through. She dropped upon a chair, and found a parcel upon it. It was addressed to herself, and had a town label upon it. Elizabeth had left it for her. She took out the contents. For the first time for years she drank a cup of decent tea, and ate until she wanted no more. Then she hid the rest of the food for the children away from Joe.

When he came home he paused on the doorstep, thinking his ears deceived him. He had fancied he heard his "old hen" as he called her, singing.

He stepped into a house a shade less dirty than usual, noticed something was different about the table, without realising what it was.

Elizabeth looked several times that evening, from the front door, to see if she had the signal to go across —the lamp set in the window—but all was peaceful gloom. She went back to the making of two pairs of pants for the Crowther lads, out of John's old ones, and wondered if John would be sober when he came in. She knew that clean houses do not make traps to keep men in, and after close scrutiny of her own soul, she knew she had not been guilty of conveying such an impression to poor Mrs. Crowther.

She had just finished stitching the buttons on the finished suits, when John Stone came in. Mary had always looked up when he came in, in a quick way, like a startled bird. He had always interpreted it for eager welcome.

Elizabeth calmly ignored his coming in, only letting him see she had noticed it, by laying down her sewing and getting up very leisurely, with an attitude that said she had been about to do so before he came.

He was dead sober. He was also in a meditative mood.

Elizabeth set him cheese, bread and a dish of salad, made as only Elizabeth could make salads, the dressing being an old recipe that was a quaint reward from a dame in Dimpleton, whose grocery bag Elizabeth had carried years ago.

Sometimes John wondered that there seemed to be so much food in the house. Elizabeth could work miracles out of what his hirelings had poured down the sink, and flung in the dustbin.

He had always been conscious of eating Mary's meals, they had called for deep thought. He ate what Elizabeth prepared with a delicate perception of comfort, and did not think of it at all.

He stared at Elizabeth as she poured out the tea.

There was bad news to tell her.

He had judged her character as one that would lose possessions very bitterly. Even her economy in his house, that elegant economy which made all the difference between those shades of poverty that weigh lightly or heavily on a man, seemed to him to partake of her being a little "near" as the village would have put it. Besides, had she not taken off Mary's ring, to save its being buried?

Elizabeth could pour tea out with an air of splendour he had not noticed in any other woman. His mother, for instance, always appeared to throw it at the cup, as if she said "take it, an' ha' done wi' it." Mary always used to slop it over, through pouring it too fast. Elizabeth poured it with the true-born tea-giver's air, which is an inheritance.

John felt sorry. He decided to break the news after Elizabeth had taken her supper. Then, as he saw her drink her tea, quite unsuspicious of what he had in store for her, he began to feel hypocritical. Besides, Jack Peel knew, and would rush in at any moment. John wanted to take the edge off the blow.

"I went through Dimpleton," observed John, as a good beginning. "There's an organ recital at the church to-morrow, Ambrose Jenkins is playing."

"I'd like to hear him," Elizabeth let slip.

Then she bit her lip.

"We'll go," said John.

Then he wished he had not proposed it. When he had told her the bad news, he felt sure she would not want to go to Dimpleton.

"Ambrose is a born genius," said John, with the regretful admiration of a man who knows he is not.

He allowed Elizabeth the comfort of another half cup of tea. He also watched her eat a half-slice of bread. Once, when he had used to attend literary societies, John had heard a passage read, a description of a lady pilgrim in Chaucer's Cavalcade to Canterbury. He had forgotten the lady pilgrim's name, but he remembered one thing about her, and never saw Elizabeth eat without the similarity haunting him, until he began to feel angry at its coming into his head. "And let no crumb drop from her mouth." It haunted him even now, when he was going to tell her that she had lost three out of her four houses that her grandmother had left her.

"There was great excitement in Dimpleton," said John, cautiously creeping towards the bad news again.

"A chimney on fire," smiled Elizabeth.

John felt he could have told her better had she not smiled. It made him feel he was going to be such a brute. A woman who could not bear the thought of a thirty-shillings wedding ring being buried with the dead, how would such a woman learn that four hundred pounds of hers had been swallowed in a night?

John grew afraid, but he was midway in his task now. There was no going back.

"Oh, more than a chimney on fire," he said, gravely.

Elizabeth was looking at him now. Her calm eyes distressed him. He wondered if she would cry, and if she did, what he would do. He believed, suddenly, that if he saw Elizabeth cry, he should not be quite responsible for his actions. Even as the thought shot at lightning speed through his brain, he knew it, with bitter self-censure, as treachery, treachery to his dead.

John made a bee-line towards breaking the news. He had lost his head.

Suppose—she should cry. He averted his gaze from her face.

"You know Jim Wild?" he said.

"He lives in one of my houses/[9] said Elizabeth.

John took a moment's reprieve. He tried to be tactful.

"He was smoking a pipe, just before going to bed, in the kitchen, you know he doesn't sleep upstairs," said John. He looked at Elizabeth now.

"He's set the place on fire," she said swiftly. "Stupid man!"

She frowned down at her cup.

Before John could continue, she asked quickly, "Is anyone burnt?"

John looked at her in wonder.

"Nobody burnt," he said.

Her sigh of relief came across to him.

"Thank the Lord for that," said Elizabeth, folding her arms.

The phrase was neither Christian praise, nor scoffing, though it could easily have been either in other women. It was just human relief—most generous human relief.

"Nobody was burnt," said John, looking at her fixedly, "because the place never got on fire. Jim Wild was smoking his pipe, when he was swallowed!"

He had to look at her now. She was staring at him as though he were crazy.

"Swallowed!" she echoed.

John nodded. He was going to tell her.

"The sand-hills!" she ejaculated.

Her eyes beseeched John's. But for her eyes, she was ghastly pale.

He nodded.

"Jim's—dead?" she queried.

Her hands were striving with each other. She was whiter even than she had been in the little parlour, when she had told him she would never marry him.

"Anyone else?" she queried, squaring herself for the blow.

Even as he realised the stuff she was made of, that she had not even thought of the financial loss, her dry, anxious eyes burnt him to the quick. He knew that she did not breathe until he answered. A mute gratitude overspread her countenance, a subdued light, when he did so.

She learnt that James Wild was dead—his wife and children only saved by a miracle, it seemed, and the tenants on each side, fled, pell-mell, far away from that row of houses built behind the sand-hills that children had played on, generation after generation, but which had now slid away from under those houses.

"I suppose the other houses are badly damaged?" quoth Elizabeth.

The colour was coming back to her face, but the wincing look with which she had heard of James Wild being swallowed, yet lingered.

"Badly," said John, "but they'll forget, and live in 'em again. The sand will have shifted all, it will. Besides the foundations can be—"

"I shall never trust the sand-hills again," said Elizabeth, quietly, but firmly. "That—that little, knocker-kneed man, sitting down to smoke his evening pipe in my house, for which he has paid rent twenty years—and—it swallowed him. My house swallowed him—alive.'

She shuddered slightly. Her voice came throatily.

"But you—"

"I feel responsible," she said, with the same shuddering look of horror. "I—I must go to see Jane—and the children. Will you look after Mary?"

John made up his mind.

"You aren't going to Dimpleton alone," he said.

He asked Mrs. Peel to come in and stay.

Mrs. Peel's great worry was whether Jane could claim compensation from Elizabeth, seeing that the sand-hills were not Elizabeth's but only the houses.

Elizabeth gave her mother one look, as she allowed John to help her into her cloak. Taking a lantern, for the way to Dimpleton was treacherous by night, they departed.

The silence of the night wrapped them about. They passed through Shirley Woods, the lantern rays falling on the ghostly larches, so badly eaten by caterpillars this year, that they looked like ragamuffins. Water glistened sometimes. Bats flew over them once, attracted by Elizabeth's white hat, and John learnt that the woman of the big courage was afraid of bats. He took off his black silk funeral muffler, and covered her head gear. Then they came out on the narrow field path, stone walls loomed black, and they passed through farm-yards with barking of curs, John always feeling that he could not go fast enough for Elizabeth.

They were approaching the stepping-stones, on the middle-most of which Mary had once screamed, going dizzy so that he had to carry her. That was how she had won his heart.

Elizabeth strode after the man carrying the lantern, whose flickering rays made the water-depths seem deeper than they actually were.

"Mind that next stone," he called to her.

The night echoes repeated his last word. He had got six paces away, when he realised that Elizabeth was not following. He fancied she could not see, and shone the lantern light in her direction. The expression of her face flashed at him at once, just as the lantern gleam caught it. Elizabeth was afraid—just as Mary had been afraid—to cross that wide gap between the two stones.

97

"Wait a minute! I'm coming," John called to her.

She seemed to realise his intention. John was coming to carry her.

"I can get across," she said, with something defensive in her voice. "It's only—the skirts."

Then, she was close behind him. But he knew she was trembling, and also what panic it was that had goaded her past her fear of the water. He had a momentary feeling of chagrin.

Then they were going along, on the straight road, to Dimpleton. The village, usually fast asleep at this hour, was yet loitering up, lights shining from the windows, people talking by the market-cross, people wondering just how far the sand did extend under their houses.

John did the inquiring.

They learnt that James Wild had been dug out, and was laid in a cottage just beyond them, where his wife, children, and old father, all dependent on the little knock-kneed wheelwright, were also housed.

"Eh, come in. Miss Peel," said the stout woman who opened the door.

Elizabeth and John entered.

James Wild's family was crowded in the tiny kitchen, with the family of their good Samaritan. The children were worn out with crying. Two slept on the settle, one was eating at table. In the inglenook was old Jonathan Wild—almost in his dotage, for James had been the "baby" of a large family. The old man was staring into the fire and did not look up or take the slightest notice even at their entry. All that he knew was that his mainstay was gone, that the workhouse awaited him.

"Where's Jane?" asked Elizabeth.

She was as calm now as ever he had seen her.

"Upstairs," said Mrs. Binns, shaking her head.

Elizabeth went up the stairs, which was merely a strong ladder, with great gaps between the rungs.

She evidently listened outside a door. Then, "it's me Jane," John heard her say.

The door opened, and the low murmur of their voices came to the kitchen.

Ten minutes later, Elizabeth came down, bringing Jane with her. She was a frail woman, quite heartbroken and incapable of speech. John noticed that she kept hold of Elizabeth's hand, without realising that she did so.

"I'll set the kettle on, Miss Peel," observed Mrs. Binns. She looked at John. "Excuse me callin' her Miss Peel," she said. "It takes a bit o' gettin out on." The old man in the nook looked up. He had caught a word. He stared round on the group assembled, and saw Elizabeth, who had collected the rent from his Jim, for twenty years. The effect was electrical. He burst into wild passion, incoherent, save as its meaning was illuminated by the blaze of his eyes—the pointing of his shaking hand—the few words that managed to jerk out, in which "murder,"—"workhouse"—"dead and still" told the accusations in his dazed brain.

In vain Jane tried to calm him down, coming out of her heart-broken dumbness to plead with him, to tell him it was nobody's fault.

"Don't worry him," said Elizabeth, gently.

She laid her hand on the old man's gansey sleeve, and raising her voice, spoke to him.

"You're not going to the workhouse, Jonathan," she called several times until it reached him.

The frenzy died out of his face, but he still mumbled and started up once again, to ask how Jim should be buried, seeing there was nothing laid by, demanding black horses with plumes and an oak coffin, much as though Elizabeth carried them about with her, thought John.

These also Elizabeth promised, and the old man subsided, chuckling anon, as one who has carried some victory.

Jane began to apologise, but Elizabeth stopped her. Mrs. Binns made tea, and Jane took a cup, also. At midnight, John and Elizabeth set out for home, Jane certainly looking more cheerful after Elizabeth's mention of setting her up in a shop. He saw that a half hint from Elizabeth was sufficient to convey that the dead man's family would not suffer economically, at least, from this blow.

They found little Mary up, quite wide-eyed, when they arrived, dressed too, and Mrs. Peel toddling her round by her finger, sleepy-eyed.

It was five o'clock when they got to bed, and Elizabeth looked on the verge of collapse.

"Let me take her in my bed," said John, as Elizabeth was going, candle in hand.

"Let me have her," said she. Then she smiled, shaking her head as he said, "You'd rest better."

John heard the baby crooning in that other room, for half-an-hour. Then he dropped to sleep.

***

A knocking on the front door aroused Elizabeth. It was too early for the milk-man on Sunday morning.

The knocking made the baby cry, tired with loss of sleep on the previous night. She heard John stirring in the next room; he ran downstairs, and as he unlocked the door and flung it open, she heard "Burnham! Come in, old man."

When she got downstairs, baby on arm, the fire was roaring up the chimney. Dick Burnham sat smoking, and John said somewhat sheepishly, "This is my wife, Dick."

"So soon," said Dick's glance, though he strove to hide it under a polite mask, murmuring congratulations. But by the time baby Mary was bathed, and the breakfast cooked, Dick had discovered that there was a curious stiffness in the attitude of John and Elizabeth for married people. It haunted him vaguely, even whilst he pulsated with regretful emotions at being in the place where she had died. He held the baby on his knee, Mary's baby, whilst John set the chairs, and Elizabeth poured the tea. He could see himself looking queerly out of the child's blue eyes, and wondered what madness had made him come to suffer this. The child took to him, gurgled "Dad-dad," at him, too, taking all men for "Dad-dads", and the haze of a deep regret covered him. Dick was doing penance. As they ate, the parrot kept calling "Mary."

John and he took the baby out. He knew it was to give Elizabeth a chance to make dinner and make the house spick and span.

When they got back from a walk through hayfields, during which John had apologised for his marriage, as they watched a man sharpening his scythe, dinner was ready, and Elizabeth was dressed.

Dick Burnham fell under the spell of Elizabeth during that meal.

The Sabbath quiet of the little village seemed to wrap the house around. He made up his mind to stay and work here, where Mary had lived and died. He learnt that Elizabeth had been with her to the end, and hoped to glean if she had mentioned him. It was a hope which he knew was not justified.

"We'll go to Dimpleton this afternoon," said John, and told him of the organist.

So while the child had a half-hour's sleep, they smoked and talked, whilst Elizabeth washed up the dinner things, then she came out and sat with them. Dick admired her more and more.

"I think I shall be able to do good work here, Stone," he confided.

"Stay as long as you like, Burnham," said John.

Dick noticed the relief on the faces of both John and Elizabeth as he said he should certainly stay a month, and, calculating the brief time they had been married, was surprised. It was not often newly-weds so soon welcomed "a shadowy third".

Elizabeth in a black hat, and the bottle-green silk dress, looked grander than ever. She was sitting putting the child's fat arms into pudgy looking sleeves, and John was holding the little white coat, that made little Mary look like a fat, white rabbit, ready for Elizabeth to take from him, when Elizabeth said sharply, "John! your mother?"

John followed the direction of Elizabeth's glance.

His mother it was, her keen, hard face, red with heat, her heavily beaded black bonnet, was seen above the yard door.

John went to open it.

He brought her in. She was so agitated that she did not notice a stranger in.

She dropped heavily on a chair. In her hand was a small box.

"John," she said, "I'm turned out of house and harbour. They want to buy the other half lease o' the farm from me, for ten shillings a week. They can't wait till I'm dead an' gone. So I said "No. I'll go to our John's, and see if he'll turn me out. He was allus th' lovingest child I had."

She looked at Elizabeth as she said this last. She had wondered at John marrying before his wife was "cowd," as Little Hareton put it. But there was that in Elizabeth's face, looking at her over the top of little Mary's yellow head, that broke her down into a softness John marvelled at.

"I'll kill the pair of 'em," said John Stone, fiercely.

His love for his mother revealed itself, like a flash of lightning.

"It's their wives," said Mrs. Stone, shaking her head, "they've gotten the lads round their little fingers."

John was walking about.

Elizabeth sat little Mary down on the creeping-rug, where she endeavoured to detach one of the blue appliqué rabbits.

As Elizabeth took off Bella Stone's hat, the old woman forgot that she had ever meant to come and inspect Elizabeth.

"Tha's gotten a good lass, John," she told her son, a little later in the day.

It was a somewhat uncomfortable tea-table party, for at intervals the old woman broke down again, and cried into her tea-cup. After tea was over, she sat in John's chair, having put on her black house-cap with the curtain down the back, and John and Elizabeth realised that she had certainly come to stay.

The keen eyes watched them both, approvingly.

She was sharp as a needle.

In a house of two up and two down, with Burnham and Bella Stone in it, how were they going to keep their secret?

"I can't sleep on hard beds," she said, that evening. "I'm used to feathers."

Elizabeth's bed was the only one with feathers.

"Mr. Burnham won't mind sleeping at my mother's?" asked Elizabeth.

Dick was quite agreeable.

"Ay. That'll be better," said the old woman.

"Our John morn't sleep on a couch. It's hard followin' their work after sleepin' on a couch."

She had not only come, she was going to take a hand in the government. John realised that his mother must be somewhat of a trial to the young wives, but it in nowise abated his anger against Ted and Charlie.

There was a tense time waiting for Bella Stone to go to bed first. They had to tire her into it. Then John made up the fire and the couch.

Elizabeth went upstairs, to that other room. John clomped up afterwards, step by step, with a racket, opened Elizabeth's door, closed it again, with a "goodnight, mother," and getting a sleepy answer, stole softly down again.

He fell asleep on the couch, with an anxious wonder as to what time Burnham would come in in the morning, a wonder which submerged itself in another wonder as to how long Elizabeth and he could carry on this sort of dodging, without getting worn down by it, and just what the end would be. Then, hutching under the clothes he had piled to keep himself warm, he put out his candlelight.

Chapter VIII

Elizabeth does not tell

Bella Stone decided when she saw Elizabeth making elderberry wine, that her John had struck a rare bargain. It may have been because Elizabeth's way of making it happened to be her way of making it, but she had certainly unbent more to Elizabeth than to anyone John had seen her with, and still stuck to her assertion that she was like the daughter she had buried.

Elizabeth, who would not stoop to wile the heart of a man, considering such behaviour a breach of natural law, had certainly had no such qualms about going out of her way to win the heart of this crusty old woman. Without knowing it, she was deepening the spell on the son, as he saw his mother respond to it. Elizabeth, gracious and warm to his mother, perplexed him with the contrast of Elizabeth ungracious and cold to himself.

He went every night to see Mary's grave, plucking off the weeds with a consciousness of other things growing up in his heart, obscuring those memories which he had once thought must fill his life to the end.

Little Mary was cutting an eye-tooth, and going mad to walk at the same time. Elizabeth had crowded days between the child and John's mother, even her big vitality suffered under the strain, whilst to that was added the anxiety lest the Stone brothers came to try and get their mother to go home and give up her half of the farm lease. She knew there would be trouble if that happened.

The matter had already got into the lawyer's hands. Acting on John's very bad advice, Bella Stone had been to a solicitor, and the whole thing was getting very complex. Whilst almost every day, just after Jack had gone back to the factory, in came Mrs. Peel to groan at Elizabeth's folly in having sent carts to convey the stones and timber of the four Dimpleton houses to the man who had bought them en bloc. Three houses gone to pay compensation that could not have been claimed legally.

"Thy granny'd turn in her grave if she knew," sighed Mrs. Peel, "an' it's robbin' John, too, an' any children yo' may have. Tha needn't smile. Childer is things as runs in families!"

"'Twould be a sin an' a shame if a gret young woman like her did ha' noan," chipped in Bella Stone, the curtain of her cap wagging. "Why yo' can't look at her without fair seein' little uns clusterin' round her."

Elizabeth would quietly stand little Mary against the dresser, coaxing her to walk a foot to her, the blue eyes of the bairn staring into her own encouraging ones. With her mother and Bella Stone she was certainly between two fires.

In the attic at the top of the house Dick Burnham worked away as long as the light lasted. A week went by in this manner. Then, the expected episode of the two brothers coming to John's house took place.

They had got the lawyer's letter, and suspected John's influence having caused it to be sent. They had suspected also that he was jealous and fearful that they were trying to get his share of the farm.

Elizabeth opened the door to them one warm evening just as she had finished a day's baking. They stared hard at her with their hard faces, that had that resemblance to John's face.

She met their suspicious gaze frankly, and without antagonism.

"Come in," she invited, opening the door wide. They followed her in.

Charlie did take off his cap, but Ted kept his on, insultingly.

"Won't ya sit down?" asked Elizabeth.

She had ushered them into the parlour, not into the kitchen, where their mother sat. Charlie sat down, but Ted ignored the invitation.

"We've come to see John," said Ted meaningly.

"Please don't shout. There's a child asleep," said Elizabeth gently.

Ted muttered something to himself.

"I thought perhaps you'd come to tell your mother you were sorry," suggested Elizabeth.

Ted almost choked as he heard the words. Elizabeth was evidently primed with the whole story.

"Sorry!" he ejaculated.

This young woman, smiling at him in the frank, sisterly way that made him feel ridiculous, seemed to think that their breed would confess even if they knew they had made a mistake.

Elizabeth laid her hand on his sleeve.

Charlie had begun to watch his brother with interest. Ted edged away.

"After all," said Elizabeth, meditatively, "the trouble is really between your mother and you lads. What you are really doing isn't breaking the farm up into pieces, it's just breaking her old heart up. Though of course, she wouldn't tell you so. You're all alike. You all like to think you haven't any feelings. Now do sit down, Ted, whilst I tell your mother you are here."

Ted looked waveringly at Charlie. Then he sat down. He sat, without having decided anything at all, until Elizabeth came back. The audacious woman carried a tray, with two glasses of home-brewed on it, and oaten cakes and cheese.

"We can't be bribed," said Charlie, who felt that Elizabeth had set him down as not worth getting round.

"I should offer refreshment to a chimpanzee that had come so far!" flashed Elizabeth.

Ted laughed at that, Elizabeth's face had been so merry as she said it. Quite sure that they were not being bribed, they drank the beer, and ate the cake.

"'Lizabeth!" called Bella Stone, quaveringly, "who is it?"

Before Elizabeth had made up her mind what to say, they heard her coming.

"She's sat worrying all week," said Elizabeth, very low. "She looks years older, and it's you lads that have done it."

Then Bella Stone looked in on them from the threshold.

The truth of what Elizabeth had said was patent to the two lads. But when Bella Stone saw them her face took on its hard look, and with a grim "Oh— you think I'll go back an' give up everything, do ya?" she walked back into the kitchen.

It was flint striking flint again.

A pathetic plea from the old woman, and the matter would have settled itself in her favour, but Bella Stone would have died before whimper.

"Come into the kitchen," said Elizabeth.

The two men went in surlily. They sat down, no one speaking, only the creak of the rocking chair Bella Stone had occupied during her stay, breaking the uncomfortable silence.

"It were our John put you up to goin' to the solicitor's, mother," said Charlie, leaning forward, and addressing Bella Stone.

She stopped rocking.

"Don't 'mother' me, lad," she asked, "when tha wanted to make me in a lodger to suit that wench o' thine."

108

Charlie looked uncomfortable. Then his face changed. The front gate had clicked.

Elizabeth knew that it was John.

John came in—saw them, and was passing into the scullery to wash his hands, when Ted leapt in front of him. Like lightning they were at grips, before Elizabeth could say a word.

The passion of a week, nursed in their separate hearts, was upon them.

Charlie was coming in to help Ted, but Elizabeth gave him a push back upon the chair, with a "one to one, Charlie."

Poor Bella Stone was wringing her hands, crying distractedly—

"Lads, take the farm, but don't feight."

Mary's old nursing chair was overturned in the struggle, and the shrill excited shouting of the parrot made a weird accompaniment to the sounds of conflict.

Ted was stockier built than John, but John had it in litheness.

Elizabeth was fully occupied in keeping Bella Stone barricaded behind her ample figure, for, at the moment no one could have separated them.

"Get him one in the leg, Ted," called Charlie.

But John prevented Ted doing any such thing.

"Couldn't you wait?" panted John, "couldn't you wait—till she was dead?"

"Lads, take it," cried Mrs. Stone.

John had got Ted under him now. He was thumping him soundly, too, but the look in his face was less savage.

Elizabeth's fingers got round his wrist.

"Give up, John," she urged.

John stared up from the fingers to the face. He realised that Elizabeth had touched him. But he gave the struggling Ted a few perfunctory blows, each lessening in energy, and allowed him to get up.

"Tha'rt a bonnie mon," said Ted to Charlie.

By stopping Charlie from fighting, too, Elizabeth had split their unity.

She dusted Ted's jacket, whilst he still looked dissatisfaction at Charlie.

"Set the kettle on, mother," said Elizabeth.

Bella Stone moved tearfully to the task, glad of something definite to do.

"We bring you up for summat," she said, trying to get back to her old loudness of tone, but her voice trembled.

"If my foot hadn't slipped, I'd ha' given thee what for!" said Ted to John.

John smiled scornfully. Elizabeth stepped quickly between them at the look on their faces, saying "Don't start again," and smiling at the same time.

Half an hour later they were all sat at supper table, "harring an' jarring," as Bella Stone put it, but in that stage of quarrelling that leads to peacemaking. Elizabeth said not a word. She merely handed round the stuff, and kept the men's glasses full, but whenever one or other of the antagonists did look at her, her look was so calm, so hospitable, so impartial, that unconsciously they responded to it.

When John and Ted parted amicably on the mat an hour and a half afterwards, Ted remarked, with uncomplimentary candour, "That wife o' thine's too good for thee, old man."

To which John said not a word. He was beginning to wish heartily that Elizabeth Peel would show some imperfections, and not make him feel so basely inferior.

Mrs. Stone, when the lads had departed, after her promise to come home by week-end, on the old footing, as mistress of half of the farm, sat rocking herself.

"You can go," she told John and Elizabeth, "I'll lock the house up."

"I'm not tired," said Elizabeth.

"Tha doesn't look it," scoffed Bella Stone, meaning that Elizabeth did look it.

But Elizabeth sat on with the old woman, John going upstairs, after taking his boots off.

"I seed th' cats at them candytufts in t' front garden," said Bella Stone, "I'll put some pepper there to-morn."

Which startled Elizabeth into paleness. If Bella Stone began to dig up and put pepper down, she might discover those love-letters set under the blue Magdalens, the place Elizabeth had selected as the most suitable place to bury them, since she had been unable to keep her promise,

"Don't bother, I'll put the pepper down," she said.

"Nay, I'll do it," said the old woman, stubbornly.

It was in vain to talk her out of it, even if Elizabeth had dared to do so. To her great relief the old woman departed soon afterwards with her candle, but she would be up by what she called "the strike o' day," and out peppering the cats, Elizabeth knew.

She believed that John Stone was sleeping upstairs this night, that that was how he meant her to interpret his meaning glance over his mother's head. This was her only chance. She made up a bed on the couch, then went softly out, with an old miner's lamp in hand, to dig up those love-letters until Bella Stone was out of the house.

John, meanwhile, only waited to hear his mother's sleeping snore, which came very soon after the exhaustion of this day of triumph, when he stole downstairs. He found the kitchen empty, and the night air blowing up the passage, then, as he heard a slight creeping sound, he stood close against the wall in the shadowy firelight of the kitchen, holding his breath.

It was Elizabeth. She came in, without the slightest suspicion that he was there.

"Oh!" she said, when she perceived him, his suspicious eyes shining on her.

Something fell on the floor. It was a box, which burst, letting out letters.

John made a savage movement towards them.

"No," she said, in an almost childishly frightened way. "Don't, they are nothing to do with you."

"Evidently not," said John.

He picked up one of the envelopes, and scrutinised it. Only "Little Hareton," could be seen in the dim fireglow, for that was written in a bigger hand, but he recognised the handwriting. It gave him a shock. It was—Dick's.

"Love letters," said John. "I heard what my mother said about peppering the cats. You were afraid —you had buried them in my garden. Why in my garden?"

"They—didn't take much room," said Elizabeth.

She held out her hand for the envelope to be put back into it. She was greatly agitated. John could see that, even in the shadowiness of the room.

Her breath of relief, as he gave the envelope back to her, her hurry to put the scattered letters into the box, all told to him a story.

It was apparent to him that in her guilty agitation, her fear lest he should read even one letter, there was something more than an innocent love story here. Elizabeth was that odious thing—a woman with something to hide.

At the moment of the revelation, John Stone realised that during these weeks he had been fighting down a growing fondness for Elizabeth.

He had desired imperfections in her. He had found them. They were not such as he should have suspected.

Elizabeth was locking up the box. She had the attitude of a child yet quivering with a past fright.

"So—it was Dick!" said John. He could not disguise the bitterness in his heart.

Elizabeth looked at him waveringly.

"Yes," she said, almost inaudibly.

She had taken upon herself the dead woman's indiscretion of keeping the letters at all.

During these past days she had perceived the change in John Stone. She had told herself she would pay him out for that insult he had done her, when her heart had been a coal of fire in its pride, but now— she suffered intensely.

"I see why he came here," said John. "He never came whilst Mary was here. So soon as you came—"

"After all," said Elizabeth, her voice very calm, "you have no right to grumble, I assure you it is all over and done with."

"I shall stand no nonsense, Elizabeth," said John, grimly. "I won't have folk talking."

Elizabeth thought of when he had lain on the path, repenting that he was marrying her, for all her world to hear, if it listed.

"I shall be very careful not to bring disgrace on you," she said, witheringly, and went past him, a dark figure, carrying the box upstairs.

John spent two hours pacing the kitchen. He felt that he could kill Burnham. He understood quite well just how Burnham would play around with a love affair, not philandering really, but struggling with his Bohemian inability to settle down.

He wondered if he could not out-rival Dick. Perhaps if he told Elizabeth that he forgave her having cared for any other man—asked her to give him a chance.

Of this demoralised acceptance of her power over him, John refused to think any more. He knew that he could never have taken this humiliating attitude about a secret affection of Mary's. But Mary, John told himself bitterly, much as she fell below Elizabeth's standard in intellect, maternal instincts, and some subtle nobility of atmosphere she carried about with her, had been second to none in loyalty and affection to himself. It carried a selfish consolation to his hurt vanity.

Chapter IX

Elizabeth is just

John did not see Elizabeth next day until dinner time. When she set the square of Yorkshire pudding on his plate, there was that in her demeanour that told she felt, however she strove to hide it, his critical condemnation of the secrecy shrouding those love-letters.

"More gravy?" asked Elizabeth.

Her face had a degree more than usual of the housewifely anxiety to do right by everyone who sat at table.

John shook his head.

Dick Burnham, looking across the table, decided that the couple had quarrelled. The opinion that they were mis-mated had been growing on him before.

Bella Stone sat at the head of the table, and also arrived at the conclusion that John and Elizabeth had quarrelled. Whilst to John, Dick's glances in Elizabeth's direction were translated out of his artist's admiration of her personality into regret at having let her slip through his fingers. For John had not been slow to perceive a graver, more wistful phase in the Dick he had known so long, since his stay here.

John was somewhat curt with Dick when they met at table during the rest of his mother's stay.

Bella Stone was driven back in state on the following Saturday, changing her mind about staying until Sunday, taking with her two of Elizabeth's currant loaves and a bottle of the elderberry wine.

Her going took away a great strain. There was now no more need of those affectations of affection that had been so hard for both John and Elizabeth to play.

Dick Burnham became more and more suspicious. Sometimes it seemed to him that there were very awkward silences in the house. He could not explain to himself why they sometimes grew so terrible that suddenly two people would break them at the same time. When John was out, he noticed that Elizabeth, though more subdued, more sad, it sometimes seemed, was yet more easy in her mind. It seemed to him that she was afraid of sitting down with empty hands.

He liked to watch the tatting-shuttle fly as she held it. The motion, he decided, was much prettier than knitting, which had in it, in his opinion, something stilted and old-maidish.

When the light was gone in that attic, he would come downstairs to watch Elizabeth working, whilst always the thought that she had been with Mary at the end, seemed to give him some intimate claim on her.

Elizabeth, disturbed by the condemnation and hard judgment she felt John had passed on her, responded to these unspoken moods of the artist. She did not feel so harshly about him for his having been unable to settle down with Mary. With an insight, that is not common in those of her temperament, she saw the shade of regret that Dick would always carry about with him. Elizabeth believed in the rod of justice, but so soon as she saw that the one it beat knew he deserved it, she began to question the rod.

Often John would find them, chatting quietly in the dusk, Elizabeth sitting by the window, Dick smoking—on the other side of the house.

I wonder how long Burnham is staying yet!" he growled, one day.

Elizabeth made no answer.

"Think on," he warned, "no fooling with him. I wonder that he had the courage to step into this house," he frowned.

Elizabeth had whitened. She was wondering what would happen if the truth that Burnham had written all those letters to Mary, leaked. John Stone, she thought fearfully, had loved Mary.

Whilst the thought that had come to John to try and win Elizabeth, to coax her out of this delusion that her heart was buried in the past, to tell her that he could forgive her anything, no matter what the letters contained, came to him again and again. His pride often wrestled with it. He grew to regard it as an obsession.

His mentality regarded it as unmanly, and even as it did so, he knew that Elizabeth had always made him feel more of a worm than any other human being.

He was haunted at his work by so many pictures of her—pictures of her, sleepy-eyed in a morning setting his bite and sup; pictures of her hushing little Mary to sleep, or rubbing the child's gums with her silver thimble, as Little Hareton believed in "helping teeth through."

Once he had caught sight of her standing at the door, looking up the street. For a moment he had fancied she was waiting there to welcome him, but her "the tea's spoiling for Mr. Burnham" knocked the hope out of his heart. Only as it flared out did he realise its intensity. Sometimes she would be sewing, waxing her thread in a very antique way, that ceased to be laughable when Elizabeth did it, mending his shirtsleeves so finely that the patching did not show, or thrusting her hand into his sock to darn the great holes, unconscious of the shame he felt at her having to do such tasks for him. But the most staggering thing that ever befell John Stone, was when he discovered that the buttons he sewed on his own clothes, proud of his skill, did not come off because Elizabeth sewed them after him. He grew afraid of the magnanimity of such a woman; He could not have imagined that any female, hearing him boast to Burnham of always sewing his own buttons on, could have held her tongue, knowing that she had sewn them after him.

It was just a week after Bella Stone's going home, when he returned from a visit to Mary's grave (he had begun to feel very self-censuring on these visits) to find Elizabeth again standing at the door. But she had not noticed his approach, until his hand touched the gate. He saw that at once.

She was staring across at Crowther's cottage, a queer expression on her face. It was less vindictive than full of hurt resolve.

"He's at it again," she said wearily.

John stared at her.

"Joe Crowther," she explained. "He's knockin' her about. She's set the light in the window."

John's glance saw now that there was a light in the window, but the distance the house stood away, it was only a glimmer.

"He's so drunk she could knock him down if she wanted," said John.

"But she can't want," said Elizabeth, with sarcasm, if so hurt a tone could pass as sarcasm. "She thinks she wants, but the truth is, she can't."

Then she wheeled round, and into the house. John followed her.

"If you like," said John, haltingly, "I'll go and bash him for you."

His obsession to tell Elizabeth that he could forgive her anything, could lie down and let her walk on him, was coming over him again, but his scorn of himself for his disloyalty to Mary, who would have been so loyal to him, overmastered it.

117

"For her—it would be for her," frowned Elizabeth.

The majesty of her splendid shadow was flung on the fire-lit walls of the kitchen, whilst he remembered that ages ago, he had seen her big shadow, praying that she would say "No" whilst he asked her to marry him, because Mary had asked him to.

"Yes—for her," said John, staring at Elizabeth like a fool. He knew he looked like a fool, and that she saw it. She moved restlessly under his gaze.

"But it's really woman's work, thrashing Crowther," he said.

A passion entered into her, a mood John had never dreamed could be hers, took her up and shook her out of herself. Five minutes later she left the house, cloaked, carrying a large, new bed-sheet, and a stout walking stick.

Elizabeth had gone to administer justice to the man whom God had left unpunished for twenty years.

John sat down in the comer of his fire-lit kitchen, and laughed. He had not the slightest fear for Elizabeth. Crowther would be up against a feminine Hercules. He would have given his ears to hearken unto the cowardly Joe, remonstrating with Elizabeth. Then he realised that Elizabeth had a paradoxical tender heart, that she would suffer most in this business.

He set the kettle on, spread the cloth, set her cup and saucer with clumsy hands, and waited for her return. He was just about to set out after her, when he heard the gate creak. She came in.

Her lips were firm, one on the other, her face a little pale, but quite calm, and the sleepy look usual to her quiet eyes was absent. They almost sparkled. But she lagged on her way to the chair. When she reached it, he realised that she was spent.

He clumsily poured her a cup of tea. She caught the glance of his eyes, and tried to pull herself together.

"He swore quite a lot—at first," she said jerkily. "He had gone to bed—and—we stitched him in the sheet. It was a fight. We covered his head first, so that he couldn't see; he thinks it was Mrs. Crowther." She laughed shakily, and took the cup of tea.

The colour came back to her cheeks as she sipped it.

"Then—he pleaded," she said, "and threatened and promised, and Mrs. Crowther was crying and looking at me, like I was a murderess. He won't be able to sit down with any degree of comfort for a week."

She laughed, but the sparkle had gone out of her eyes. The hand holding the cup trembled.

"He had been left to God twenty years," she said, as if answering some inner self-condemnation.

"Perhaps," said John, "Nemesis used you, after the twenty years."

Elizabeth set the cup down.

"It—it was like thrashing a child, a big, bad, cowardly child, not a man," she confessed, waveringly.

To John's utter consternation she leaned her head on the table and wept. For every weal she had dealt Joe Crowther, there was a smart "where nobody could put salve on," as Mrs. Peel spoke of the hurts of the mind.

John struggled for a moment with that scorn of his disloyalty to Mary, then, quite like a fool, was drawn irresistibly towards the sob-shaken Elizabeth.

Immediately his hand touched her shoulder, she sprang up. Her face twisted itself into an attempt to smile. But John stood before her.

"Elizabeth," he began, and then realised that he did not know anything else to say.

His obsession took him in its grip. Her eyes, wet yet shining, like northern streams with the sun on them, met his, their old serenity dawning again. The humiliating confession that he did not care how many men she had cared for, provided he was in the

119

running, trembled on his lips. Then his pride just managed to save him, but it was a close shave, so close that he felt as though someone had poured cold water down his spine, even as he sat down, to be seemingly buried in the local newspaper.

Dick Burnham came in to supper, but he did not stay up to-night watching Elizabeth tatt the collar for Letty. John stayed, doing that in an absentminded, foolish sort of way. John Stone was realising that, when Dick went, the struggle to make ends meet would be harder for Elizabeth. He was beginning to feel ashamed of his poverty, to wish that he had things to shower on her, splendours to share with her. He had always shared with Mary, but Mary had never made him discontented with his position, though he had tried to invent something to prevent men being gassed when the "monkey" opened unexpectedly when they were shuttering the ore to be blasted. Mary, tired with pots and pans at the close of the day, had thought him wasting his time. He was conscious that Elizabeth inspired him, as she was doubtless inspiring Burnham.

He got out the old box with his ideas half worked out, and spread them on the table.

Elizabeth was making the ivory shuttle fly. He could see the motion from his sideway position, without appearing to look. Elizabeth was at the turning of the shamrock's third leaf in Letty's collar, and John had forgotten that she was there, save for a peaceful perception of quiet companionship, when a knock came to the door.

"I'll go," said the man of the house.

He looked at the clock. It was late for Little Hareton.

There had been rumours of bold robberies in town. John was amused that Elizabeth followed him as far as the door of the passage, looking down the dimness after him. He opened the door, letting in the smell from the hayfields, and the glimmer of stars.

"Does Miss Peel live here?" asked a man's voice.

"Mrs. Stone lives here," John said.

"What used to be Miss Peel, then," said the voice.

"Ask him in, John," came Elizabeth's voice from the kitchen."

John asked him inside.

As the light from the kitchen shone on the man, John Stone saw that he was what Little Hareton termed a "swaddy"—a red-coated member of the militia. Such is the difference clothes make, he did not recognise the soldier as the lad who had ruined and left Melia Young, until Elizabeth said "Sit down".

Then John saw that for the second time this night, Elizabeth was called on to administer justice.

Joe Briggs sat down on the chair Elizabeth pointed him to, looking about as comfortable as a man who expects being electrocuted thereon. Apparently, he expected Elizabeth to speak, but since she did not, he was perforce compelled to.

"I've sin them as telled me you was with her," he said at last, with halting painfulness of speech.

Elizabeth nodded.

"I—I meant to do square by her," he began. Then his gaze flickered as he met Elizabeth's. He grew sullen.

"Honest truth, I did," he protested, "but—they thought I was too young—"

Elizabeth evidently knew who "they" were.

"I didn't know that she'd—"

"Die," said Elizabeth.

"Lots of women die—" said Joe, as though, asking her not to say something.

There was a tragic silence.

"You broke her heart, Joe," said Elizabeth, out of the silence.

The red-coat stared across at her. No one passing court martial sentence on a man could have appeared less moved than Elizabeth.

121

Joe's face grew gray for so young a man's.

"Then it wasn't the child?," he said, asking her not to say it, to give reprieve.

"You left her to it—and the burden was too much," said Elizabeth, simply.

The clock ticked several times. Then there was the sound of a man sobbing. John took a walk down the passage. He was telling himself that Elizabeth was too brutally just, even whilst he knew that the tenderness she had felt for Melia had engendered this harshness.

He opened the door, and passed to the gate. When he finally got courage to come in, he found Joe sitting dry-eyed, looking like a criminal. Evidently Elizabeth had made him feel the enormity of his omission.

"And—did she—forgive me?" asked the young man.

John felt a strong sympathy with his craven humility before Elizabeth.

Elizabeth's brow lightened, lost its frown. Even so, some judge, having given the impression of being made of flint, might suddenly become human.

"Her last words were," said Elizabeth: "Tell Joe I never stopped lovin' him, an' there's nothin' to forgive!'"

Which message, coming as it did as though the dead had spoken it gave Joe agony of another kind. His face contorted itself strangely. He mumbled something about never forgiving himself, and saying "Thanks" in a very strangled voice, rose to his feet.

Then he sat down again, and asked Elizabeth if she thought Melia would have been glad to know if he set a stone at the head of the grave, and Elizabeth, very human once more, discussed the kind of stone, and said that at least it would show he stood by her, though rather late in the day.

He went out, at last, and John realised that to the end of his days Joe Briggs would carry with him a new humility in his bearing towards a woman, that Elizabeth had helped to make a man of him.

"You winced more at walloping Crowther's hide than you did at stripping Joe's soul," said John, after a pause.

Elizabeth came out of a brown study.

"Crowther hurt his wife, but he never left her," she said, swiftly.

John realised that loyalty was Elizabeth's cardinal human virtue.

Another barrier had been put up against his telling her that he was in love with her, and forgetting his dead. Whilst he knew that, though it was too late, she would be loyal in her innermost thoughts to— Dick Burnham, or rather to the Dick Burnham of the past, when she was young.

The child waking and crying, she hurried upstairs, carrying the milk. John pretended to stamp after her, opened the room door, and gave it a good slam to—to convince Burnham.

At least Burnham should regret to the full his lost opportunity, thought John savagely. The next moment the spark of vindictiveness was swallowed in the weary wonder of how long things would go on like this.

Making the couch up, he tried to read, but he could not. At last he fell asleep.

Something moving on the staircase awoke him. He got up, seized the couch-clothes and stumbled under the stairs, closing the door after him, just as Burnham came down, candle in hand.

John held his breath. He could see the glimmer of the moving candle through the crack in the door. The little hole under the stairs was strongly scented with polishes and with paraffin. Trying to get a more comfortable position, John's hand touched something which was dislocated. Then he tried to catch it, he missed it by an inch, banged his head, and down came half-a-dozen loaf-tins, with a rattle that seemed enough, to John, to have awakened all Little Hareton.

The knob turned, and Dick Burnham, candle in hand, shone the light on John's dazzled eyes. Whilst John was wondering what to say, Dick burst out laughing.

He had seen the couch clothes on the floor.

"Do you sleep on the coals?" he asked.

"If you don't shut up, Burnham, I'll choke you!" said John.

Dick laughed again.

"I didn't think you'd stand that," he said.

This genial tone of impersonal amusement struck John as too natural to be assumed. John could only come to the conclusion that Dick, like Elizabeth, also regarded that old love affair as a beautiful dream of the past. But Dick thought John's manner strange as his situation, and John did not explain.

John left Dick up, reading. Dick said he had been unable to sleep. When he came down to light the fire in the morning, Dick's book was on the table, the leaf of the page he had been reading turned down.

John read Browning's "Statue and the Bust" through before lighting the fire. He made out the simple, poignant story of the two lovers who never came together, promising it always to themselves tomorrow, until they grew old.

Dick's pencil mark was set by the triplet that told he considered the words expressed what he had felt—

"And weeks grew months, years, gleam by gleam,
The glory dropped from their youths' love,
And both perceived they had dreamed a dream."

"At least," John told himself savagely, as he fanned up the fire with a folded newspaper, "if he has got the dream, I've got the substance."

From that he grew to pondering how much Elizabeth weighed, and thence to praising his own trust of her, to go out to work and leave her in with Burnham. It dawned on him that Elizabeth was the most loyal woman he knew. She was being loyal to the "dream" and to the man in whose house she was only a hireling.

"How much do you weigh, Elizabeth?" asked John, irrelevantly, as she passed his coffee.

Elizabeth was off guard by the suddenness of the query.

"My normal weight is seven score," she said, "but I'm a bit under just now." She stopped herself then.

John Stone realised that he was not imagining that Elizabeth was thinner.

"How much?" asked John.

"Oh—a pound or two," she said lightly. "It's the hot weather."

John took her hand unexpectedly, as she was holding out a plate of sweet-loaf slices to him.

She looked at him in the proud, yet frightened way with which she quieted any of his rough attempts at familiarity.

"Keep still," he said, calmly.

His pulses were beating at the touch of her soft hand, prisoned in his. It was like holding a wild bird, only the sensations were stronger. He held her hand in such a position that the finger tips pointed straight down at the table. The ring slid down, and would have come off, the ring which he had passed with such difficulty over her plump finger not long ago.

"You must have lost nearly a stone," he told her. "You must be very unhappy here to lose flesh like that."

"It's just the summer," said Elizabeth, smiling frank denial.

But he was not convinced. Had it been Mary, he would have asked Conrad to call in and see her. He could not do things like that with Elizabeth.

Chapter X

Sitting up

Bella Stone had no sooner got settled again on her own hearthstone than she wrote to John, saying she thought it time that there was a house-warming, so that all the family could meet Elizabeth. Really, she meant the family to inspect Elizabeth. Bella Stone was proud of her daughter-in-law.

John wrote and asked his mother to arrange it, and informed Elizabeth. Dick Burnham, hearing of it, fled, going for a week at Dimpleton, which was near the moors.

John had faced out to himself, at last, what he had at first set down with hard self-accusation as disloyalty. He understood now why he could not forbear that shuddering pity that would dive down into the grave, to the decay covered by flowers. His love for Mary had begun in protectiveness, a form of pity. It had ended in the way in which it begun. The grief in his heart for his dead wife was rather a pitying grief for a dead child left out in the dark and the wet, than a strong man's agony for his mate, whom he could always meet equally. Another phase of suffering was entered on with his realisation that his affection for Mary had been less than he had deemed it.

His grief, he knew, would last, a hazy regret to the end of his days. Not even Elizabeth could oust it. But it was not that grief which is at once the thundercloud that darkens the earth and the lightning that parts the heavens, and lets the soul look through.

He knew that only Elizabeth could inspire such grief in him, that his antagonism to her had been subconscious protest against her spell.

It was at the close of one of those wet days that justify the Italians in terming our country a box of wet moss, that John and Elizabeth sat alone. They had a constrained consciousness that they were alone together, yet cut off from each other. Mrs. Peel had not been in in her usual way, having a cold.

Elizabeth was dressing little Mary for bed.

The child was staring at her with two round eyes blue as the beads on its own dimpled neck. John was staring at the pair of them. The house had that warm moistness consequent on Mary's bath, the doors being closed. Something had gone wrong with the gas. Two candles were lit on the table. These and the light from the fire made the only attempt to beat down the shadows.

In one of those moments all mothers watch for— the little one smiled. The smile started in its eyes and, finally, it seemed that the entire baby smiled from head to foot, for the little pink toes wagged, too, in its ecstasy of delight at being alive. Or so it seems to purblind grown-ups.

With the widening of the smile, Elizabeth smiled.

Her face grew lighter, trembled into an almost gay tenderness. The light lessened and died out from her face as the baby's smile lessened. She looked up just in time to catch the tag-end of a similar smile on John's face.

Then Elizabeth set the baby on John's knee whilst she took the bath-tin away—"cleared the deck," as John expressed it to himself. She always set the child on his knee with an almost imperceptible attempt to lengthen her long arms, so that she would keep far enough away from him.

As she took the child, holding her for him to kiss, John had the maddest desire to kiss that other mouth. So strong was it that he felt that Elizabeth must have perceived it. Whilst the thought sprang up in his mind that if he kissed Elizabeth her eyes would just be level with his.

When Elizabeth came downstairs she found him seated by the table bending over his model. It was the second time he had pondered on it with Elizabeth present. Her presence helped him in some peculiar way.

He worked at it until nine o'clock, their usual week-day supper hour. There was a weak spot in his invention—a weak spot he had struggled to overcome scores of hours and had not yet surmounted.

Elizabeth was making a new bonnet for the child. When he put his work aside, she cleared her own off and made supper. They sat down.

They ate the meal in utter silence, without any awkwardness, and none of the constraint that had characterised their silence before. The baby had smiled, Elizabeth had smiled, and he had smiled.

He had never dared to be silent long with Mary. She had always thought something was wrong.

"Have you thought that it's Little Hareton Feast next week?" he asked her, looking up from his plate.

Elizabeth came out of a big planning for the cleaning through. The candle shed a soft lustre about her. Her grey eyes looked full of dreams. He imagined them to be thoughts of that man she had loved. She was really turning the parlour inside out!

"Yes, John," she answered.

He had heard that 'Yes, John,' once or twice in his dreams and had wakened, smiling at the irony of it.

"I wish," he said, desperately, "you wouldn't say, 'Yes, John'. Well, then, what are we going to do about it? I suppose we shall be expected to go away? If we don't go away—Mary and I never missed a holiday. Your mother would think I was mean with you. I won't be thought mean. There's the holiday money to draw."

So it was decided.

They had just agreed on Blackpool, because of the grand sea, when the door opened and Burnham came in, returned from Dimpleton unexpectedly.

Elizabeth made him his supper.

"Going to bed, Elizabeth?" asked John.

Elizabeth nodded assent.

The night dews on Burnham's hair glistened in the light of the candle near his elbow. He had that wild, moody look which sometimes clouded him. He ate with the affectation of the man who pretends to disdain food.

"You needn't wait up for me, Mrs. Stone," he said to Elizabeth. "I'll lock up the doors."

But Elizabeth did not intend to give him the run of the house.

"I've got a few things to do," she said, quite truthfully, and set about doing them. Whilst it seemed to her that Burnham would never have finished his meal. When he had finished, to her utter horror, he pulled out a little volume from his pocket and began to read.

"We have only those two bits of candles," she told him, apologetically, but with meaning.

She went down the passage and locked the door.

She had given John a bottle of milk to take up for baby. It was a little homely domestic touch capable of deceiving many.

"I really don't mind. I can sit in the dark," said Burnham, unmoved, thinking only of her reference as it affected him.

Elizabeth sat down, waiting, with the calm dignity of the mistress of the little house.

To allow their lodger the right to monopolise the kitchen would place them in a queer position. She did not know of his discovery of John under the stairs.

Burnham read on.

The ticking of the clock became at length a monstrosity to Elizabeth.

"Mr. Burnham," she said, "I am waiting."

He looked up quickly.

"Oh, sorry," he said, apologetically. "Borrow— have you read George Borrow?"

The provincial woman shook her head.

"'There is likewise,'" repeated Burnham, dreamily, "' there is likewise a wind on the heath.'"

Then he paused, like one listening to the wind, racing over the bents, the little dark pools.

"You should read Borrow," he told her, rising. Then he said, hurriedly, "Nay, why should you? It is for folk like me who forget, who get apart, you know. Why should you read Borrow?"

Elizabeth was looking at him in wondering fascination.

"Oh, by the way," he said,"I found this this morning, on the stairs."

He held out a tiny scrap of paper.

Elizabeth held out her hand for it.

Then—her cheeks flamed.

She had recognised the colour and shape of that paper. It was that used by John and herself in their weekly making out of household accounts. Had Dick Burnham read it?

She glanced at his face.

He was looking at her scrutinisingly.

Then he spoke.

"You are worthy," he said, gravely, "of a man who would not reckon you up to a penny halfpenny."

She realised that Burnham had half-realised the situation, mis-reading it because he did not know the whole.

She remembered what John had told her of Dick's philandering—those spiritual bigamies that enabled him to put a soul into his pictures, just as some men have to drink.

But all that she saw in the man before her was a certain cold, clear-cut indignation against John. He was judging John.

"Thanks for my little household paper," she said. "Please, believe me, you are quite mistaken in your reading of your friend's character."

But so shaken was she at the thought of having no explanation to give that would not make the thing seem worse—the paper shook also.

He smiled, discrediting all she had said, all she could say.

Since she could not defend John, she seized the moment to attack him. Moreover, she had felt that this was the fit and proper course to take—only her common sense had shrunk from it as unnecessary and painful. But now circumstances had forced it upon her.

He was turning to go.

"Just a moment," she said.

Surprised, he watched her go to a drawer, unlock it, take out a box. When she spoke her voice had sunk to a tone that would not convey her words to John.

"I think," she said, "that these are your letters. I found them, and was afraid John would be upset. I—didn't like to burn them, you see. They weren't mine. They were Mary's. John's mother might have found them. So I—buried them. Then—Mrs. Stone was going to put cayenne down for the cats. I dug them up. John would be so upset. And I should not like that. For we are very happy."

In the speaking of the lie at the end of the truth Elizabeth was not provincial, but a consummate actress.

Burnham stared at her dazedly, then down at the letters. It seemed to Elizabeth that he could not speak for a moment.

When he did break the awkward silence, despite his restraint, his voice shook. He sat down.

"So—she kept them. She cared," he mumbled, rather to himself than to Elizabeth.

She stood in the centre of the kitchen, realising vaguely that she had given to Dick Burnham joy that should have been John's.

He looked up to see her there, at last—this rather conventional provincial, with her narrow, deep judgments.

"Thanks," he said, very humbly. Then he added, "It is like Mary coming back into my life."

Elizabeth's attitude told that she stood there as John's representative, prejudiced on that account.

He felt a fear of her.

"Did she—mention me, at the end?" he asked.

It was the thing he had come to ask, and had dallied with, these weeks.

Elizabeth sat down. She did not throw aside her attitude of being John's representative. As he listened to the conscientiously, uncoloured sentences, it was very like hearing a Blue Book read. Dick Burnham read between the lines. He knew it all—Mary's heartache, and her poor chaotic thoughts, turning to him at the last. He was more hurt, more humbled, and yet more happy than he had dreamed he could be on that day when he had seen Elizabeth, in a black dress, pouring him out funeral wine. He knew now that she had known, then.

"Thanks, Mrs. Stone," he said again.

Then he realised the rareness of Elizabeth.

She rose and crossed the hearth, and held out her large hand. It was a warm, impulsive side to her nature he had not suspected.

Dick gripped it as he would have gripped a man's. He was going to say something to this woman whom he knew had smoothed Mary's way for her passing when he saw John Stone on the threshold, the child in his arm.

"The child's got croup," said John.

He had seen Elizabeth take her hand from Burnham's in a swift, awkward way. She was quite crimson as though she knew what he was thinking. Then she was quite pale.

Dick, he noticed, had not turned a hair. John wanted to choke him.

The house was soon in a bustle, the fire roaring, whilst ever came that curious little croak.

Elizabeth took a seat by the fire, talking soothingly to the child, an d getting her to swallow "ippypec," as Mrs. Peel called it.

Dick Burnham left John and Elizabeth struggling with the child after two hours' watching. He went to bed, telling them to call him if they needed him.

"Conrad," suggested John, after another half hour.

"He could only tell us to do this," said Elizabeth, calmly.

Then she said, "Fill the bath-tin, John. Let us try that."

John Stone looked at her. But she had not noticed her slip of the tongue.

The woman whom he had seen snatch her hands from Dick's, in the panic of a child caught in a misdeed, who had handed her old love-letters into his charge (John had not been there to see the box), now spoke of herself as one with him, in his grief, it was bewildering.

But he obeyed, and they soon had the child up to her plump little neck in the hot water, struggling and crying wheezily for "Issabeth."

"The phlegm's broken," said Elizabeth, as she took her out. "Keep the doors tinned, John. I'll bed the child on the couch. She'd be bad again if I took her upstairs."

She meant it as his dismissal. He had an insane anger against the idea of being dismissed.

"I'll stay and watch, too," he said.

"She's out of danger now," said Elizabeth. "Unless she gets another cold."

But John did not budge. He watched her put the child snug upon the couch, patting and pulling the clothes to keep off the tiniest draught.

"Why don't you teach her to call you 'mother'?" asked John, frowning. He spoke as if the thing was dragged out of him.

Elizabeth was surprised out of herself.

"Because—" she said, and then shut up.

"Because what?" said John.

She saw the resemblance to his brother Ted when he looked like this. She did not reply.

"Can't you be straight out and frank, for once in your life?" asked John.

He had touched her to the quick now, and saw it with mad joy. She looked like the woman who had said "No" to him in the parlour. He was reminding her of what he had seen when he brought the child downstairs.

"My position here is not frank and open," she said, and he saw the dark passion in her eyes. "But if you want to know, I don't teach her to call me mother—" Here she wavered, conscious of having been weak enough once or twice to indulge the guilty fancy.

John was looking at her, defying her to go on.

"Because I'm not her mother," said Elizabeth.

"It's simple enough. Shall I teach her to call me mother—when I'm not?"

It was at once the essence of truth, and of pride, against taking the tiniest atom of the ground that was holy ground, belonging to Mary.

"There are women," said John, "who could take another woman's child and believe it was their own."

Her glance trembled slightly.

"Possibly," she admitted, not claiming place with them.

She mechanically pulled up the rug around the child. Her look evaded John's. She would not defend her attitude.

He was plainly out to wound her.

She sat in his chair, a big gray shawl round her shoulders, plaiting her hair in two thick plaits, so that her head could rest comfortably against the back of it.

"I'm tired, I want to sleep," she said, spiking his guns against a further attack.

"You'd have been better on the couch," he said.

She stiffened as though a strange passenger with her in a third-class carriage had suggested that she lie down and sleep on the seat. John felt a grim sense of humour wake up in him.

"Oh, all right," he said, nonchalantly.

She did not sleep at once. He had hurt her too much.

Sundry sighs and movements convinced John, who was foxing at being asleep, that she was troubled. He thought once that he caught the glitter of a tear-drop on her lashes. The little hearthstone was scarcely longer across than the space of a cradle, and the fire was bright. But, at last, she ceased tossing about, and with the shawl halfway across her face, as though fearing it might reveal her soul, she slept. She had put out one hand to the couch, so that if the child stirred she would feel it. The shawl fell away from her face. John gently stirred up the fire. She did not move. She was fast asleep. Her features had a tired calm, a soft look that they had not in her waking hours—as if a mask had fallen away. The child at her side did not look more innocent.

John leaned forward in his chair and looked at her. If he had not thought Elizabeth beautiful before, he could not but think so now, though it was an unpopular style of beauty.

She drew a tired breath, like a child, worn with a burden almost too heavy. It came across to him like a reproach.

But for him, he told himself, Elizabeth would have married Dick Burnham. He thought of his slight on the care she had bestowed on his child, his stinging words that she let the child call her "Issabeth".

He was madly in love with her, and he could not tell her so, because any move he made in that direction she always put down as common sense philosophy in making the best of a bad job. Besides—there was Dick, Dick who had been clutching at her hand, and looking at her as though she was an angel.

John turned his face from the contemplation of Elizabeth asleep. There was something in her face that made him ashamed to look at her when she did not know it and could not be proud and resentful.

After smoking a pipe he dropped asleep, to waken as a big cinder flopped on to the hearth. Elizabeth was still asleep. So was the child. Elizabeth's hand had fallen limply by the side of the couch. He hovered about the couch, listening to little Mary's breathing. He would not acknowledge to himself that he was drawn irresistibly near Elizabeth. Mary had never had steel in her, Elizabeth had. She was nearly all steel. Therefore she drew steel.

"Have we—overslept?" she inquired, starting up in self-reproach two hours later, as the foundry hooter blew.

John was again bewildered by the "we."

"It's only the first one," he said, turning from the window, a big black ghost, dressed ready for toil, even to the cap.

He handed her a cup of tea.

She stared down, to find her feet on a buffet.

"I—put them there," said John, grimly. "In good society men sometimes do so much, even for other men's wives."

The warfare had opened again. Elizabeth knew it as she sipped the tea.

Between a married couple it would have been bickering. Between them—it was a buffeting up against barriers she could not help to push away without—a confession of her own impulse to move towards John Stone's life, an impulse as irresistible as the laws of chemistry, and without a breach of faith to the dying.

"'Do not tell John."

The childishly frightened plea rung in her memory. She did not answer John's taunt.

"The child's better," she said, bending over the couch.

He noticed that her cup trembled in her hand, when she sat back to drink the tea. It reminded him that Mary's cup had always shaken a little. But Mary had been a frail thing.

He drank his own tea, standing with his back to the fire. Then he walked over to the window looking on the garden, beginning to glow under the growing light.

"If I see Dick holding your hand again," he stated, turning up his coat collar, and pulling down his cap neb foundryman-like, "I shall kick him out of the house."

Her lips half parted, as to speak, then closed again in the old stubborn lines. She assented to his verdict, his interpretation.

He made a half move to the door.

"What about the house-warming?" he asked.

"The child has the croup," said Elizabeth.

He realised that she shrank from the ordeal of the farce of house-warming a house that was not a home to her, of being embraced into a family not hers.

"If the doors are kept closed," he said, "we can manage it. I'll write them."

She bent her head.

He went out, towards the foundry, walking with down-bent head. He had begun to detest his work, and the scene of it. Elizabeth had made him realise his humble position. Dick could lie in bed till ten, and earn twenty times as much as he could, and travel—and be superior.

As he was crossing the yard, purple black with its powder of iron-ore, and the great barrows waiting for men to wheel them, he saw a figure standing, a craven outline, against the timekeeper's cabin, with its lighted window showing the timekeeper having something to drink before the day's work began.

John stared at the figure by the cabin as though he had some optical delusion.

"Joe?" he hazarded.

"Ay. It's me," said Joe Crowther's voice.

John began to understand.

"What arta after, Joe?" he asked. He invariably spoke broad dialect with Joe.

"Wark," said Joe.

John assumed surprise.

"What's ta want with wark?" he asked. "It's only fools an' horses wark, isn't it?"

Joe came up to him.

"Hesta a chew?" he asked, disconsolately.

John gave him a piece of twist.

"It's the missus," explained Joe. "She's gone barmy, clean barmy. Sets me empty plates an' quotes Scripture about not eating if you don't work. An'—she's had three homin' pigeons worth a quid each, their necks screwed, an' made pies on 'em for th' childer, an' says th' lot are goin' if I don't shape. An' one night she thumped me atween two sheets, an' she said she would again, if I didn't get work. I'se ha' to work, chewsheaw!"

Joe looked despairingly at John.

"Then she wants that ground making into a garden, to grow potatoes,' said Joe. "Somebody's puttin' her up to it, I think."

John had hard work to keep his face straight at this.

"I'll come up an' give thee a hand at turnin' ground," he said.

Joe brightened.

John went into the timekeeper's lodge.

"Yon's Joe Crowther come after work," he said, enjoying the joke.

"Potty?" asked the timekeeper, with sarcasm.

"His wife's turned on him," said John.

"What!" yapped the timekeeper, as though he had heard a hare had turned on a lurcher.

"Well, fact is stranger than fiction," said the timekeeper.

John nodded. He was thinking about the strange life he and Elizabeth led, and what Little Hareton would have thought of those facts.

Later, a sweating giant, in shirt and trousers, he was wheeling his barrow to have the ore weighed, before conveying it to the basket, to go up with him to that dizzy, narrow-railed height where it would shutter down, with a noise like thunder, and a blaze like hell, to be blasted.

"I've got on," came an excited shout, that sounded to come from the clouds.

John stared up. Leaning against the narrow rails was Joe Crowther, a very marionette. John nodded, to show that the far-off shout had reached him.

Then he set his load into the basket, and stepped in after it, giving the cry almost before he had got his head clear. It swung up as he readjusted himself.

The young "boss" was passing and saw the incident.

"Who was that?" he asked a barrow-wheeler, standing near, ready to weigh.

"Stone," said the man.

The boss nodded.

"That's twice I've seen him do that," he said. "One of these days he'll have no head on."

"He's too cool to happen aught," said the man with the barrow.

Five minutes later John Stone came down in the basket, holding Joe Crowther up, a dead weight against him. The "monkey" had not closed soon enough when the ore shuttered. Joe had been near and got the gas fumes. It was not very often it happened.

They laid him out on a strip of grass just beyond the purple-black yard. John and another mate fanned him with their dusty caps until he revived. It took him an hour to recover.

John had much ado to persuade him to resume work. He did it for Elizabeth. It was helping the work of her hands. There was a humility in assisting her influence to work in behalf of that half-famished woman and her brood.

As he watched Crowther crawl away, yet dizzy, he thought of the finer specimens he had seen lie on that stone-scattered bit of grass, and then crawl away like that, to continue again. A deep unrest, foreign to him, clothed him till noon, an unrest in which he hated the clothes he wore, the barrow he wheeled, even his mates, dusty with the iron-powder. It seemed to him that he had been a slave until now. Now—he wanted a world to give away, and to lay it at Elizabeth's feet, he, a foundryman, who could only give her seven shillings a week.

He had asked her to bring his dinner, or send it, if the child was not fit for Mrs. Peel to stay with. There was overtime. The question as to whether she would bring it or send it was sandwiched in between his unrest.

"Stone, there's a lady asking for thee," said one of the men.

"Whoo—a lady?" chaffed another man.

They were sitting down in the purple-black yard, eating their dinners in five minutes, ready to begin again.

John went out to the gates.

It was Elizabeth. She had dressed herself neatly to bring his dinner. She wore a little black velvet bonnet, with a wreath of artificial ivy leaves. He had seen her sewing at it at home. She held up her dark dress clear of the iron-dust, and kept her gaze for that of the staring dinner-eaters.

"Baby's better," she said. "The croup's quite gone."

She handed John his dinner. He took it silently. There was nothing more to be said. She had just brought his dinner, and the good news.

But all the way back to that line of dinner-eaters he saw a little picture of her, in the new bonnet, and the joy in her eyes to be able to tell him that the child was quite safe.

"Stone knew where to hang his cap up," said a huge man, peeping familiarly into John's dinner basket.

Elizabeth had sent him a meal fit for a king. A bottle of the home-brewed beer, too.

He did not reply to the big man's jest.

For a moment it had seemed an insult to Elizabeth, that anyone should be able to believe he had married her because she could cook. She could cook. He was glad of it. But if she had peeled potatoes with a tin lid, like a Maori, and had baked cakes as impossible as Mary's, he knew he would have been humbly grateful, and have appeased his hunger in pie-sprees in the town. Which shows the high- water mark of his love for Elizabeth. As it was, he certainly enjoyed the rissoles, the pie, and the ale. Whilst he added a fame to Elizabeth by giving out her little cakes, and feeling quite glorified himself by the praise they received.

Chapter XI

A house-warming

Dick Burnham fled to Dimpleton again, just in time to dodge the house-warming.

Elizabeth noticed that he took with him a parcel, curiously alike in size and shape to the box of love-letters. He said he was going over the tops. Going that way he would cross a waste of moorland. Something told Elizabeth that he was going to leave those letters under the heather, where curlews and wet winds wandered.

John Stone had sat indoors night after night, since that episode when he had surprised Elizabeth with her hand in Dick's. His attitude was curiously like someone's on guard. He had never spoken to Burnham when he could help it since that night. Even Dick, preoccupied as he was in that maze of regret, which at times was not all sad, since Mary had come back to him, had felt it at last. The reason of it he could not tell. He was certainly very far from the true solution. The nearest guess he made was that he was outstaying his welcome, that John wanted to have the house to himself, though, if this were true, he was puzzled to account for the mutual relief evidently felt by both John and Elizabeth, when he came in to save them from the solitude they shared.

They were alone together now, struggling in that same net of absurdly awkward feeling that had increased since that night when they had sat up with little Mary. The child slept in her cot, brought down into the ingle-nook. She went up to bed when Elizabeth did now, until she was quite recovered from the attack. The big woman crept about with that utter quietness characteristic of her. Yet John was disturbed by her, irritated by her, as he had been disturbed and irritated by no previous woman. He had wanted to work at his patent, helped by her friendly presence, as she had helped him before. But that time was gone. Always now, he was conscious of the barrier of the flesh, risen between him and Elizabeth. In sheer disgust at his inability to work in Elizabeth's kitchen, he went off into the parlour. There he could work a little better. But a subconscious self listened to the tiniest sound from that kitchen, and his brain was haunted by the picture of Elizabeth, frying-pan in hand, a most dignified culinary goddess, frying the meat and onions ready for the gigantic shepherd's pie that was to be the king dish of the evening. This was Elizabeth's test night, when she would be inspected by his family.

He came out of the parlour, having solved one knotty point that had long evaded him. Elizabeth was just taking out half a hundred cheese-tarts from the oven.

She had the tray in her hands, and was getting it out when he came to sit down in the corner. His glance appeared to disturb her. But he did not realise she was burnt, until she had carried the tray of tarts into the scullery, rather more hurriedly than usual, and had returned.

"Would you mind reaching the carron-oil?" she asked politely. Her brow was a little puckered, that was all.

John reached down the oil bottle that Elizabeth had got in the house in the first week of her coming, to have ready should little Mary have scald or burn.

He took her hand in his, and poured generously with the other hand. He noticed she was eager enough to get it from the touch of his. Against her will, he bandaged it up with lint.

"There is a score of potatoes to peel," she said.

"And—they'll be here—in an hour."

"I'll peel the potatoes," said John.

"I'm sure I could do it," she said, "when the smarting's gone?'"

"Do you think independence is a virtue?"

She stared across the fire-lit kitchen at him. He was attacking her again.

"I never thought about it," she said, in a tone that ought to have frozen him.

"These helpers, and good givers, and strong folk, generally—have you ever noticed how they resent being helped, and how impossible they are to deal with when they ought to take a gift graciously? For instance, now, if I should take it into my head to black your boots—"

Elizabeth's figure stiffened at the mere idea of John Stone cleaning her shoes.

"Mary cleaned mine," said John. "And—I wasn't hurt. Why shouldn't I clean yours? Besides, Ted told me I wasn't fit to black your boots."

He was trying to make her out a Pharisee, and she knew it. Whilst his tone suggested that Ted did not know everything—not about those letters and the "dead past," and holding Burnham's hand, for instance.

Elizabeth rose from her chair. She took a big spoon in her left hand and stirred the meat and onions in the pan on the "crow."

"I don't know why you keep talking like this," she remarked. "But if you are doing it to hurt me, you can't."

John tossed a potato into a brown dish full of water at his side.

"I shall never let you have a minute's peace," he told her, smiling grimly, "until you send Burnham out of the house, and say 'John, I love you'."

He was picking an eye out of a potato, as though he poked Dick Burnham out of Elizabeth's heart.

There was a moment's silence.

"I shall never do that," said Elizabeth very quietly, but, oh, how destructively firmly.

Woman-like, she was thinking of the will of John to bring her to his elbow, like a pet lamb. John, on his side, was thinking of Dick having to go.

"Never is a long while," smiled John.

He drowned another potato.

"I'm very fond of you, Elizabeth," said John. It cost him ten thousand pangs to acknowledge the fact. His heart thumped against his ribs as he made the admission. But his brain was very cool. Elizabeth had the effect of a whetstone on him. She sharpened his wits.

"Most men are fond of people who make them comfortable," said Elizabeth, as if they discussed some general topic.

"You don't make me comfortable," said John.

Elizabeth gave him an indignant look. The practical woman had taken him literally.

What she would have said he could only surmise. The first knock came to herald the arrival of their folk, representatives of both families come to embrace each other, to cement the happy union.

The relief on Elizabeth's countenance was a blow to John. He was beginning to want her to himself, so that he could hound her down.

Elizabeth pulled off the lint as she went down the passage, and opened the door to Uncle Ned Stone, whom she had ever remembered as robbing the dead of pickled onions.

"Come in," John heard her say, genially.

Uncle Ned came into the fire-lit kitchen, with its smell of baking.

"Oh, hello, John! I see tha'rt livin' in Good Husband Street, yet," he joked. Then he turned to Elizabeth. "He'll alter, lass," he warned her, "when he's bin wed to thee as long as I have to mine."

"I daresay," said Elizabeth comfortably, as though the prospect did not appal her. And—the man peeling potatoes in the ingle-nook got the idea that she was laughing at him, that, knowing he knew how impossible it was that he could ever grow careless from such intimacy, she was having a dry joke to herself at the comedy he and she enacted before their relatives. He had heard her father was a droll man.

Men and dogs hate being laughed at. The idea buzzed in John's brain. As he peeled the rest of the potatoes he was laying a trap for Elizabeth, a trap to go off this very night.

The ethics of the thing did not trouble him. He was the strong man of the north, who would not ask "Yea" or "Nay."

"Well, tha knows how to kick up a good smell, lass," said Uncle Ned, as Elizabeth took the dish with the onions and meat out of the oven.

Uncle Ned had only visited John once whilst Mary was alive, and had conveyed to the rest of the family his belief that she fed John on bananas and corned beef. The old belly-god, hands on fat knees, was registering the opinion that he would come and see John oftener.

John got up and followed Elizabeth into the little scullery. The gas was too far from the table to give the light there required. She had lit a candle. She was stirring up the stuff in the dish with her left hand. John took the spoon from her commandingly.

"Let me!" he said.

"Mind your own business," said Elizabeth.

He was doing her out of earning her wages.

She showed a degree of mad-hatterishness that delighted him.

But she had spoken beneath her breath. Uncle Ned was sitting only a few yards away.

"Let me see," quoth John.

Quick as lightning he had seized her burnt hand, and inspected it by the candlelight. It had blistered between the large fingers of the large hand he had once thought unwomanly, with its great, knotted joints and outline suggesting vigour.

"Put something on it, or—I'll make the pie," threatened John.

She was cornered. She could not fight with Uncle Ned sitting only a stone's throw away.

For the first time since that night when she had told him of his having repented on the garden path of marrying her, and he had cringed before her—he felt a man.

"Burnt thee, lass?" John heard Uncle Ned say, as she applied oil in the kitchen.

"Just a bit," said Elizabeth.

She came back into the scullery to light the jet and set the pan of water on to boil the potatoes.

"This place is too small for us both," she announced to John, in a mild voice.

He was not quite clear as to whether she meant the house, or merely the small scullery.

John was sitting on the scullery table, his feet scraping the floor, as he took away the potatoe-eyes he had missed in the dim kitchen light.

"Other people quarrel after marriage," he whispered at her, as she came near him for the salt. "We're doing ours—before."

He grinned genially at her.

"These kind of tactics—" began Elizabeth.

"All women have to be pursued," said John.

Her large scorn flashed at him.

"Those that are—sheep," she said.

In the candlelight she looked leonine.

She put one lot of potatoes into the pan. But he was so leisurely with handing the rest over to her that she had to wait, chafing all the time to return to Uncle Ned.

As she came near him for the last lot, John seized her hand roughly. He looked cautiously at the door between themselves and Uncle Ned.

"Elizabeth," he begged, humble all at once, "let us have this for a real house-warming."

She looked at him quite calmly.

The spiritual rage he had seen roused in her by Crowther, and Melia's lover, was upon her.

"I'm not—a sheep," she said. "No. I—hate you, John Stone, as you hated me, because she asked you. I couldn't let myself go to anyone that could forget a woman you liked as you liked Mary—at least forget her so soon. It's just because I happened to come here, that's all."

She jumbled the words, so that Uncle Ned would not be able to make moss or sand of their echo. But John heard them. He wilted under them. And even as he wilted he saw the swift remorse that followed the flame of her anger, an anger that kindled in him an answering anger, that strangest and maddest of angers against one who loved as he now loved this big, human, perfect, and yet most imperfect, woman.

"I—I didn't—I oughtn't to have said that," said Elizabeth.

He was sitting with bent head, hearing the trickle of the rain down the scullery windows. It was falling on Mary's grave. Elizabeth had just reminded him of his fickleness.

"There, come out o' there," called Uncle Ned.

"You've bin spoonin' long enough."

Elizabeth entered the kitchen, lit the gas. Uncle Ned looked at her.

"Wedding doesn't look to ha' agreed in thee, lass," he said solicitously, much as if the wedding state was diet that gave indigestion to some.

Her swift anger against John Stone's high-handed tactics had burst out. He had tried to drive her as a sheep into love's fold. She felt tired and looked it.

John came out of the kitchen, looking guilty, despite his efforts at unconcern. Uncle Ned gave him the wink.

"These young married couples," he said, shaking his head at them, knowingly.

Then he and John began to discuss family topics, dipping right back to John's boyhood, Uncle Ned even going as far back as John's christening in the old font at Dimpleton Church.

"He screamed heavens high," confided Uncle Ned to Elizabeth. "Didn't like the water on his face."

He smiled so genially, looking at John also, and seeing the great man as a tiny baby, that Elizabeth was called on to smile also.

John realised that Elizabeth's smiles were always conscious smiles—made ones, though very good imitations, which only he could recognise as spurious. Why could she not be happy, and smile without knowing it, as she only did when the baby smiled at her. The truth burst in on him as he pondered. She didn't believe in his affection, because he had forgotten the first one so soon!

Elizabeth, on her part, was suffering for having told John the truth, even as she had suffered in beating Crowther. The idea of John as a baby, a small baby, was a new strange one. She wished Uncle Ned had not given her the idea. It appealed against her pride— her pride not to surrender until every fort was gone, every gun shattered, every ditch taken.

Charlie and Ned, called after his uncle, arrived next with their respective wives.

"We've met before," said one of them, tactlessly, as John introduced his "wife".

"Oh—ay, at th' funeral," said Uncle Ned. Then looked as though he would like to kick himself.

John reddened, and Elizabeth felt the sting. He saw she did, he only. They saw in her a wearer of a dead woman's shoes. Whereas he knew that she had taught the child to call her "Elizabeth" when she wanted to be called "mother".

Uncle Ned took a great interest in the making of the shepherd's pie. For Elizabeth quite unconventionally mashed the potatoes in sight of the company before she popped the dish into the oven.

Mrs. Charles and Mrs. Ned Stone helped Elizabeth to set the table. John noticed that both together they contrived to do much less than Elizabeth.

Bella Stone had called on Elizabeth's mother. They came in together, with Jack and Letty following a little afterwards, and chatted accordingly. These three people represented Elizabeth's family. It was not a big turn-up, but Elizabeth took pains to explain to Uncle Ned that most of her folk lived away.

"Oh—they'll turn up for the christening," chaffed Uncle Ned, with a knowing wink.

John's relations continued to pour in. Each one, as they came, took stock of Elizabeth.

"Tha's a bit o' summat to get howd on thear, John," chaffed one, as Elizabeth disappeared into the scullery.

He nodded assent. There was certainly quite a good deal of Elizabeth.

"Jerry Young's bringin' his fiddle," said Charlie watching his mother put on her house-cap.

"Elizabeth, dost think thy oven's hot enough?" questioned Mrs. Peel anxiously. "Where's thy sticks?"

"Bottom drawer," called Elizabeth. Then; unerringly, "Not many, mother."

Mrs. Peel pushed the sticks under the oven with a satisfied air. She felt that she had done something towards the pie. Whilst Bella Stone thought that this example of filial bending (nobody believed that the oven couldn't have done without those two puny sticks) gave both her son's wives a much-needed lesson.

"Tha shouldn't poke anybody's fire until tha's known 'em seven years, unless tha does it with thy finger," one old man told Uncle Ned. For Uncle Ned showed a disposition to have a finger in the pie, too.

"I've known our John twenty-seven years," said Uncle Ned. "And our Elizabeth—well, I feel I've known her all my life."

Which made Elizabeth smile as she came out of the scullery with a dish of raspberries.

Rat-tat!

"It'll be Jerry," said several voices.

John went to let in the very old man of the young name. He was Little Hareton's pride. His father had lived to be one hundred and three. Jerry was over ninety, and since he had gone ninety always bragged that he was "creeping on towards a hundred," as proud of his age, as jealous of being thought younger than he was, as any woman is proud of her youth.

"Well, how are we, Jerry?" asked Uncle Ned.

He had to repeat the question twice.

"As well as ever we were," answered Jerry, vain as a peacock.

He set his fiddle, in its green baize case, on the floor. Uncle Ned shook his head at someone when Jerry was not looking.

Elizabeth came and smiled him a welcome. They began to watch what Elizabeth was doing.

"It's years sin I've sin that done," said Uncle Ned.

"My father allus had it for a nightcap," said Bella Stone, the curtain of her cap wagging approval.

Elizabeth poured the ale into the shining copper warmer, digging its pyramidal shape into the bright heart of the fire.

"I'm fain tha'rt not t-t, lass," smiled Uncle Ned.

It was beyond Uncle Ned's conception that any tea- drinking female could warm ale as gloriously as Elizabeth did it. John smiled to himself.

"This for me, lass?" shouted Jerry Young, pleased surprise, as she handed him the warm ale.

Elizabeth nodded.

Jerry's other hand slid down to his fiddle.

"Make that at home, somewhere," he begged.

"Elizabeth," said Uncle Ned plaintively, "when I'm creeping on towards a hundred will ta make some ale-posset for me?"

Which set everyone laughing.

"I'm a bit of a gay dog," acknowledged Uncle Ned, looking as innocent as a fat pink daisy as he boasted of his gay-doggishness.

How "at home" everyone was.

Charlie was counting up chairs and trying to discover if they would all go round, whereupon Uncle Ned volunteered to sit on the dresser, if there was not room elsewhere.

"I asked Joe Crowther and his wife," Elizabeth told John in an aside, amidst the general buzz of conversation. She was seated by him now, looking wifely duty and industry, until the pie was ready to come out.

John realised that it was the half-apology of a woman who has no right to invite guests. He nodded. But he did not know it was an excuse to speak to him —a pang of remorse lest she had been too severe in the scullery.

"It's all right," he said.

152

The next moment the door opened and Joe and his wife came in. Joe's new "goodness" made him look extremely guilty. John recognised a pair of pants Joe wore as having been his own, and as Joe came near him, he recognised the patching as Elizabeth's handiwork, because it was so difficult to detect. Mrs. Crowther had on a new blouse. He recalled having seen Elizabeth embroidering it, and realised the delicacy of Elizabeth in not giving Mrs. Crowther an old garment, recognisable by all Little Hareton as a "cast-off" of her own. Generous, noble and fine—with all but himself. Always this bitterness came home to him.

Charlie was telegraphing to his brother that someone would have to sit on the dresser now. Which actually happened.

"'Shepherd's pie', dost call that, lass?" roared Uncle Ned, viewing it on the landscape of the table below him. "Well, by gum. I'll turn shepherd, I think, if it is, for it smells right grand."

"Behave thysel,' Ned," chided Bella Stone. "She'll think we're a lot o' gormands."

"Sit thee down, 'Lizabeth," said Mrs. Peel. "Here. There's a chear aside o' John. I'll serve out."

But Elizabeth plainly did not intend to sit down. It was John's brother Ned who placed his great hands on his sister-in-law's shoulders, and thrust her down beside John by main force.

Through the cloud of steam from the pie in the centre of the table she saw the faces across the table—Ned, Charlie, the two wives, Joe Crowther, digging into his pie as though he had never eaten since he was born, and poor Mrs. Crowther terrified lest she drop anything on the glory of her blouse. Everybody looked happy. The families had married each other. Only—the individuals had not.

"Did ta ha' some o' this pie afore tha wed her, John?" chaffed an old fellow.

There was a general laugh.

"Nay, tha needn't glance at me like that, John," he was told.

Elizabeth felt sick. Her very efficiency became an insult to her. She wished vehemently that she had cooked pies suggestive of the Stone Age. Whilst she toyed with the food on her plate.

"Well, tha'll not be out of pocket wi' what she clears off," chaffed another. Which almost made John jump off his chair.

It was all honest, northern fun—quite decent if they had been what they were thought to be. But with their mutual knowledge the badinage held stings their friends did not think of.

"Let 'em alone. Let 'em alone; they'll eat in a bit," shouted Uncle Ned, waving his fork, as he showed an empty plate from the dresser. "They're livin' off luv. Charlie and I will join at an' egg as the young lady said at the Hotel Majestic when the waiter asked what they'd 'ave."

Quite suddenly, Elizabeth wanted to laugh; was it possible that her cooking had gone to the depths of John's heart? Had she waited thirty years for that?

After the pie, whose only fault Uncle Ned had set down as "it was moarish," came the pudding and the raspberries, and the cheese tarts, and the coffee, whose berries Elizabeth ground ready for the pot as the kettle boiled. John realised that Elizabeth's fine economy only had made it possible to serve such a houseful of folk such a spread.

"'Tilda," called Charlie to his wife, "tha must get her to show tha how to make these." Tilda smiled, without resentment.

All the women folk shared in clearing away and washing up, with the exception of Mrs. Peel and Bella Stone, who sat chin-wagging whilst Jerry Young made weird noises as he tuned his fiddle. A young girl whom he greeted as "Annie" came in, with a shawl on her head, and sat down by the old man.

"Somebody'll have to sit on somebody's knee now," said Charlie.

Elizabeth, having packed the pots away, was the last to wander towards that hearthstone circle, where every chair was touching the next.

She looked for a seat. The next moment she was pulled on John's knee. John was living and learning. He knew that she wanted to kill him, as they all laughed at the joke. He knew her pride was putting her into torments, and it filled him with malicious delight.

"She's trying to look as if she doesn't like it," said Uncle Ned. "Eh, these women!"

Jerry Young was still struggling with the E string, making all kinds of faces, and, quite suddenly, as she stared across at the old man, the strain Elizabeth had been conscious of all the evening culminated in an almost imperative desire to laugh hysterically. She never achieved anything so hardly, as holding down that desire to laugh, whilst unconsciously she knew that, like a cough, the more it was struggled against, the worse it would be when it did come.

"What shall I play?" asked Jerry Young, cuddling his fiddle under his chin. He shouted the query out from his walls of shut-in-deafness. Then, without waiting for an answer, he began to play. Rigs and jigs, and croony Irish melodies and old ballads he played. The deafness had not yet eaten its way into his music.

Whilst John, trembling within, but bold enough without, slid his arm around Elizabeth's waist, whilst Uncle Ned nudged Charlie, and John's eyes said, "Well, why shouldn't I?"

He was glad that he could not see Elizabeth's eyes. He knew he could not have done it if he had, whilst he felt that excitement a man might feel at having a mountain lioness on a string.

"Come on, Annie," nudged Jerry. He had evidently asked the young girl to come and sing. Sing she could.

"That's it! Let's ha' some o' th' owd' uns," said Uncle Ned, as Jerry struck up the accompaniment to "Annie Laurie."

"An' for bonnie Annie Laurie I wad lie me down— an' dee."

John gave Elizabeth's waist a faint squeeze. He knew she was boiling with rage.

"'Lizabeth! The child's wakened," said Mrs. Peel.

It was Elizabeth's opportunity. She took the child and its wrappings from the cot, and Charlie gave her his seat. John could see her face now, It was quite pale at the indignity she had suffered. The child stared at the assembly with round, wide-awake eyes, and they looked for protection to Elizabeth.

When Charlie sang "The Full Ones don't care what the Empty Ones feel" (with his waistcoat quite tight, as Uncle Ned said), his glance fixed bashfully on the centre of the ceiling, Jerry Young packed his fiddle, and Annie put on her shawl.

"Wait a bit. There's a speech to make," said another crony, catching Jerry by the button.

"A—what?" he yelled back.

"A—spee—ech," said the other.

Oh, said Jerry, and sat down. For a moment he thought it was more ale-posset coming along.

Uncle Ned mounted upon the strongest of the kitchen chairs.

"There's nowt in being low down in the world," he said with a beaming smile. Then he rambled on about the happiness he could see in Elizabeth and John, and was sure he expressed the sentiments of everybody there when he hoped all their troubles would be "little ones," with a sly emphasis on the

156

words, as though anyone could mistake his meaning, with that knowing twinkle in his eye. He sat down amidst great applause. People began to talk of going. But Mrs. Peel, in answer to Elizabeth's eye, made cocoa, and handed cups round. Some of them had a fair distance to travel.

One by one they went off into the night. Mrs. Stone, Charlie and Ned, and their wives went off in a trap. Uncle Ned loitered amongst the last four.

Thunder, by God!" he said, as he was buttoning up his coat. Thunder it was.

In five minutes, during which they waited, with northern optimism, for it to pass, the storm was raging across the country-side.

"What'll ta do, Jerry?" asked Uncle Ned.

He was really wondering what he should do himself.

"You can't go in this," John told the old man.

Elizabeth seconded him rather faintly.

A mile in the rain that would follow might give old Jerry his death.

"Ninety-five an' not out yet," said Jerry, "an' not a bit waur, not a bit waur."

"Thar't goin' to ha' to put us up, John," said Uncle Ned, with a good assumption of reluctance.

"It can't last long like this," said Elizabeth hopefully.

"I've slept on a sofa afore," said Uncle Ned.

"I've slept in fish-carts afore to-night," said a little bandy-legged man, whose relationship to John nobody seemed to know.

With varying hope and despair Elizabeth stood in the passage, watching the storm. The child was asleep again.

When the clock struck twelve it was too late to ask if it would still clear up. Jerry Young was locked out. Elizabeth made the couch comfortable for him. Uncle Ned prepared to lie down on the rug, and said he wanted to be turning in. The girl in the little shawl—she was a problem.

"I'm freetened o' th' leetnin'," was all she would sob. "They'll not expect me home in this."

Elizabeth gave her a nightdress and led her to the room usually occupied by Dick Burnham, Then, taking her candle and the sleeping child, she also retired.

John Stone went upstairs, after dawdling as long as he could. He pushed into the room that had been Burnham's, thinking it was empty. Whereupon he got a vision of a half-dressed girl plaiting her hair by candlelight. There arose a penetrating scream.

"What the Hanover—" came from below stairs, in Uncle Ned's voice.

John stumbled out upon the yard-square bit of landing between the two bedrooms.

"It's only John got into the wrong room," came Elizabeth's laughing voice. She had to open her door to shout.

"More mistakes nor beef-steaks," called Uncle Ned back again. "Good-neet to everybody."

Elizabeth was closing the door on John. But he put his foot in at the door.

"I can't sleep—on the mat," he said doggedly.

"You can't sleep in the housekeeper's room," she told him in a low voice.

He shouldered his way into the dimness of the room. It had a holy look to him, the candles lit, the flowers in glasses, the clean sweetness of it—and Elizabeth, quite forgetful of her bare neck shimmering through her hair, as she said, with stiff lips, "You can't sleep here, John Stone."

She was trapped. Downstairs were the house-warmers. He advanced a step towards her. She retreated one—with wide, frightened eyes.

John stared at her for a moment, then his eye caught sight of a little drawing stuck on the wall with pins.

It was a sketch of Dick Burnham, by himself. John smiled.

"Oh, that's it, is it?" he said lightly.

Then he saw the glitter of tears in her eyes. She half-opened her lips to speak.

"You are quite mistaken, John," she murmured.

Dick had given her that sketch as a memento of his gratitude for her soothing of Mary's last hours. It was another proof to John Stone that Elizabeth had a passion for his friend.

"When I see eggs I can guess shells," said John, not noticing his transposition in his agitation. For he was agitated, more startled than by anything that had befallen him.

He had not meant to intrude upon Elizabeth. A mad whim had urged him to test her, to scare her, to do anything but let her remain proud and unshaken. Before he had seen Burnham's picture he had repented of it.

"You are quite wrong, John," said Elizabeth, shakily.

Uncle Ned with his picture of John as a baby, had struck a great blow at Elizabeth's forte of pride.

John did not remember until he was up in the attic that Elizabeth had followed him to the door, her face quite pale. To him it was a weighing of guilt and fear he saw in her face.

It was really the struggle of her soul to shake itself free from that promise to the dead— "Don't tell John."

She was beginning to believe that John Stone cared. She was beginning to cease to care how it had come about, and whether he had liked Mary more, or differently, or all those things that are details. As for herself—

There was not another man in the universe for whom she would have suffered these indignities peculiar to their strange life.

She had even acknowledged to herself, with burnings of shamed pride, that she had actually gone through the mockery of that service, not merely to save being talked about, but to be able to serve him more, serve him who had actually despised her as he lay drunk, talking on the garden path.

She had anathematised herself as allied to the dogs that lick the boots of those who kick them.

"I shall kill Burnham if he stays here long," John told himself, as he tried to sleep.

Then he seemed to feel the wavering, timid touch on his sleeve as she said, "You are quite wrong, John." He rolled a velvet coat of Dick Burnham's angrily into a pillow for his head, and slept at length, unwittingly that in the pockets of it were several of the letters Dick had left out from those he had gone to bury.

Chapter XII

John eats humble pie

When John came downstairs in the morning, his guests were gone. He was stiff, and the sense of humiliation from last night clung to him. He rattled at the fire-grate so vengefully that Elizabeth feared he would bring the house down. This thought was mildly chronicled on her face, as John turned his countenance in her direction when she entered the kitchen. He got the absurd feeling that she was laughing at him again. Things were reaching a crisis, psychologically. John felt he was being laughed at. The calm Elizabeth was losing her nerve.

In utter silence John blew up the fire with the bellows, whilst Elizabeth made tea and set cake.

"I'm going to Dimpleton to-day to help Jane Wild open her shop," announced Elizabeth. "She asked me to show her how to make rhubarb wine for sale."

She cut his cake as he spoke.

John had the irritated feeling that would come of her asking for a holiday like a conscientious hireling. How rigidly she stuck to the very letter of her bargain. "I will keep house for you, John Stone." It was he who had striven to break the contract.

His antagonism now was of a different calibre from that old one. Elizabeth could not be bent.

"Taking the child?" he asked, whilst he was wondering how to break her.

"I—hadn't decided," she answered.

Elizabeth was usually decisive.

There was something evasive about her, for a moment—a troubled something he could not account for. But it soon faded away.

John went out to work carrying his food basket, discontented with himself and the world. It was going to be a very hot day. The haze told of it.

Elizabeth would not be bringing his dinner.

"Mornin'," he said, casually, before closing the door.

"Mornin'," said Elizabeth, already commencing her day's work in conscientious discharge of her seven shillings' pay.

"I must get out of this poverty puddle," mused John, frowning at the shimmering beauty of the dawn. "I must take the work away from her—make her dependent. Then she'll have to move."

That night, in the quiet of his kitchen, John solved the problem of his invention. It was solved in a fury of effort to drive Elizabeth from her stronghold of pride. Only as he completed his task and looked at the clock did he realise that Elizabeth was late. Mrs. Peel brought in the baby and put her to bed before Elizabeth came.

"You needn't have waited supper," she remarked, and winced.

For John had prepared the meal. He poured out her tea and waited on her, watching her reluctance to be served, with quiet malicious satisfaction. He had got his cue.

"How's the shop gone on?" he asked.

Elizabeth glowed.

"Splendidly!" she said. "It will be a success. Jane isn't the least bit afraid."

She had not realised that Jane's courage was the effect of her own personality. John realised it and her almost incredulous modesty.

"Oh—don't!" she exclaimed, as he got up to pour her a second cup of tea.

But John did. He had got the right cue at last. She had come to keep house; he could corner her by robbing her of her duties. First of all he must get his invention going.

The path for John's success was easy for three reasons. There was a long-felt need supplied by his machine; it was cheap to produce, needing no complicated plant; whilst it saved the men in health and risk it saved the employer compensation claims, and was also an economiser.

Young Manners, the foundry owner, was sufficiently impressed with it to get John to promise to see no other firm about it for a week. He promised that if it worked on its secret trial, that he himself would put up plant. It could be one of the articles they produced and their own monopoly, John being partner in all profits made. John, with the suspicion engendered by the difference in the house Manners lived in and his own, carried away with him a written promise not to infringe.

During the next fortnight, great things happened in the Stone household. Little Mary set off walking, "all by herself," as Mrs. Peel wonderingly put it. Dick Burnham went back to London, but left a warning that he should return soon, after assuring himself that Chelsea was still there. Mrs. Peel knelt on a tin-tack and venomed her knee so that she could not kneel down to wash floors, which meant that Elizabeth worked in both John Stone's house and her mother's. Mrs. Peel had extra work to be done. Whilst Elizabeth, little Mary toddling unsteadily after her, needing to be watched from falling, was setting her mother's house in order, each evening John was maliciously doing "odd jobs" for Elizabeth. Her pride was sorely tried.

At last the struggle culminated.

"I can't mind two houses, mother," said Elizabeth, "you must get somebody in—and I'll pay for the work doing."

"John can take pot-luck for a bit," said Mrs. Peel in surprise. "It isn't as if he isn't used to roughing it."

To let John "rough it" was exactly what Elizabeth could not let John do. Her only justification for being in John's house was her domestic service to him.

John grinned to himself when he saw Mrs. Crowther come over to help Mrs. Peel. He was quite convinced things would have to be worse before they were better. For the moment he was resolutely content to let Dick Burnham stand out of the picture entirely.

Within the next month Manners put up the plant for the making of John's machine. Humidifiers and a few other iron goods were their specialities. The gas-safety was apparently going to play second fiddle to none of their productions. But John knew that its chief interest to employers lay in its being cheaper to have one than to have the yearly expenditure on compensation claims.

"Orders are pouring in already, Stone," he was told, as he crossed the yard one morning. "There's going to be no doubt about it."

Neither was there.

Its success was assured on the basis of economy to the employer, and the notices of its advent in the Mechanical Times and similar journals, giving its appearance on the market a philanthropic use to suffering humanity, made John smile with the inner knowledge of a man who has worked for low wages for twenty of his goldenest years.

"Tha'll be leaving the foundry," was a common cry in these days, and as he walked through the village it had much pride in him, and some wonder that for all these years he had passed himself off as a somewhat stupid man.

Elizabeth, meanwhile, was daily gathering up rose-leaves, as they fell, in John's garden (and her mother's). She was going to give a couple of pot-pourri bowls to the bazaar.

Apparently, she was quite unimpressed by the sudden fame that cast the limelight on John.

A reporter called one day, asking for a photograph of John, and Elizabeth sent him round to the foundry. But that did not prevent him giving a detailed description of the house, garden, and the foundryman's "comely and amiable partner."

"You haven't a family photograph, have you?" the reporter had said, before passing forth.

"I haven't," said Elizabeth, in a tone the news vulture could not mistake. He had heard it too often.

John went on wheeling his barrow to the weighing place, without thought of changing his job, until Manners put it into his head that he might do better. He jumped at the position of foreman, since it would leave him considerably more energy for brain-work.

If you've any other ideas for improvements," said young Manners; "trot 'em out." Then, "This is going to make you a tidy little fortune, Stone. I've waited until I'm quite sure. They're booming your invention in The Mechanic this week."

Which made John go hot and cold.

His discontent had been a smouldering affair; now, its flames leaped sky-high. But the essence of his triumph was—he could hound Elizabeth from her lair of pride.

That week, acquainting her with his good luck, he paid Elizabeth ten shillings instead of seven, quarrelled with little Mary's Sunday dress, ordering Elizabeth to get the child a silk one—and came back from town with a huge snake gold-framed brooch for Elizabeth.

She accepted it after a brief hesitation, as too small a matter to worry about.

"If things go on as they should," said John, cheerfully, "we'll leave this little house, and live better." Elizabeth tried to hide her discomposure.

She was sewing a fine seam. John had boldly planted his chair near to hers. He was close enough to see the eye of her needle, but he might have been a thousand miles away, for what notice she gave to him.

"This house is quite large enough for me to keep clean," she said, some time afterwards, as she rethreaded her needle.

"You can have help," said John.

She looked up from her fine seam.

Her gaze met his quizzical one.

She had perceived his drift.

He was out to make her either less—or more—than a hireling.

On the morrow John went to work whistling cheerfully. He could not help feeling excited, and he had put on cloth trousers to mark his rising position in the world.

Elizabeth was bringing his dinner to-day, too. That was always something to look forward to.

"Who was that jumped into the basket, then?" frowned the boss, at eleven o'clock.

The timekeeper looked down from his window.

"The foreman, sir," he said.

"Oh!" said Manners, but still frowning. "Some men value life very lightly."

John laughed when the timekeeper acquainted him with the incident.

He knew whether he valued life lightly or not. In another hour he should see Elizabeth.

"He's got that accident of Vernon's on the brain," he said, laughingly.

"I should be careful, Stone," said the timekeeper. "He'll be putting fines on the others, else."

Which did touch John's conscience, though he still thought Manners somewhat of an old woman in his nervousness. John had gone up and down in that basket thousands of times, each time barely giving the hauler up time to miss dashing his brains out against the chimney-tunnel.

He walked across the yard, whistling, and then, sitting down on an upturned tub, drew something in the ore-dust with a stick. Now that his brain had got working, it seemed as if he could not stop it producing other ideas. Whilst he knew that his real inspiration lay in Elizabeth—always busy, always impelling the best in others, from Joe Crowther's wife, in her ramshackle home, to Dick Burnham, with his art school training.

Raking the purple dust over his drawing, he sauntered to the foundry-gates. He told himself that he was looking at the river, shining in the sun as it wound between the banks, but really he was looking for Elizabeth. Then, he fell to picturing her. He could always picture her at any hour of any day. She was very methodical. She would be peeping in the oven, now, with little Mary toddling after her and maybe she was saying "burny-burn" in her gravely warning way.

He had another chat with the timekeeper, and settled a dispute between two men, who both wanted to claim the same barrow. Then, his aimless wandering towards the gates began again—until, realising it, he swung round, checking himself.

"Hungry to-day, old man?" quoth the timekeeper, grinning, having noticed the attraction of the gates.

He wondered afterwards why John flushed so. After all, there was nothing to be ashamed of in being hungry.

It was just a quarter to twelve when John got the idea of going up in the basket, for a chat with Crowther on his domestic circumstances.. For John had heard that Mrs. Crowther in her new-fledged mother-courage was making pies of Joe's pigeons— saying her children had gone hungry long enough.

There was humour in it, to John—for he saw what Joe did not—the hand of Elizabeth pulling the strings. He went towards the basket.

"Seen Stone anywhere about?" Manners asked the timekeeper, a minute later.

Gone up," said the timekeeper.

At this moment a white-faced workman came hurrying towards the boss. It was Jim Dooley—but a shaky Jim Dooley, unlike the man who was always quarrelling about wrong barrows.

The boss looked at him.

"Accident?" asked the boss, laconically,

Jim nodded.

"Yessir!" he said, hoarsely.

"Who is it this time?" asked Manners. Involuntarily, he moved towards the hoist. "Stone," said Jim.

He walked unsteadily away.

There was no man with whom Dooley had quarrelled more about barrows. Indeed, they had come near to fighting once or twice.

"I reckon Stone's got a pretty hard knock," said the timekeeper, trying to make his voice callous; "Remember Vernon?"

"The damned fools!" said the boss, savagely. "Come on, Riley!"

Riley realised that the boss wanted the human comfort of his company, and forgot that Manners had had an education.

They went.

They saw.

Joe Crowther, reiterating that John had shouted "Up with it!" before he had got into the basket, and that he must have jumped in when it was a foot from the ground, was a pitiful ghost, who followed in their wake.

"Phone Conrad," said Manners to Riley. "And—the constable."

The timekeeper went into the office.

" 'Up with it,' he says," said Joe, shuddering. "So I up with it. How was I to know?"

The boss was looking at the path leading up to the foundry-gate. A woman carrying a baby, and a dinner, was approaching. He was almost sure it was Elizabeth. Though he had not seen her at close range, he had once noticed her in church. She had almost fallen asleep during a rendering of Bach's Fugues, played by a famous organist. But her smiling face had been so good to look at, that Manners had found himself forgetting the Fugue.

"Isn't that Mrs. Stone?" he asked Crowther.

Crowther gave one glance—and bolted.

"The doctor's out at a confinement," said Riley popping his head out of the office. "But the assistant's coming—and he's ordering the ambulance from town." Then he followed the direction of the young boss's gaze.

"She's fetched his dinner!" said Riley, and followed Crowther's example.

Manners advanced towards Elizabeth, who was telling the baby something about "Dadda".

She was already looking for John.

As Manners got nearer to her, he lost his fear that she might faint and let the baby fall when he broke the news.

"Bringing John's dinner?" he asked.

She nodded.

"Sit in the office a moment," he said.

He led her to the little room.

Baby Mary was trying to eat her hat.

She evidently sat there under the impression that the boss would fetch John to her.

The telephone bell began to ring.

"Excuse me a moment," said Manners.

It was the ambulance station.

"Yes. The accident is here," called Manners.

"Hurry. Concussion, we believe, and minor injuries."

Elizabeth was looking at him, and the baby was really getting a good chance to devour the hat, when he hung up the receiver.

"So someone is hurt?" she asked.

She was trembling a little.

Her voice was more beautiful than might have been expected of a woman who fell asleep during an organ recital.

She had set the dinner basket down on the floor. It assumed pathetic meanings Manners had not supposed a dinner-basket to hold.

"Didn't you think it strange, my bringing you to wait in here?" asked Manners.

The baby actually dragged a red rose, with a gurgle of delight, into biting range.

Elizabeth was looking at him dumbly:

"He jumped into the basket without giving due warning," went on Manners, noting her closely. "He's very badly hurt, Mrs. Stone. Very badly hurt, indeed."

They heard the sound of Conrad's trap.

"Where is he?" asked Elizabeth.

He was scarcely recognisable.

She was trembling violently now.

But she was mechanically rescuing the rose from the intentions of the baby to eat it, and die.

She was dry-eyed.

But her look hurt the boss.

"Over there, on a bit of grass,' he said, pointing. "Two men are with him. One has done ambulance work."

He watched her lug the fat baby across towards the bit of grass. She was trying to walk as though nothing was the matter. She did not walk quite straight.

"A fine" answered the boss. "A damned heavy fine!"

Then he turned to lead the doctor's assistant to John's aid.

When they reached the bit of grass they found the baby sitting on it, too. Elizabeth was standing waiting. She had put her handkerchief under John's head, where the blood was oozing.

"How—did she take it?" asked the boss, of one of the men in a whisper.

"She's just stood there, like that—all the time," he said, in a low voice. "When we saw her coming I said, 'Now for it!' But—she's guts!" he added, in foundryman's language.

"The miracle is he has a head on at all!" said Conrad's assistant, rising. Then "Are you his wife?" Elizabeth nodded.

She had an hysterical desire to laugh, to cry, to scream. She felt that she was only saved because she couldn't do three things at once.

"Operation," said the assistant, to Elizabeth. "But whilst there's life there's hope. The ambulance—"

"At home," said Elizabeth.

She picked up the baby from the grass.

"You mean he'll be operated on at home?" queried the assistant.

Elizabeth nodded.

"Twenty pounds," said the assistant.

"Home," asserted Elizabeth.

The foundrymen watched the ambulance-van drive away, with Elizabeth and the baby in it.

"Well, it's only natural. They've not bin wed long. But mine wouldn't pay twenty pence to keep me at home."

Such was the humorous statement of Riley, the timekeeper.

"Eh, tha never knows a woman," said another darkly.

In another hour, John was laid on the big bed that had held Mary. Mrs. Peel was rocking herself in

Mary's rocking chair, ostensibly come to help, but in reality doing quite the opposite. Elizabeth and she had drunk strong tea three times within the hour.

Upstairs was the doctor, and a nurse.

"She were very soft," said Mrs. Peel, out of the depths of some thought.

"Soft?" asked Elizabeth, stupidly.

Upstairs John's life hung on a thread.

Mrs. Peel would talk on, until, as she said herself sometimes, they stopped her mouth with earth.

"Mary, when she were dying," explained Mrs. Peel.

"She was none that soft," said Elizabeth, swiftly.

"Well, I weren't saying—" began Mrs. Peel.

"He'll get better," said Elizabeth, stubbornly.

Her mother looked at her for a moment.

Then she said, shaking her head sadly, "Well, I hope so, lass. An' if he doesn't, tha mun make the best of a bad job. Anyhow, tha's done thy duty. It's cost clean twenty pounds." After a pause, she added, "How will you go on—whilst he's not workin'?"

For Elizabeth had lent her brother all her savings, so that he could marry Letty at last. Letty was getting restive, and there had been a few quarrels lately.

"I shall sell the house," said Elizabeth calmly.

"The—th' last house tha has?" gasped Mrs. Peel. "Thy—thy granny'd turn in her grave."

"H—sh!" said Elizabeth.

The impatient look on her face faded away into an intentness of listening.

"It's over," she said, rising from her chair.

They were coming down.

The assistant was met at the foot of the stairs by Elizabeth. She was silent.

"We can't tell for twenty-four hours," he said, and gave instructions.

"I'll take the child out of the way," suggested Mrs. Peel.

Elizabeth's face had touched her.

Even her loquacity failed a little.

She remembered Elizabeth's sympathy when James Peel was brought home from the quarry, and she had dimly perceived a little how Elizabeth had hidden her own grief in the depths of her heart.

"An'—whatever comes or goes, it'll be a comfort to thee to know tha's bin a good wife to him!" she said.

Elizabeth looked at her in that dazed stupid way.

As the door closed behind her mother and the baby, she burst into hysterical tears.

She only remembered—that she had slapped his face! That she had nursed titanic pride, that until now, whenever she had thought of him lying on the garden path and repenting of having asked her to marry him, she had not forgiven him. "The mark of the cloven hoof," Elizabeth told herself, fiercely. "What had I to be proud of, anyhow?"

All through that weary day, and still wearier night, Elizabeth brewed tea. Never afterwards could she look at the brown enamel teapot with the white painted lily on it without a human feeling that it knew things about her, which she had never told anyone, that it could speak, if it would, of utter demoralisation and panic, when all her world tottered, and even faith was an empty thing.

At last it was over.

John Stone would live.

With that strange feeling of additional age, and yet additional youth, Elizabeth sat by the bedside, waiting for him to open his eyes.

The district nurse was gone.

Measles had broken out in Dimpleton.

She had much to do.

Elizabeth had just finished the last rose in Letty's tatted collar, when she saw that John was coining back to consciousness.

The joy of it.

"I shall—get rid of the parrot!" was John's first remark.

He was staring wildly at Elizabeth.

Her radiant hope flickered down.

The stupidly, helpless feeling she had had whilst waiting downstairs came to her again.

"Yes, John," she said, soothingly.

Then John was staring at her, gathering up the threads, or trying to, where he had left off.

"The—basket," he said, and tried to raise his splintered arm to his head.

Elizabeth soothed him, made all clear.

She did not go away.

John realised that.

"My mother," he asked, after a while.

"I wrote her," said Elizabeth.

There was another pause.

Then—"Are you very sorry, Elizabeth?" asked John.

"Sorry?" she queried.

"That I'm getting—better?" queried John.

Elizabeth struggled.

She had meant John to go on his bended knees before she gave in. Then—she had thought him dying. Now—he was out of danger. He was better. And—she could not give in. Besides—

The thoughts of the buried letters further confused her.

"If—I'd gone out, you could have married Burnham," said John.

Elizabeth gave up the hopeless struggle.

She could not explain Burnham away without explaining—Mary.

"I—don't want to marry Burnham," she said.

Marry him! She was sick of his name, and his muddle, and the hole he had helped to put her in, or at least to keep her in.

"You let him hold your hand, said John. Why did you do it?"

"I—was sorry for him,"' said Elizabeth, her pride fainting again under the pallor of his look.

John struggled with the same pride.

"Be sorry for me, like that!" he begged.

He put out his uninjured hand, feebly. Elizabeth wavered. Then her fingers touched his.

"Let me hold it, for a minute!" said John.

He was holding Elizabeth's hand.

It trembled more than anyone would suppose Elizabeth's hand could tremble.

Elizabeth was watching the clock on the little mantelpiece, with the rosy pot apples, one on each side of it. Something was breaking up in her. It was her pride. With every tick of the clock it was going, moving like an avalanche—going to crash, at a mile a second. She was realising things as John's hand held hers, entreatingly, so it seemed, yet commandingly too. His hand, the hand of her man, the hand of a toiler, as he had always been a toiler, held hers. He needed her. She stared deep into the depths of her own heart, and did not flinch.

"I was jealous—because she came first," she acknowledged to herself, at last.

This took about half of John's minute.

He was looking at her averted face.

The avalanche was nearing two miles a second, now. Pride was going. And, unfortunately, with it, conscience, "I have no right to bear her burden of shortcomings," said something in Elizabeth.

"You—are very kind, Elizabeth," said John, humbly grateful that she did not draw her hand away.

She started guiltily at the sound of his voice. Kind!

At that moment she had felt cattish.

The tears sprang to her eyes.

That was what Mary had murmured once, in her chaotic last breath.

"The—the minute is up," said Elizabeth.

Her voice was shaken.

175

She could not hide her emotion from John.

"Thanks," he said, relinquishing her hand, slowly. "I—I didn't think I could have asked a woman to let me hold her hand—when I knew it—hurt her. We don't know what we have to come to, do we?" with an attempt at jocularity.

She looked at him, shaking her head in assent almost stupidly.

Elizabeth was reaching the limit of her endurance. She knew it, too.

"I'll fetch you something to drink," she said, as an excuse for going downstairs.

She tried to think out the situation after five cups of strong tea, but could find no solution. Elizabeth could not walk to John's side over a broken promise to the dead, who had thought her kind. Moreover, she could not bear to think John should think harshly of Mary.

To tell the whole truth was to let him know that for two years he had lived with a woman whose heart still clung to a former affection. The letters would tell that.

As she went up with John's beef tea, the door opened and closed.

"Only me," came Dick Burnham's voice.

So he had heard of the accident.

John had heard the door open and close. Burnham was back.

He came upstairs, as Elizabeth was letting John drink from the boat, which Mary had not long ago drunk from.

"We can't kill thee off, then," he said, jocularly.

Elizabeth's arm was under John's pillow.

Burnham had spoken in deep concern at John's accident.

"No," said John, dryly. "They say God'll not have given stuff. So—tha'll ha' to wait a bit yet, Burnham."

Beneath the retort there was a meaning Dick could not mistake.

He pondered.

"Seems so," he said at length, diplomatically.

"I think you'd best go down," said Elizabeth, fearfully.

John read her uneasiness. He looked at her reassuringly.

When Elizabeth went down to make Burnham his tea, that young man remarked: "I say—is the doctor sure his brain will be all right?"

"Perfectly sure,' said Elizabeth.

The sense of the ludicrousness of it all came to her.

Sitting down in Mary's chair, without realising that she was doing so, she began to laugh. She laughed until she saw Burnham looking at her, not sure of her brain having been turned. Which made her laugh more.

Upstairs John heard her laughing—laughing as she had not laughed since she had come to his house.

"She can laugh when he comes back," he thought, moodily.

He sulked at the next beef tea she took him up. Then he ate humble pie again. He was always eating humble pie these days. As he thought of it, another idea entered his head.

"Good Lord!" he startled himself with. "What shall we live on this next six months?" Compensation pay would be a living, he thought, if he should get it. There would be nothing from his patent for six months.

Next day his mother came.

Which he knew meant a family diversion.

He put out feelers as to borrowing money.

"Everybody's fast as thieves now," said Bella Stone. "What's tha want th' brass for, John?"

He told her.

She opened her eyes.

"Why—hasn't Elizabeth told thee?" she asked. "She's sold her house. A hundred an' fort—y!"

Never had John been so irritated at his mother's way of saying fort—y.

Humble pie.

Only two days before he had been going to bring down the proud Elizabeth by moving her into a fine house with a housekeeper. Now—

He was beginning to live on the bricks and mortar of her last house.

Chapter XIII

Burnham dispels an illusion

Bella Stone left no doubts of her intention to stay at least a week with John and Elizabeth. By that time they would have got the hay in at the farm, and she would change the bed-ticks against the winter. So she comfortably told them.

The old problem of hiding a secret in a house of two up, two down, was upon them. It came in an intensified form this time, for Mrs. Stone was not blinded by agitated grief, as before. Dick Burnham made a shake-down on the attic floor in preference to being talked to death each morning before breakfast by Mrs. Peel. Bella Stone slept in the little room.

When they had thus settled themselves, Elizabeth was left downstairs to consider, whilst she made John's barley and lemon water, where she should sleep. John was not well enough to be left unattended all night, even if she had dared to run the risk of that poking early-bird of an old dame coming down to the horror of finding her sleeping downstairs. If she slept outside the door, Dick or Bella Stone might discover her. For Elizabeth was very tired with the past week of strain. She had broken almost as many pots during the past three days as placed her a good second after the girl whom John had had, who had said that it was good for the pot trade. She caught herself nodding sometimes in the daytime.

John awoke to hear the jink of the jug with the cup set inside it, and to see Elizabeth with the candle.

She had something over her arm, too. On close scrutiny it proved to be the sheepskin rug from the parlour.

"I've got to sleep in here," said Elizabeth with dignity and never a blush. She did not even move the candle light from her countenance.

She was indeed a spiritual Amazon. There was a moment's silence.

"It's hard on you, Elizabeth," said John, sympathetically.

"My pay has gone up," said Elizabeth.

It was out before she realised it. She was dimly amazed at the return of the cattish mood she had felt when she let John hold her hand, remembering her promise to Mary.

John was looking at her. He took the blow without flinching. But his fingers moved a little as if he were trying to play the piano.

"I didn't think the post would have been so difficult," he said, merely.

Elizabeth had not thought so, either.

It was becoming more difficult, more bitter, more impossible every day. And the reason was—she was afraid, living in dread that John Stone would discover that she was in love with him.

Little Mary smiled in her sleep when Elizabeth tucked her up.

John watched Elizabeth's shadow on the wall, as she plaited her hair. At least there was no ban against that. He was waiting for his customary drink.

Elizabeth brought the cup, holding him up, her arm under the pillow.

"Good-night," said John, as she set the cup inside the jug once more.

"Good-night," answered Elizabeth.

He was staring up at her. Quite suddenly it dawned on her that he was struggling against a desire to kiss her.

Elizabeth turned her back. What she was really saying to herself was, "Get thee behind me, Satan."

The road of love to Elizabeth was becoming a path of disloyalty to Mary Stone. Once the barrier between herself and John broke down, she feared she could but tell him all, and clear herself of the least suspicion that she had cared for any other.

John saw, in that back-view of Elizabeth, only a determination not to be disloyal—to Dick.

She laid herself down in her clothes on that sheepskin rug, hidden from John by the pink curtains draping the bed-foot, and was fast asleep within a minute.

"Elizabeth!" woke her.

She was dimly aware she had fancied she heard someone calling her several times before, but had been unable to answer.

Dawn was pouring into the room.

"Did you call? asked Elizabeth, on reaching John's bedside.

"Parched up," he told her.

"I'm so sorry," she said, with a sudden warmth flashing out on him, like the rising sun.

For a moment, Elizabeth had forgotten that a barrier existed. She had touched his hand with the half-caress that only love employs. John drank greedily.

"That's—heaven!" he said, gratefully.

The twittering of birds came up to them.

Elizabeth laid him down again and looked at the clock. Scarcely five. It was too early to wake the house yet. The hush and holiness of a new day wrapped them round. Everything was a pearly shimmer. There were two bright bars of light on the bedroom wall-paper with the horseshoes of roses on it and the blue lovers.

Elizabeth walked to the window and held the blind away a little, making the two bars of light rush into a triangular patch, and a sudden radiance fell on a square yard of the generous roses.

"It's a lovely morning," she remarked. Then she put the blind to again, gently.

"It's good to be alive," said John, following her with his eyes.

"I'd best dress your hand," said Elizabeth.

"It will do after breakfast," said John. "Don't spoil this hour, Elizabeth."

She perceived that he, also, had felt the beauty of these moments.

"Sit and read something, Elizabeth," asked John.

Elizabeth took something out of the dressing- table drawer, and sitting down, read it out. John was torn between two joys, the joy of listening to her voice and the very earthly joy of trying to grasp all that the words she read meant to him. It was the "boom" in the Mechanical Times.

"So you needn't worry about my having sold the house," smiled Elizabeth, "you can pay me back."

Even as the sting of this from the woman he had been gloatingly thinking he would make dependent, came to him, he was conscious of the gate of the morning's holy beauty slamming on his face with a dull sound. The magic was gone. Elizabeth, nobly though she had done it, had brought up a sordid barrier, and they stood apart, self-sufficing, proud, balance sheet in hand.

Elizabeth also perceived that the glory was departed.

"Shall I do your hand now?" she asked.

"You might as well," said John, spiritlessly for a man whose fortune was prophesied in the Mechanical Times.

Elizabeth took off the bandages and dressed his hand. He noticed that she winced once or twice at the pain she caused, and laughed. She was a curious blend of hardness and softness, this woman who could stitch a man up in a sheet, and make herself the instrument of Providence.

The drip of the water into the bowl sounded loud in the stillness of the room. As she held his hand in hers, whilst she put on clean lint and bandage, a momentary gleam of the glory and the dream came back to them.

"That's Dick moving," said John, sombrely.

The shadow fell again.

Dick came whistling his way down out of the attic.

It was one of his carelessly selfish traits, the same one which, on an enlarged scale, had made him shirk "settling down" with Mary Bussey, though he had known he ought to.

He awoke the baby. There was a loud, expostulating cry. And then the house woke up.

Soon Mrs. Stone in the other room was getting into her clothes.

The bustle of the day began.

The first lull that fell upon it was just after ten, when Conrad's trap came up to the little house.

"Morning, Elizabeth," he said, as she opened the door.

He spoke without his usual smile. Elizabeth guessed. His last son was dead, despite Swiss hydros, and pine forest air. It was the Doctor's burden.

"Are they going to get their hay in?" he asked, and tapped the weather-glass to see.

Elizabeth followed him upstairs.

John began to agitate about getting down.

"Well—perhaps for a few hours towards week-end," said the Doctor. "Anyhow, Elizabeth'll keep you in order."

When he got downstairs he admired the apples in the blue and white dish on the table, entered into a conversation with Elizabeth on the relative merits of Newtown pippins and russets. Elizabeth regarded him gravely, meanwhile, as he was well aware.

He reached the little vestibule.

"Doctor!" said Elizabeth.

She came down the passage with the apples in a bag.

"Please take them," said the provincial, "I—I feel like I want to give you something."

Behind the big woman Conrad caught a glimpse of the child who had come to have the tooth drawn twenty years ago. Outside its own family, Elizabeth was the first to know of that last son taken away. She had guessed.

"Thanks, Elizabeth," murmured the doctor. Then, "You're a good girl."

Carrying the hag of apples rather clumsily, he stepped into the trap.

Elizabeth was behind the scullery door, rubbing her face vigorously on the towel.

"Hast bin cryin', lass?" said Bella Stone, sharply. "Is our John worse?"

Elizabeth explained.

"Man is born to sorrow as 't sparks fly upwards," said Bella Stone, the curtain of her cap wagging.

Then she asked cheerfully, "What's to make for dinner to-day?"

"John's beans are ready to pull," said Elizabeth. "And Joe Crowther found a pile of mushrooms, and brought some last night. So—if I go out and get a piece of meat—"

"We shall do nicely," said Bella Stone. "I can pull the beans, Elizabeth."

Which she was doing, ten minutes later, performing weird gymnastics with her long, tight-sleeved arms, to keep the midges from biting her.

Elizabeth watched her for some minutes, thinking of her quotation from the Bible.

"But a bit of joy goes a long way, like spice," thought Elizabeth, contradictorily.

She was recalling that half minute when she had let John hold her hand, he thinking it hurt her. Then the front door opened. It was Dick Burnham. He had been out viewing the morning sky from the top of the village.

"It's no use," thought Elizabeth. "I can't tell. John would never speak to Dick again."

She had begun to guess, in a curious intuitive way, the kind of love John had had for Mary. He had, so he thought, sheltered her. He would never forgive Dick if he knew, whilst the blow to his man's pride, to know that all those two years, during which he had kissed her before going to work, her heart was with Dick!

Elizabeth shuddered at the prospect of such a blow falling on John, whose pride was almost a match for her own.

Whilst she was cooking dinner, with some of the spiritlessness that seemed catching, Mrs. Crowther called.

"How's Joe?" asked Elizabeth, smiling.

"A changed man," replied Joe's wife.

There was a short pause. "Thanks very much," she said, gratefully.

She began to unwrap a little parcel.

"It's the sheet," she whispered, even as Elizabeth guessed.

"How's your husband?" she asked.

"Getting better," said Elizabeth.

Mrs. Crowther was staring out into the garden, where John's mother was toddling the child round.

"I've got mine to turn the ground over," she said, dreamily. "Next year, happen we'll have our own vegetables."

Which reminded Elizabeth to pull some of John's peas for her, and to give her a huge cauliflower.

"Ay! He's a changed man," reiterated Mrs. Crowther, from the doorstep.

Then, "Who'd think it'd make all that difference in 'em?"

"It wouldn't do for 'em all," said Elizabeth, hastily, for she was confused by Mrs. Crowther lumping "'em" all together.

Then she burst out laughing at the thought of anyone stitching John up in a sheet and beating him.

Upstairs, John heard that burst of fresh, heart-sprung laughter.

"She laughs more since Burnham came back," he thought, morosely.

After shutting the gate on Mrs. Crowther, Elizabeth decided to go in and see how her mother's knee was.

"It aches a bit, Elizabeth," said Mrs. Peel.

Elizabeth looked at it.

"It's going the wrong way, mother," she avowed. "I shall ask the doctor to look at it when he calls in to see John."

The doctor called in that very afternoon, not to see John, but Elizabeth. He had a call only four doors away, and Mrs. Conrad wished to be remembered to Elizabeth. The doctor had told her of the apples and how, somehow, if he'd had a daughter, he would have wished her to be like Elizabeth. Perhaps Mrs. Conrad had been a little misunderstandingly jealous of the big village woman, perhaps the apple gift touched her, for the dead lad had always brought home pockets full in days when all life stretched seemingly sunnily before the young brood. Anyhow, she wished to be remembered.

Elizabeth marshalled the doctor in to see her mother's knee.

"Yes, yes," he said to the flow of talk from Mrs. Peel.

Elizabeth was watching him. She followed him to the door.

"What has she—?" he asked.

Elizabeth stood looking at him very solemn-eyed.

"I told her to use Condy's," she said, "but she would use Bluefly ointment."

Bluefly was a local remedy.

"Bluefly be damned," said the doctor, vigorously. "This is going to be serious. You'd better get her into your house and lay the law down. The knee is poisoned."

Then he relented as he saw Elizabeth's worried look.

"I know it's not your fault," he said. Take her in and rule her with a rod of iron. And—burn the 'Bluefly'!"

Elizabeth told her mother.

"But I can't," expostulated Mrs. Peel, "our Jack's wed in a fortnight."

"He must be wed from John's house," said poor Elizabeth, thinking with a blend of humour and horror of John's mother, and her own mother in the same house.

"Well," acknowledged Mrs. Peel, "it would take a load off my mind, Elizabeth. I've found the housework almost too much lately."

Elizabeth gave her one look.

"You come an' be nursed up," she said, decisively.

Mrs. Peel wiped her eyes on her apron.

"Eh, 'Lizabeth, tha art like James," she remarked.

It was the first time Elizabeth had heard her mother say that with so tender a meaning.

Thus was Elizabeth toppled into all the bustle and excitement of running a house with two determined mothers in it, of looking after John, and a baby that wanted to eat pins amongst other incidentals, with a wedding coming down full sail upon her.

There was a big gathering at supper that evening, for Jack and Letty came, and Dick was back from Dimpleton—getting to be a favourite place of his, as Elizabeth had noticed.

"He goes a lot to Dimpleton," somebody chaffed Dick.

"There's nice lasses at Dimpleton," said Bella Stone, looking sprightly for her sixty years.

Then Elizabeth changed the subject, for Dick looked confused.

"Ay, look after the lame an' the lazy," said Jack, as Elizabeth set the tray for John's supper.

"Nay," Elizabeth heard protestingly from Dick, as she set the spoon in John's saucer, amidst a burst of laughter.

Then, with the swiftness of a thunderbolt, it came.

"I'm getting back to the city to-morrow," said Dick. "I've wanted to see Dimpleton to-day because I used to court a lass there."

Then he saw Elizabeth's eyes, and stopped.

"Stop!" said her look.

She was quaking as she dropped the sugar lump in John's cup. Who knew but what the name of the girl might come out sometime, when some of the family were talking to old Dimpleton natives?

At this moment she knew she could never have broken her promise to the dead, nor have given John's heart that blow.

"Oh—oh!" laughed Jack. Then, "An' is she wed now?"

"And—worried?" asked Mrs. Peel, meaning children.

"Dead," said Dick, soberly.

Which caused the conversation to stop, and turn into a different channel.

"Oh!" said Bella Stone.

"Poor thing!" said Mrs. Peel, sympathetically, and without the slightest presentiment.

Elizabeth carried up the dainty tray.

John was lying awake.

"What'll you do with two like them, Elizabeth?" he asked, whimsically, waving his spoon towards downstairs.

He alluded to the mothers. An answering smile dawned on Elizabeth's face.

"They're sleeping together," she said, in a confidential whisper.

John whistled.

"Mother'll go home to-morrow," he said, cheerfully. "She's used to a feather bed all to herself."

When Elizabeth got downstairs, Jack and Letty were going, Jack to take his sweetheart to Dimpleton. For then, the moon was rising.

Elizabeth put the two mothers to bed, after dressing her mother's knee with the ointment Conrad had sent. She was very tired. When the last task was done, she crawled wearily upstairs.

"Good-night," she said at the door of the two mothers. Their candle was yet burning. They were talking—talking—talking. But for one of them, there was not much more talking to do, and Mrs. Peel always held that everybody had so much of everything to do before their time came, poor things.

Elizabeth slept so soundly upon the sheepskin rug, she did not see the glimmer of candlelight through the door-chink, nor hear the creak of the stairs under Bella Stone's foot. Mrs. Peel could not sleep for the pain in her knee. John's mother was gone for first-aid, by way of the bag of blue left over from washing-day. Thus did destiny conspire against Elizabeth and the good doctor.

When Elizabeth went downstairs next morning, Dick was nursing the fire and had the kettle boiling.

"You won't be sorry to be rid of me," he said, jestingly.

"I hope you've enjoyed your stay," said Elizabeth, courteously, striving against a feeling that she was being a hypocrite. It had felt hard, recently, to see the man whose selfishness had thrown the onus of John's suspicions upon her.

There was a moment's silence. Then Dick spoke with the nervousness that was a compliment to Elizabeth.

"There—excuse me—but no one could live in the house without seeing it—there is something wrong between yourself and John. You see I owe you so much, I want—is it anything I can set right?"

Elizabeth met his sympathetic look with a frigid one.

"I'm afraid your imagination runs away with you, Mr. Burnham," she told him.

Dick almost crumpled up for a moment. Then a spark of antagonism at her pushing aside his fellowship flamed out in him.

"When I found your husband hiding under the stairs," he said, with sarcasm, "I couldn't but believe my imagination."

Elizabeth turned faint. The shock was great. Why had John not warned her that Burnham had discovered his ignominy?

"I didn't mean to hurt," said Dick, with compunction, "I wanted to help."

"It's nothing anyone can help in," said Elizabeth, and went into the scullery for the frying pan. At which point, Bella Stone came downstairs, and Mrs. Peel was heard stirring and groaning, and a child's cry rang out impatiently.

Dick could say no more. He packed up after breakfast.

"Still alive?" he queried, peeping in at John's door, when the packing was done.

"Come in," said John.

Then he saw the Railway Guide in Dick's hand.

"Off back," said Dick.

"For good?" quoth John.

Dick balanced himself on the cane chair.

"That chair's been broken," said John, warningly.

Dick was not listening.

"Can't stay here any longer—waiting for you to kick the bucket, old man," he said, seriously.

John's silence with him since that unexpected coming into the kitchen, when Elizabeth had taken his hand in a moment's sympathy, had worried Dick. Dick was guessing at things now.

"No. It doesn't seem worth it," said John.

There was a spark in his eye that filled Dick with amazement.

"Do you mean to say, Stone?" queried Dick, very serious now, "that you've been jealous of me?"

John struggled with himself. Then his pent wrath burst.

"When a man knows another man has written love-letters to his wife, even before she was his wife, and that she kept them years, and even buried them to be safe, and—then he comes along and lodges with them, don't you think it all looks rather—well, not usual?"

John's fury was working.

Dick's face stared at him in an expression of utter demoralised agony.

"If I could punch you, Burnham, just for five minutes, I'd die happy," said John.

Dick struggled from the spell that was making him dumb.

"But—man alive—she was as much to blame as me," he stuttered.

Which threw John into speechless frenzy. There was so much menace in his eye, that Dick shrunk away. It was the slightest almost imperceptible movement, but it lost him his balance. He fell and the chair crashed with him.

Elizabeth came running upstairs. She peeped in on them with wide, fearful eyes.

"An accident—I'm afraid I've ruined the chair," laughed Dick.

"I thought—" said Elizabeth, and stared childishly at John, in the way that was so paradoxical with her usual dignity.

"It's all right, Elizabeth," John reassured her.

He determinedly took the old-fashioned attitude of regarding Elizabeth as being an innocent puppet in Dick's hands, now. In that way it left him a chance.

Elizabeth withdrew.

Dick got up and examined the chair.

"Beyond repair," he said, regretfully.

Then he met John's look. His own had become stronger. He was on his defence at the bar of friendship. If he had wavered in love, he had never wavered in friendship.

"But, how did I know she'd marry you?" he asked, wonderingly. "We were sweethearts two years and I always meant to marry her. She, she married you. If she kept the letters for love of me, I couldn't help it."

"Do you mean to say you walked out with Elizabeth, —courted her, two years—and—threw her over?" asked John.

He had flung himself up into a sitting position.

"Elizabeth—Elizabeth?" queried Dick.

Then a great light burst on him. "It—it was your wife, Mary, I courted," said Dick, humbly.

John toppled suddenly down amongst the pillows.

"Mary?" he gasped, incredulously.

There was silence. Then, "Did I understand you to say it was Mary?" asked John, weakly.

Dick bent his head.

"You—deserve—hanging!" gasped John, bitterly.

"Mary. Little Mary."

Yet, even as he spoke, a great relief was struggling up in him. He felt that he owed Dick some explanation.

"There was some man whom Elizabeth once cared for," said John. "I jumped that it was you."

Dick shook his head. "I never saw Mrs. Stone until she opened the door for me at Mary's funeral," he said.

John was thinking. Things he had misinterpreted were taking their true meaning. The shy way Mary had had of turning her face on one side for his kiss, the fact that she often seemed downhearted, until he chaffed her, the apologetic look that he sometimes surprised on her face, all became part and parcel of the horribly humiliating truth. She had been caring for this waverer all the time. It was bitter.

"She must have asked Elizabeth to bury the letters," said Dick.

Immediately John recalled Elizabeth asking for the box. What else had Mary asked Elizabeth?

But he shook hands with Dick, when Dick came to say good-bye an hour later.

"If it had been Elizabeth, I shouldn't have done this," said John, his hand in his friend's. Then, "But there is someone she cares for."

Dick shook John's hand warmly in both his, an almost un-English way he had sometimes.

"If there is anyone, I'm sure it's John Stone," he said.

John shook his head, but hope was springing up in his heart.

"Good-bye," sang Dick, and went down the stairs.

John heard the door close behind him, soon afterwards, after a chorus of good-byes and the talk of Mrs. Peel following him out, right to the last.

In the chaotic thoughts that were his, John heard Elizabeth setting his tray, bringing up the "biting on" that was to tide him over the long time between breakfast and dinner.

She came into the room, large, fair, and diffusing graciousness, but not the especial graciousness of a wife to a sick husband.

"Elizabeth," said John, without warning, "did Mary ask you to take her ring off?"

Elizabeth, white to the lips, just saved the tray. She had confessed without a word, his supposition.

"Did she ask you to marry me?" asked John. He spoke swiftly as the thoughts came.

She shook her head, smiling dazedly. Elizabeth was trying to deceive him.

The strained look on his face was heart-breaking to her. She misinterpreted its meaning. Somehow or other, he had found out. But, at least, he could not possibly know that, for that lay between the dead and herself.

"So—you married me because she asked you," said John, feebly. "And she asked you to take her wedding ring oft. I am very unsuccessful as a married man."

The bitterness of the weak-toned voice throbbed on the silence of the little room.

The thought that Elizabeth had married him because Mary had trapped her, as she had trapped himself, through that indulgence the living have to the whims of the dying, had come to him as a flash, bringing a new misery.

Elizabeth did not speak. It was useless. He had realised the truth. Nothing she could say could undo it.

"Where are the letters?" he asked, after a short pause.

"Dick told you?" said Elizabeth.

She was feeling anger, unreasonable anger that Dick had given John this pain. For pain it was—mighty pain, which he could not disguise. She thought it was at the disillusionment in Mary.

"Dick took them, he buried them somewhere on the moor, I think," she said, in a low voice.

"Those kind of letters, too!" ejaculated John.

Then he looked up and saw Elizabeth.

He had eaten so much humble pie that it seemed another mouthful or so would not choke him.

"Elizabeth," he said, "if we had started straight, if no one had asked you to marry me, and I had come —would you—?"

The softness faded out of Elizabeth. She was only being hard on the instincts of her own heart, to run

194

to John and tell him that she loved him even if he did not care twopence for her.

"If no one had asked you, you wouldn't have thought of me in that light," she said, coldly and practically.

It was like a blow falling on a bare, quivering patch of flesh. John had put all his pride down in that throw of the dice, that appeal.

"No," he said slowly, "I don't suppose I should. You are not one of the most lovable sort, Elizabeth."

Whilst even he did not realise how cruelly that came to Elizabeth.

Midway down the stairs she wiped her eyes on the back of her hand, as though something clouded her vision.

Her mother was sitting rocking in the chair, little Mary on her knee. Mrs. Peel was looking ill. John's mother was spreading the cloth for dinner.

"How are you, mother?" asked Elizabeth.

"I think I'd ha' been better keepin' on the Bluefly ointment," said Mrs. Peel.

Whereupon Elizabeth shook her head, smiling.

Which difference of opinion was quite sufficient to set off Bella Stone quarrelling with doctors, and with Elizabeth, and with everyone who differed from herself. Bella had not slept well. Mrs. Peel had tossed about a great deal.

She looked up, after the silence that fell after her tirade.

Elizabeth was leaning over the fire, stirring the stew round in the pan.

"'Lizabeth," said Bella.

Elizabeth turned a kindly, unruffled face on her mother-in-law.

"I didn't mean to hurt thy feelings," began Bella.

"You didn't," said Elizabeth.

She smiled.

"Tha'rt a lovin' lass," said Bella Stone, suddenly.

195

To her horrified surprise Elizabeth's countenance quivered, broke into tearful agitation, and then, sitting down, Elizabeth wept heartily.

"She's run down. That's what it is," said Bella Stone, two minutes later. "I'll tell our John."

But Elizabeth would not hear of John being told, it would worry him, she said.

The old barrier, consequent on John's jealous feelings about Burnham, was gone. In its place had risen another—a two-fold wall of human pride, dividing these two creatures. John Stone was quivering under the same shock which Elizabeth had quivered under on the night when she had overheard him repenting of having asked her to marry him. Every meal Elizabeth carried up felt to choke him. Bought with her bricks and mortar.

His mother went home after three days more of the restless sleeping, promising to send ointment from Hilltop Farm, sure to cure Mrs. Peel's leg.

As Elizabeth was fastening her cape-strings she bent her mouth close to Elizabeth's ear, and whispered into it.

Elizabeth started and flushed.

"No, no, nothing of the kind," she said.

Bella Stone laughed.

"Oh, well, there's time yet?" she replied, wagging her head. "I thought wi' thee bein' a bit downhearted th' other day—"

She went off.

True to promise a box of the renowned ointment from Hilltop Farm came by post. By this time Elizabeth was grown determined enough for anything. She undid the box—went off immediately to Doctor Conrad's, and got him to change it.

Mrs. Peel was down late that morning.

"Oh, Bella's sent it," she said, and took it up.

"Tha did right to open it, Elizabeth."

She applied Conrad's remedy conscientiously, three times a day. But it was too late. Bluefly ointment, blue-bay from the washing, and unfaith in doctors, had all worked against Mrs. Peel.

She got a great deal of pleasure in discussing her pain with the stream of neighbours who began to flow in and out of Elizabeth's house, since the one next door was shut up. The little procession of gossips was ever coming and going. When John Stone got downstairs, which was ten days later than Conrad had promised, as he had not got strength so swiftly as he might have done, Elizabeth put him into the parlour, to ensure him quiet peace away from the clatter of old women's tongues.

As she did so she apologised.

"She—she likes to talk," said the big, quiet young woman, nodding her head towards the kitchen, "and —I don't like to tell her to cool them off. Doctor Conrad told me to-day it's either her leg or her life. She doesn't know yet. But it will be her life. She'll never have anything cut."

John Stone stared into the calm, but tired-looking face. Elizabeth's hair was tumbling down, and she didn't know it. The worried look took the beauty out of her countenance.

"Let them come all they like," he said, kindly. "But—is that why you moved me in here?"

Elizabeth nodded.

His words, nay the tone, had taken a load off her mind. For she could not forget that it was John's house.

He moved into the kitchen, and was so gossipy with the gossips, that he scared none away. His chair faced Mrs. Peel's. Every morning they chaffed each other on their condition. Mrs. Peel was a better sufferer than had appeared likely. In all her pleasant life she had experienced nothing like this. After six days John broke the news to her. He had asked Elizabeth if she would rather he did. It was something in return for all the indignities and pain she had suffered through his clumsy blindness.

Elizabeth, to his amazement, accepted the offer. She took little Mary out shopping. When she came in, her mother's colourless face told that the blow had fallen.

"I'll never hop round on one leg," said Mrs. Peel, firmly. "Elizabeth, I'm going to be a heap o' trouble to thee."

Whereupon Elizabeth turned white also, and said if her mother ever mentioned that it was trouble again, she would never speak to her, and then kissed her.

Mrs. Peel never did mention the "trouble" again. She talked rather less during the next few days, and did not appear so glad to see folk. There was something almost clinging in her attitude towards her daughter, now. As for Elizabeth, she never went out without bringing in all the news she could gather up, and she bought her mother a new cape to add to those dozen others. Mrs. Peel turned the news and the cape over and over.

Then she said, "All is vanity, Elizabeth."

But all the same the cape had to be shown to everyone who came.

"I'll be wearin' it one of these days," she said, proudly. "Ay! It's mendin'. I've less pain. I can sleep, now."

Mortification was setting in.

To all appeals Mrs. Peel was deaf.

She had been born with two legs, and would die with two legs.

Jack once more postponed his much-delayed wedding.

John began to creep out into the sunshine, and do little commissions for Elizabeth. In the evenings the little kitchen was very pleasant. Elizabeth sewed by her mother's couch, and gossiped as though she had been born with the gift.

"I'm glad she's settled in life," said Mrs. Peel, once. "But I did miss her sorely in the house—at first, John."

She smiled.

There was always that past tense in her speech, now. But she was very cheerful, astonishing all by her patience.

John, meanwhile, having recovered from the shock of knowing Mary had asked Elizabeth to marry him, was going on with his scheme for making Elizabeth dependent on him. Manners had advanced him money. Overlooking the village was a big house. John was going to move into that big house. But not until Mrs. Peel had moved into that narrow one which is quite big enough at last. He was very secretive in his movements in connection with it. Jack married, Mrs. Peel dead (though he was sincerely sorry and wished from his heart she had been able to live many years), Elizabeth in a new house, robbed of her housekeeping position, would either settle or quit.

Kind as he was, unselfish as he was, in those evenings when he and Elizabeth sat by her mother's couch, these were some of his thoughts. The summit of his hopes was the gaining of his wife. All else had become subservient to that hope.

Chapter XIV

Mrs. Peel fulfils a "sign" and John gets on the trail

Mrs Peel, to use Letty Fairbody's phrase, did not dally long. Only twice did she refer to the shadows closing around her. On the first occasion she asked her daughter if she thought it necessary to have the minister pray with her, and was immensely relieved when Elizabeth said she did not see that it made any difference. She probably felt that she had not much courage, and was afraid of losing what she had. On the second occasion it was a reference to what things she would like Jack to have, and what she would like Elizabeth to have.

"I'd like thee to hav' my wedding ring, 'Lizabeth," she observed, "for tha's bin as dear as James to me. It's gettin' a bit thin towart's middle, but I know tha'll tak' care on it."

Thus she handed her wedding ring over to Elizabeth.

Jack Peel and his sweetheart were sitting with her whilst Elizabeth shopped, that evening his mother cheerfully told him that there would be room in the family grave for one, yet, when she had gone into it.

Jack neither smiled nor flinched. It was his mother's way to plan things out beforehand.

The sign of the great change coming showed itself in a desire on Mrs. Peel's part, for quietness.

They moved her upstairs.

"She wants to be quiet,'" Elizabeth told people who came, firmly.

Occasionally, Mrs. Peel would call out, "Let her come up, Elizabeth," then the gossip was admitted.

No Pope exercised more sovereign power than Mrs. Peel.

"I'm so fain she's settled in life, John," she observed more than once, in the hearing of Elizabeth. "I'd ha' felt bad about leaving her. An' I know you've bin happy together, I don't think you've ever had a wrong word, have yo'?"

"We've been as happy as two birds," John told her.

Elizabeth smoothed the sheet down.

Mrs. Peel was satisfied.

She died on a windy, stormy sunset in early autumn, saying only in a surprised kind of way, "James!"

Doctor Conrad said she was not conscious.

But Letty Fairbody, who was in the room at the passing, swore that the dying woman "saw summat," And was so convinced of it as an actual proof of the immortality of the soul that she did not dare go out on an errand after dark, for many weeks.

The same little shroud-maker who had measured Mary, measured Mrs. Peel.

"I didn't think I'd be here again so soon," she observed to Elizabeth. "But the other one was soft. How will you have her hair?"

"As she wore it," said Elizabeth,

"Let me see—she had a little curl each side her forehead?" queried the woman.

Elizabeth made the two curls.

"You are not afraid," remarked the little shroud-maker, in a pleased way.

Elizabeth merely murmured, "No."

She had slept alone in that room, with the dead, for two nights, despite the protests of John and Jack. She had guessed her mother's poor courage, and the curious streak of paganism in the good Church woman said, "stay with her."

201

They buried Mrs. Peel on the third day, quietly, as she had wished, as she said, she was "tir't."

Three weeks after that Jack Peel was married, also according to his mother's wish. Letty and he set up in Dimpleton.

Elizabeth and John were left alone.

It was strange to feel that they had no longer any need to act a part before anyone. It was both sad and strange to miss the sound of Mrs. Peel, knocking on the wall when she wanted her daughter to "slip in for a minute," or coming to bring the baby back, shouting at the child as she came.

Elizabeth did not sew for a fortnight after her mother's death. John saw a dusty patch on the dresser one day, and on another occasion, she put too much salt in the porridge, whilst her eyes had the look of one with a bad headache.

"She suffers," John told himself.

He allowed a truce.

There was more tragedy to him in these little tokens of Elisabeth's mortal weakness, than had she wept bucketsful of tears.

"You're pale, Elizabeth," he said one day. "Let's go over the moors to see my mother. There'll be a fine old breeze up to-day. Baby hasn't been out, either, for a while. It will do her good."

Which he really believed was the decisive factor in Elizabeth's getting ready.

They took bread and cheese sandwiches.

It was barely after breakfast.

A few women were sweeping the flagstones. They had the look in their eyes, as they nodded at Elizabeth, in her black attire, that told she inspired them with feelings of awe, and scared their sympathy, though they could have sought hers.

John noticed it.

"Why is she so self-contained?" he thought, irritably.

The truce was over.

When they sat down, beside a grey Stone wall, on a cushion of bilberry, to eat bread and cheese, he remarked, suddenly, "Who was that man you love, then, Elizabeth—since it is not Burnham?"

Elizabeth had the baby on her lap.

She became very red.

Fear flashed out of her eyes.

"I shall never tell you," she said, speaking in an unusually rapid way.

"Mo'—mo'!" begged little Mary, roaming after the sandwiches.

"A piece—half a piece," said Elizabeth to John, speaking in her usual tones.

He broke the bread.

"I shall find out," said John.

Elizabeth smiled.

She was paler, now, and breathed quickly.

"Who is it?" queried John.

Elizabeth's smile died away.

"Dad—dad—dad-da!" gurgled little Mary.

"I shall find out," said John, blindly.

They finished the meal.

It was as they were walking on over the springy heather, that Dick Burnham's suggestion that it could be himself Elizabeth cared for, came to him, perhaps caused by the subconscious memory awakened by little Mary's innocent "Dad-dad," coming in just when it did.

John was carrying the child.

Elizabeth walked immediately behind, following in his footsteps, for in some places the ground was very soft; she walked so close that when he stopped she was almost tripped up over his heels.

"Am I the man, Elizabeth?" asked John.

Everything was very still, save for the low sough of the breeze in the heather, the rusty voice of the bracken, the murmur of a little stream that sang in two voices, one minor, one major, the change being made by a tumble over a stone.

John's expression was a laughing one.

But no hawk, ready to swoop on its prey, was keener. "Is it likely?" queried Elizabeth, smiling also.

She asked it whimsically, without a change of colour.

"You might confide in me, Elizabeth?" asked John, humbly.

The moor had suddenly changed into a waste to him. He went on again, carrying the child, and missed seeing the relief that leapt into Elizabeth's eyes, or how, for a moment, under her cape, her hand was pressed against her heart.

"I should die if he knew," she thought.

For, now that the need for sheltering Mary had gone, she knew that, despite her irritation at being suspected of a "part," it had, after all, been an excuse; she could not confess that she cared for John Stone, because of all the humiliating circumstances which had accompanied her coming to him, and because, to her deep shame, self-analysis had revealed to her the fact that she had cared for this man, even before his wife was put into the earth.

"Whosoever looketh upon a woman to lust after her hath committed adultery with her already in his heart," the Scripture said.

Elizabeth, in whom the virtues came near to making her a Spartan, applied these words to herself. Had she not watched from an upper window, John Stone pruning his bushes, when first they came to live next door, and then retired quickly behind the curtains, with a sudden fear that he may look up and "catch her," and whenever she had seen the couple out together, a vague envy had stirred her. With a harshness as severe as that felt by the man who had broken Amelia

Young's heart, she judged herself, without mercy, without humour, and recognised the truth.

The recollection of John's warning "I shall find out," gave her palpitation. But with the calmness of her nature, she made herself enjoy that moor walk, and the prospect of the wide sky.

They called at Dimpleton on their way to Hilltop Farm. It was just noon when they dropped in upon Letty, who was black-leading, and whose face was so round, so red, and fantastically smudged, as to give her a resemblance to a black-barred rising sun,

"Eh—'Lizabeth!" she exclaimed.

Her joy was a fine thing to see.

She had so much to show Elizabeth, and they were peeping inside boxes, and looking at clothes, with little Mary toddling up and down after them, that John felt quite out of it, sitting in the kitchen, ostensibly reading. Sometimes Elizabeth's laugh came to him from parlour, and bedroom, or her quiet "H'm!" of approval, or her "It looks right nice, Letty. It couldn't look better," or her startled exclamation, whenever she thought little Mary on the point of falling, which made John think that she had plenty of demonstrative emotion where youngsters were concerned.

She was freer, easier when out of his presence, he mused, miserably angry. No, it certainly was not likely that he was the man.

"Jack and me'll pay you back as soon as we get on our feet," said Letty, addressing the couple, when they were about to go on their way, after dinner. She referred to the loan that had enabled this "set up."

"Oh, any time," said Elizabeth.

John said nothing.

He had no right to say anything.

But from the fact of his silence sprung up one of those peculiar misunderstandings difficult to beat down.

"He didn't say 'any time'," mused Letty.

It was five minutes after they had gone, and as she was washing her plump neck, with great gusto, and a spattering of soap bubbled on her chemise top, the door re-opened.

Letty gave a cry. It was only John. But she hurriedly flung the long towel around her bare, wet neck and shoulders, blushing at any man seeing her so, with the exception of Jack.

"I was just havin' a bit of a wash," she explained, struggling with her confusion.

John scarcely noticed it, or her bare neck either.

He had made a great decision as he came back to get Elizabeth's parcel of sandwiches, which had been forgotten.

"Letty," he said.

The young woman who weighed fifteen stone, stared at him. She was still endeavouring to cover her neck and bosom with the towel, without giving the idea that she was doing so, always a difficult thing to do.

"Oh, ay, she's left her sandwiches," said Letty, with sudden inspiration.

She endeavoured to rub a bit of neck dry, without revealing any other portion, and to move towards the sandwiches at the same time. But John forestalled her, pocketing the sandwiches. To her surprise he did not go.

He was quite pale, and his eyes had a strange gleam.

"Letty," he said, again.

Then, as she was about to say that if he would wait a minute she would put her bodice on, he spat out what he was after.

"Has Elizabeth ever gone with anybody?" queried John.

It had required a frightful effort to say it, and when he saw Letty's face, over the folds of the roller towel, which he now realised for the first time as irresistibly droll, he wished he had not asked her.

"Not as I know of," said Letty. She had forgotten her neck, and the towel had slid away from it.

She had large china-blue eyes, and her mouth had slightly opened.

"Think!" urged John.

Letty gave a subconscious dab at her neck with the towel. A steam was rising around her, for the kitchen was hot, aftermath of a baking.

"Whatever's the matter, John?" she asked at length.

"I want to find out a man Elizabeth cares for," explained John. "If he's alive, Letty, I'll smash him up. If he's dead—well, I can't do much."

The chagrin, the disappointment, the ludicrous humiliations he had experienced since Elizabeth came to him, from the moment when she had told him she would never marry him, to the time when Burnham had discovered him under the stairs, throbbed in his voice. To Letty he did not appear quite sane.

Or, if sane, he was jealous, and to Letty jealousy was a terrible thing indeed.

"I never heard tell, John," she said nervously.

In for a penny, in for a pound, now, according to John's mood. The cat was out.

"A young woman like Elizabeth must have had admirers," he said, with determination, and an utter forgetfulness of the time when he had thought Elizabeth was the last person in the world whom he should have thought of in that light.

"There were Tim Hardacre," faltered Letty, hypnotised by his steady glare, for it appeared nothing less to her. She was devoutly thankful the knives were locked up.

"She wouldn't care for a fool like that," said John decisively.

Letty was getting anxious to get into her bodice, and to shut the door on John Stone.

"An' there were that farmer fellow picked her up in his arms, once, at a fair to let her look over th' folks' heads," she said.

"Was he good-looking?" queried John.

Letty nodded.

"Jack said he ne'er saw a handsomer man," said Letty.

John's hands clenched.

"Where does he live?" quoth John.

Letty faltered the address, though conscious that she was getting into a dilemma.

"Did she—did she ever walk out with him?" quoth John.

"She took tea with his mother once," admitted Letty in frightened tones. "An' his mother told her she might go far an' fare worse. An' he coom once to see her, but she told him she'd never leave her mother, whilst she lived, and—he got married after four or five years."

John nodded at the details.

"He was very good-looking?" he queried again.

"Like a picter," said Letty.

She watched in horrified wonder whilst John Stone wrote down the name and address.

"You won't say a word that I've asked this of you to anyone?" quoth John.

He was moving towards the door as he spoke. Letty was by this time a bundle of nerves, sorry for Elizabeth, afraid of John, and wondering what would happen when John Stone got up to Bullgate Farm, for Ebenezer Ridehalgh, besides being handsome, was a miracle of strength, it being said he could ring a bull by himself.

"Not a word," said Letty, just as she would have soothed a lunatic.

"Thanks," said John, and took the door-hole. As for Letty, she flopped into a chair and had what she called "a good yell," out of sympathy for Elizabeth and what she must have to put up with, living with a man as jealous as that.

Elizabeth was patiently waiting, baby on lap, seated on a milestone, when John reached her. The baby had got a little restive. She said so.

"We'll take the train," said John, and they did so, arriving half a mile from Hilltop Farm just as the church clock struck three, "Eh! It's our John's wife," came Bella Stone's surprised welcome, as they pushed back the gate twenty minutes later.

Another old woman in a black cap with a curtain to it, which gave her an odd resemblance to her friend, unlike as they really were, was rising from the ingle-nook.

"Don't get up," said Elizabeth, with a smile. The smile set the old woman easy. She dropped back into the chair.

"Bethsheba, this is our John's wife," said Bella Stone, proudly.

"She's a rare big lass," said her friend. She was eighty, and to her Elizabeth was probably no more than a lass. "An' a bonnie lass," she added, shyly, noticing John's look at his wife.

"I said she'd say so," quoth Bella Stone. "Ay, she's th' flower o' th' flock, our John's wife. An' if ever I'm put out of house an' harbour, I should go to our John's, an' know I'd be done right to."

Which made Elizabeth feel a little embarrassed, being in the nature of a slight on the wives of Charlie and Ned. Bella Stone had evidently not recovered entirely from the domestic upset which had cast her, for a short time, upon John.

The kettle was on the hook, so the two old dames sat down to finish the task of putting the cleaned flocks into newly-washed bed-ticks. Elizabeth, after pulling off her outdoor garments, took a hand.

"An' such a worker," said Bella Stone to her friend.

Bella's friend proved to be a little deaf.—

"I said she were a worker," shouted Bella, across the tick.

John Stone was seated in the chair that had been his father's, watching the little comedy, Elizabeth's embarrassment at being publicly praised, the deaf old woman, and his persistent mother.

"Is that a't' family you have?" asked the pleasant old dame, looking at John.

John nodded.

"She's his second wife!"

Mrs. Stone gave the information in a loud key adding, "That's not her bairn," in the same key.

"Well," said the old woman, addressing Elizabeth, "they say th' second allus sits on the right knee. I hope tha's found it true."

Then she said irrelevantly, "An' there's time yet."

"They're so soft nowadays,", said Mrs. Stone, contemptuously. "Here am I, at my age, stuck wi' one grandchild—"

Then she said, swiftly, "I'm not referring to thee, Elizabeth. For tha's time yet, as she says."

Elizabeth went on pulling the clotted flocks into nice, tidy pieces, and casting them into the open sack, Little Mary was mimicking her. Once, John saw Elizabeth's smile dawn and fade away, seeing the motion of the little hands, womanlike in their motion —-comic, yet touching. Yes, Elizabeth had a woman's heart, but it was occupied.

"An' so tha buried thy mother, Elizabeth!" said Mrs. Stone, sadly, as they took tea.

Elizabeth bent her head.

Consolation is difficult for some natures to accept graciously. It was intensely so, in Elizabeth's case, yet John witnessed the fact of Elizabeth receiving it from his mother, his mother of all folk in the world, with her many sharp corners. It ought to have told him the truth but did not.

"Ay, if only she'd kept on wi' that ointment I sent, happen she'd be here, now," said Mrs. Stone, having entirely forgotten that for ten minutes she had been trying to show Elizabeth that this was a good world to get out of.

Baby Mary went to bed at seven.

"It's only a single bed, but you'll manage," said Mrs. Stone, as Elizabeth carried the child up. "Our John'll have to sleep wi' Charlie, an' Charlie's wife wi' me. Though I don't believe in it. His father," she jerked her thumb in the direction of the photograph of John's dead father, "an' me were never separated a single neet—till they put him to bed wi' a spade."

Elizabeth escaped.

Once within the little room, with its whitewashed walls, red and white striped bed-spread, and the picture of the Last Supper over the fireplace, she acted in a strange manner. Laying the child down on the bed, she walked to the other end of the room, to the bed again, and suddenly gagged herself with her handkerchief. The bed shook, her shoulders worked, and, the baby not understanding, began to cry, which brought Elizabeth to herself. Tears yet trembled on her lashes, but they were tears of laughter, the first laughter that had shook her heart since her mother died. There had suddenly come to her a picture of deaf Mrs. Crane asking if they had any family, and saying the second wife sat on the right knee. Moreover, laughter and misery were beginning to shake her alternately, lately.

John went out that evening.

Elizabeth helped John's mother to make supper ready, and then sat down to turn the heel of a stocking which the old dame had said worried her.

Whilst she was busy with it, Bella Stone went out of the room. She came downstairs just as Elizabeth was wondering where she had vanished to. She carried an old-fashioned japanned box, which she set down on the table. Her face had a soft look Elizabeth had never seen on it before.

"Come here, lass!" she commanded Elizabeth.

Elizabeth set down the stocking carefully, and advanced to the table with its oil-cloth cover, and the lamp set in the centre.

She wondered whatever could be inside the box. Bella Stone opened it very gently.

"Them were our John's little clothes," she said, "I'd like thee to have 'em, an' not either o' yon two. They're a bit yellow, but I know thee can whiten 'em. His father used to sit in that chair whilst I made 'em, an'—ay, them nicks int' sleeves o' them skips were when we had to cut 'em. His fists wouldn't go through, when he were born. He was a big lad, allus, our John. I'd to save up at sixpence a week to buy that linen. We were poor in them days. An'—well, I laid awake thinkin' th' other neet, 'I'll give em our John's wife, she'll appreciate 'em.'"

"Thanks," said Elizabeth.

She did not want to laugh now. The old woman's words had touched her. The sight of the old hands, fumbling amongst the ridiculously small clothes, the sheen of the worn wedding ring on the shrivelled finger, brought tears to her eyes.

"Eh, tha'rt welcome," said Bella Stone, fondly.

The clock ticked solemnly.

"I like thee, Elizabeth," she said, laying her hands on Elizabeth's shoulders.

Elizabeth found the keen, loving look hard to bear. She had an hysterical desire, for one mad minute, to tell Bella Stone everything. But she knew it for very madness.

"And—I like you," she said, slowly, and quite suddenly took the hard-featured old face between the palms of her two hands, and kissed her on the cheek.

The undemonstrative Elizabeth had kissed the undemonstrative Bella Stone. For a moment one was as startled as the other.

Then, "Bless thee," said Bella Stone, fervently.

Five minutes later both were knitting, and chatting, when the outer door opened.

"Mind th' lamp," called Bella Stone, in her normally sharp way.

For the draught had almost made the light flare to the top of the chimney.

Charlie, Ned, and their two better halves came in.

"I'd a job to shut th' door," explained Ned. "It's like a great beast pushin' against it."

"Why," said his mother, "it's snowin'."

"Hello, Elizabeth," said Ned.

"Good evening," said his wife, who had pretentions to educated manners.

"Where's our John?" asked Charlie.

"Gone for a bit of a blow," said his mother.

"Well, he'll get one," grinned Charlie.

He came over near the fire and sat by Elizabeth. The sight of her black clothes scared him a little, but after a few glances, he came to the conclusion that she was not one of the mournful sort. It was quite a jolly family party that was gathered round the red, roaring fire, when John Stone got back into the house.

Mrs. Stone was dishing out potato-hash from a huge brown pot set in the centre, with seven plates set round that, her black cap appearing fantastically magnified by the steam.

"Eh, John, wherever hasta bin, lad?" she queried.

John mumbled something.

He had been locating Bullgate Farm, also gaining information about the paragon of a farmer from people at the inns. The farmer had had a "disappointment" he had ascertained, and about the same time that he had "come after" Elizabeth. His wife was now dead.

John had found the farm wrapped in darkness and locked up. He had also walked into a horse-trough, which had increased his irritation. But he sat with his eyes in the shadow, and got down to the table as soon as possible, hoping his wet condition would not be discovered.

The wind was rising, and hail and snow blew alternately against the windows of the bleakly-set house.

"That's a grand sound," observed John, who sat by Elizabeth, when the wind gave one of its deep, wild organ blasts of Beethoven, like gloom and glory. She shook her head in disagreement.

All the rest were chattering, making little privacy for these two.

"I thought you'd like it," said John in surprise.

Elizabeth did not seem so far away from him tonight, he did not know the reason why.

"It reminds me of my father lyin' dead in the house," she said. "Every night it was like that. I hated it then, an'—I hate it now."

"Hand thy plate over, Elizabeth," called Ned. She handed it mechanically.

"We cannot live with the dead, Elizabeth," observed John, in a low voice.

Then they both started.

Elizabeth had spoken those same words once.

"I know," said Elizabeth, cheerful again, "it's only when th' wind makes that racket."

She had hidden herself again, behind that bright repose of hers—hidden a passionate heart, with its loyalty to old affections, its loyalty that was John Stone's admiration and aggravation at once. She was incapable of ever forgetting when she had loved. It was like his doom.

"It'll be a foot deep int' mornin'," said Mrs. Stone, prophetically, referring to the snow.

It was as she had foretold. When John came down in the morning, his was the first foot to descend the stairs. Elizabeth evidently waited until his mother came down, before descending. John smiled grimly to himself.

"Good morning," he greeted his wife.

He kissed her. She had to submit.

"Na then—noan o' that here!" laughingly said Mrs. Stone.

Elizabeth managed to smile.

"I'll tell yo' what, yo' two," she said, after breakfast, "get off as far as Dimpleton an' back before dinner. Our John were christened there. I'll look after th' child. Elizabeth'll be fain of a walk, freehanded."

Elizabeth demurred.

"Sh—I can look after th' child," said Bella Stone. They were overruled.

Neither John nor Elizabeth had wanted to go, John because he was not a churchgoer, Elizabeth because—she did not want to see the font where both she and John Stone had been christened. She had dreamed as a result of Bella Stone's gift of baby-clothes last night. She had dreamed that she was carrying a baby in her arms, hers and John Stone's—the feel of it against her was different even from the warm maternity little Mary awakened.

John pulled her arm through his.

The bells rang out as they came in sight of the quaint church, perched like a martin's nest, almost, on the hillside. Dimpleton boasted a peal. The sound of bells ringing over snow is always a sound unlike any other sound.

"Upstairs or down?" queried John, as they reached the gates.

Unconsciously his voice had lowered itself.

"Up," said Elizabeth.

"Let's walk round, first," said John.

So they walked along the paths between the graves, snow-covered, and the quaint epitaphs on the gravestones, ridged with snow on their projections, were read.

Elizabeth's arm hung less woodenly within John's.

They had paused before a very old tombstone, bearing the date 18 something. Snow had blown against the two last figures. The stone itself was slightly tilted. Elizabeth and John were reading the epitaph together.

"Friend after friend must part,
Who hath not lost a friend?
There is no union here on earth
That hath not here an end."

When John stole a look at his companion's face, he saw that her lips were moving, saying over the words to herself, and her expression was one that showed she was touched by the sad truth of the epitaph over the bed of the blacksmith of Dimpleton, laid to rest so long ago.

"Life is indeed very short," said John.

His voice sounded loud in the crisp morning stillness, broken only by the twitter of a bird in a rose- tree where the faded roses were looking down through the snow. Elizabeth's face told that she had heard him.

He remembered suddenly, with an incongruous mixture of humour and self-irritation, that he had once thought it very long and had wanted to be done with it. They sauntered on again.

Despondency fell on him. He was asking himself the question which millions of human beings must have asked themselves, whether there was such a thing as absolute loyalty, when Elizabeth stopped, and he stopped also.

"Ay, I remember this gravestone," he said in answer to her unspoken question. "There was a lot of fuss; the parson—he's dead, too—didn't want these words put on, and the chap had told his children he'd haunt them if they weren't."

Elizabeth's grave face had broken into a smile.

John rubbed away a veil of snow that covered the words of the famous tombstone.

"Life is a city full of crooked streets;
Death is the market place where all men meet ;
If life were merchandise that men could buy,
The rich would live and none but the poor would die."

"After all," said John, as they walked away, "the parson was probably in the right. Has a chap any business to ha' things written on his gravestone that'll start a debate inside every thinking person?" But Elizabeth would not debate that, either.

They walked along the snowy paths between the graves, until the bells clashed out again. The Dimpleton ringers were the best within forty miles and made good music.

The couple made towards the door of the old stone porch. The last time John had been inside a church it was to be married, but Elizabeth's face did not say if she recalled that fact. He pulled off his hat with the sheepishness of a man who does not go to church, and as he followed Elizabeth, noticed a warning against measles and the announcement of a mothers' tea-party, side by side. They passed the little octagonal stone font where they had both been christened, and each caught the other looking at it, with the same thought.

Then Elizabeth went up the steps into the gallery. John followed.

They entered a pew where sat a middle-aged man and two red-coated, cherry-cheeked children, and Elizabeth knelt down.

John knelt, too, but he felt a hypocrite to be there at all, and particularly so beside Elizabeth. Though he had a malicious comfort in the thought that Elizabeth was a very proud woman to be saying that she had erred like a "lost sheep." He was very glad, though, when she got up, and to see her glance across at the far gallery, where the sun was winking golden lights out of the gilt of the organ pipes.

Yes, life was very short to be wasting its sweetness as they were doing. When she leaned forward he could see her profile against the dull blue of the gallery wall.

He felt like a little, awkward boy as she found the first collect for him, so awkward that the prayer book almost slid from his hand, and he saved it by an acrobatic feat that was an inspiration. But as the pages fluttered, he read upon the fly-leaf—"Ebenezer Ridehalgh, Bullgate Farm, Dimpleton," and, horror of horrors!—it was in Elizabeth's handwriting, and the date—he was reckoning off how old she would be when she gave the handsome farmer that book. He could have gnashed his teeth at the end of the sum. Elizabeth—Elizabeth would be twenty-two, sweet twenty-two. What did Elizabeth look like at twenty-two? Yes, he could certainly kill Ebenezer Ridehalgh.

This was evidently the pew the man sat in.

All through that beautiful service John Stone was divining means of meeting Ebenezer Ridehalgh naturally, and of provoking a quarrel, naturally, and then of giving him a good hiding, also naturally, but he dimly groped his way to the "places," by Elizabeth's aid, and was tugged at by her, when he had to kneel down.

They went out again into the wide world, with the sunshine beating down on the snow-covered graves, so strongly now that, as they passed the fading rose-tree with its weight of snow and roses, it was all ashimmer with big, pellucid drops that, when they fell, made round marks on the smooth, snow-palled mound below, and there were marks of birds' feet about.

It seemed to John that Elizabeth also felt relief to step into that large, sunshiny world, where the bird voices were so unashamedly loud, and to whisper seemed all wrong.

As they were passing the grave of the blacksmith of the sad, sweet epitaph, John said, bending his head close to Elizabeth's, "What words did you pray in, Elizabeth, when we entered the church?"

She gave him a half-startled, wholly dignified look.

"Mind your own business," was, he knew, what another woman would have said.

"I—I should like to know," he pressed.

He tucked her hand within his arm.

She smiled, in a whimsical, yet wistful way, it seemed to John.

They were passing a gravestone they had noticed that morning, where slept seven children, all aged less than two years, with little name after little name set down pathetically—some parents' tragedy—for there were yet flowers for the last laid on the snow,

"I was praying," said Elizabeth calmly (and it seemed to John that she stepped more gently on the path past that grave) "to have the mark of the cloven-hoof taken from me. I was askin' to be made a good woman."

The smile yet lingered, but her eyelashes flickered a little.

"You!" exclaimed John.

"Me!" said Elizabeth, with the same sad, humorous smile. "I have really a very wicked heart."

She was not joking.

"What—what have you ever done wrong?" quoth John. "Ever drunk, stolen, envied, lied—"

His tone was contemptuous.

"I have done worse than any of those things," avowed Elizabeth, emphatically nodding her head at him. He had never seen this mixture of gravity and bantering guilt in her before, nor seen her nod her head like that.

He was about to ask her if she had murdered anyone, or what the terrible crime was, when he saw her looking straight before her in an intense way.

At the turn of the white road, where the bare black bows of trees forked a pattern across a brilliantly blue sky, was a man.

"Someone you know?" asked John.

"Yes—no—that is, a little,' said Elizabeth.

Her embarrassment grew as they approached that figure, standing out darkly against the snow. Even before they reached him, John had guessed who this was.

The man was surveying the sky in a dreamy way. He had autumn leaves and wore red berries in his buttonhole. At the sound of their approaching steps, he half-turned, evidently disturbed by them—not curious. John could see that. He looked them over casually. Then he seemed to come alive.

"Elizabeth!" he said.

"It's a lovely morning," said Elizabeth, smiling.

Then she added, "This is my husband."

"Husband!" ejaculated the farmer. "Thy husband!"

The absolute dumbfoundedness of his look was a picture. Had she said, "Here's my monkey or my elephant, or my tame, performing flea," John felt sure Ebenezer Ridehalgh would not have been more surprised.

"We've been married quite a long time, haven't we, John?" queried Elizabeth, demurely.

John nodded.

Anyone finding himself lassooed could have looked not more surly.

"Well, she's a bonny lass," said Ebenezer, frankly, "and—tha'rt lucky."

"I know about it," said John.

Ebenezer looked at him. "Hello! hello! Jealous, is he?" he thought.

In his younger days he had been a practical joker. "I see you have the prayer book yet," said Elizabeth. She was walking between them. "We sat in your pew," she explained.

Ebenezer looked at her, then across her at John. The moody-looking youngster roused his old desires for a prank.

"I asked her to wed me," he confessed humorously, "an' she said 'No,' but to brook the blow she gave me a little present of consolation, a prayer book."

He looked at John as much as to ask him what he thought of that.

Elizabeth laughed.

"I was very young then," she pleaded.

And John—

John winced, winced at not having known Elizabeth when she was two and twenty, before he had known Mary Bassey. Who knew? Perhaps he and Elizabeth—

"Ay, she's livin' yet, mother is," said the handsome man. "Come and see her, Elizabeth."

Of very intent he did not include John in the invitation, and his risibility was further stirred to see the effect.

"Mrs. Stone hasn't much time," said John, stiffly, "And—"

Elizabeth looked him over.

"Tell Mrs. Ridehalgh," she said, in her ordinary kindly tones, "that I will come along to see her before the winter closes in. I—I want very much to see her."

"Now, what's ta think o' that?" said Ridehalgh's look, as they parted.

Whilst John's said "Murder."

"What did you say you would go for?" he ripped out, as soon as they were out of earshot. "Look how you've let me down! A husband—and not invited with his wife."

Elizabeth flushed.

"A housekeeper," she said, with dignity, "does not cart her employer in her wake."

John mumbled something.

It sounded like, "Smash his jaw."

Elizabeth took no notice.

Then, ahead of them they saw a church spire. It appeared to make her remember something. She slid her arm in his.

"I'm sorry, John," she said.

Her face had a troubled, soul-disturbed look.

"Then you won't go?" asked John, dominantly.

"I want to go and see Mrs. Ridehalgh very much," she said, gently.

They walked back, and on to Hilltop Farm.

"Well, tha doesn't look much like a saint," chaffed Charlie.

"Two words, and I'll pitch thee through t' window," said John, shortly.

"Well, by gum!" said Ned.

But his mother gave him an indignant look.

They departed after dinner, Elizabeth carrying a little parcel, and John the baby, calling on their way through the village to see Jane Walsh in her little shop.

"What's in there?" queried John, an hour later, as they went over the moor. "Anything to eat? I'm hungry."

"Nothing to eat," said Elizabeth.

She stuck more tightly to the parcel. Her voice was very quiet and musing.

They reached home in time for tea.

There were letters under the door.

"Well, we'll get ready to leave here," said John, triumphantly. "I've got that house, and the boss has sent an advance on the patent. We are going to be grand folk, Elizabeth."

Elizabeth was saying, "Chin-up," and untying little Mary's bonnet strings.

"And we're going to have a housekeeper," said John. That stirred her.

She looked at him, with the same scared childish look with which she had turned her face when he discovered her with those love letters in her hand.

"Chin-up," she said, in a rather shaky voice to the child.

Then, "And what shall I do, John Stone, when you get a housekeeper in?"

"You will have an easy time," said John.

She looked at him in a vague, helpless way. She knew that he knew he was making it hard for her, and that he knew that she knew it.

Her face steadied itself suddenly.

It became the same face whose proud mouth had said to him, "Never," in the little parlour. And though she had said, "Never," yet had married him. She set the child down.

"Did you ever know my father?" she asked, irrelevantly.

John shook his head. His eyes never left her.

"Well," said Elizabeth smiling, "in some ways I'm like him. You try to drive me, John Stone—"

Which made John wonder what the dead James Peel could have been like, when he was getting cornered.

Chapter XV

Into the big house

Ten days later they moved into the "big house." with its twelve rooms instead of five. Elizabeth gave no outward sign of regret at leaving that little row of houses, in one of which she had grown up. It seemed to John after her warning that she was like her father, that Elizabeth became more and more of an enigma. He did, however, allow her to get settled before introducing a housekeeper, and this time he engaged one by official means, going to a servants' registry office.

She arrived on the edge of dark, just as Elizabeth was pouring out tea. John had asked Elizabeth not to light up. There was something of a household vestal's look about Elizabeth, in the firelight.

John answered the knock.

"Does Mr. John Stone live here?" queried a refined voice.

"Come in," said John.

She followed him into the kitchen, and introduced herself briefly. After five minutes of conversation John engaged her. Elizabeth, meanwhile, had hit two of the lights of the great showy chandelier.

Elizabeth gave her tea, after asking her to take off her things. She showed perfect courtesy to the woman who had come to oust her from the place she had filled so well and—so cheaply.

"For hours and wages, you must arrange with Mrs. Stone," said John.

The young woman smiled assent. She was handsome, capable and genial.

"Come this way," said Elizabeth.

She took the housekeeper into the room that was to be the drawing-room, where a fire was already burning, to air it for the fine furniture soon to arrive from town.

The question of hours and wages was soon settled.

"I hope you will be quite happy here," said Elizabeth, smiling, just as though she was mistress of this big house, and not feeling a miserable outcast unable to classify herself.

Mrs. Weydale was quite sure she should be "at home" with them.

"What do you think of her?" quoth John of the housekeeper, late that evening. Mrs. Weydale was unpacking upstairs.

"She is very nice," admitted Elizabeth.

Personally, she did not like Mrs. Weydale, but in her big way set it down to her own miserable feelings.

"We shall be able to go out more now," said John. Elizabeth was neither defiant nor enthusiastic. But late that night, in her own room, she sat writing the letter that was to give colour to Letty's idea that John Stone would be glad to have them pay back what Elizabeth had lent them. On one point Elizabeth was determined. If she was not to housekeep for John Stone—she would eat no crumb of his. Hence she wrote to Jack asking if he could let her have ten pounds of the money she had lent to them, so soon as they could, without pinching themselves.

She posted it at mid-day, on the following day.

Mrs. Weydale was a wonderful woman.

She left little or nothing for Elizabeth to do; if John had personally instructed her to thrust Elizabeth out of every field, nay, even to make her feel that she was rather a nuisance in the kitchen, or, indeed, in the house at all, the effect could not have been more clever. In four days Elizabeth was looking a shade of the deep misery she was experiencing. John had returned to the foundry, and things were forging ahead with the patent. A big order had again come to hand, and another sum in advance.

Mrs. Weydale was doing out the drawing-room, ready for the arrival of the furniture on the morrow, when John came in with the money.

He listened to the sound of Mrs. Weydale's movements.

"I can pay you back that money you lent me, Elizabeth," he said, in a voice keyed low, so as not to be heard by Mrs. Weydale.

He pushed Elizabeth the money she had got for the sale of that last house—the house she had sold for a mere song to help him out.

"Thank you, John," she said, calmly.

She did not count it.

Gathering it up, swiftly, she was leaving the room.

"'Lizabeth!"

Subconsciously he was thinking of Mrs. Peel. He said "'Lizabeth" just as she had used to do in consequence.

Elizabeth turned, with an oddly rapid movement. The little accidental saying of her name as her mother had used to say it had brought the tears up from her heart to her eyes. She saw John Stone through a swimming mist, in which the chandelier lights magnified themselves.

"We'll go out to-morrow night," said John. Then, a little lamely, "I think you'll find the money right."

She nodded. "But I shan't go out," she said, in a very low voice. "I'm only a lodger here, now. And—I mean to pay money into your account for all the food I eat."

"You mind Mary," said John, meaning that Elizabeth tended the child.

She smiled sarcastically.

"Do you think I want paying for that?" she asked.

No storm of the heart was ever so quietly expressed. But her pale face, the gleam of the eyes, the set of the firm mouth—it was all told there. Whilst the tears yet clung to her, called forth by that old name she had used to hear from lips now cold.

Had Mrs. Peel been living it is probable Elizabeth would have gone home there and then despite her pride. But there was no haven.

Thus began the final rounds of the struggle between these two proud hearts. Elizabeth began to pay money into John's account at the bank, every week, and—John began to shower outrageous gifts on Elizabeth, to keep the balance, all presented before the face of Mrs. Weydale. But how the couple would have stared had they known that that young woman was now familiar with every in and out of their domestic life—that their very quietest conversations were heard, by her—by aid of a tumbler glass—and that when Elizabeth innocently remarked that her ear was very red, on some days, and she confessed to having been afflicted with a tenderness thereabouts since her childhood, even she had winced a little.

It was on a wet, wild evening that John arrived home with a present for Elizabeth, destined to play a part in their struggle.

As he came up to his own gate he saw several shadows thrown on the fire-lit window-blind and recognised one as belonging to Jack Peel, but the other was unfamiliar. But as he opened the door, he recognised a voice—that of the man they had met only three weeks ago.

"They're allus welcome guests that invite themselves," smiled Ebenezer, as John came in wet through.

Ebenezer looked very comfortable, sitting in John's chair, with John's slippers on his feet, and a coat of

John's on also, having evidently been wet when he himself had arrived. Jack Peel was puffing at a pipe, Letty's wedding gift to himself. He gave John a hard look as he came in.

"Get me some dry clothes," said John.

He addressed Mrs. Weydale, not Elizabeth. Jack Peel noticed this.

Mrs. Weydale said, very humbly, that they were aired in the next room.

John flung a heap of parcels upon the table, then went to change himself. When he re-entered the kitchen, he had tea by himself, at one corner of the table. Mrs. Weydale watched his cup, and hovered near with the teapot, which was also duly noted by Jack. Jack read nothing but the News of the World, and there had been a good many sensational divorce cases latterly, so it was perhaps not unnatural that adding the fact of what Letty had told him to the fact of what he supposed he saw now, he drew a very outrageous conclusion. He set his mouth firmly, kept his eyes open, and calmed himself with the thought that he could, if he liked, smash his brother-in-law up quite easily, for Jack was no infant in the athlete's art.

His meal ended, John wheeled his chair round. Elizabeth had lit up. Jack saw his sister more distinctly than he had done this afternoon, for it had been dark with rain. There was certainly something the matter with Elizabeth. Calm as she was, cheerful as she tried to be, Jack saw a distressing change in her. Love is not always blind.

John began to unwrap the parcels.

"These wives," he winked at Jack, "they cost a bonnie penny."

Out from several wrappings he took a dress, a superb dress of black velvet.

"How do you like that?" he asked Elizabeth.

His eyes met hers.

Jack was watching them both.

Ebenezer Ridehalgh, apparently, was taken up with watching the antics of the parrot, set in its cage on a small table by his elbow, and viciously watching his fat finger, which tantalisingly thrust itself between the wires.

"You haven't bought that for me, John?" queried Elizabeth.

John nodded.

"But—I've frocks enough," she expostulated.

Jack Peel was acutely conscious that this was not what she would have said had she and her husband been alone together.

"May I see the bill?" she inquired, in a lighter tone.

"I tore it up," John told her.

"It's a very nice dress," said Elizabeth.

It certainly was. Then she said, laughingly, "But — oh, what buttons!"

There were certainly a lot of buttons all down the back.

"Oh, when Mrs. Weydale is out I can fasten you up in it," said John.

Elizabeth flushed, but not happily.

Jack was all at sea now.

"Oh, by the way, Stone," he said, "I've brought some of that money Elizabeth an' thee lent us."

John was undoing another box.

He looked up, off his guard.

"Oh—that's Elizabeth's affair," he said, impatiently, and Jack told himself that Letty had more imagination than he would have given her credit for.

"But—" said Jack.

"I'm not needing the money just now. Save it for me, Jack," said Elizabeth.

"Oh, all right," said Jack, and scratched his head, puzzled, for he had not yet got Elizabeth's letter, telling him not to bother sending the ten pounds, as they did not need it.

"Those are a bit of all right, aren't they?" asked John of Jack, holding a pair of pearl earrings out for Jack's inspection.

"For our Elizabeth?" queried Jack.

"Who else?" asked John.

Jack's theory that John had been "sparring" Letty about old admirers of Elizabeth's, in order to get a divorce, fell clean through.

"An' she shall walk in silk attire,
An' siller ha' to spare."

Sang John, suddenly.

The look that passed between Elizabeth and John was not understood in the least by Jack. But, like his mother (and Jack Peel had a lot of his mother in him), he meant to get to know.

"Oh—" yelled Ebenezer, suddenly.

Polly had caught him at last.

Elizabeth leaped up and ran towards the cage and the swearing man who was banging furiously at the cage with his fist so that it threatened to roll off the table at every bang.

"Stop it, somebody!" he yelled, in agony.

Elizabeth seized a sugar lump and opened the cage door.

"Poll! Pretty Poll!" she crooned.

"Pretty—" began Ebenezer.

Polly had let go. She hopped out, and Ebenezer saw, to his infinite horror, the passion-ruffled bird walk on Elizabeth's hand, thence on to her shoulder and take the sugar lump. It took rather longer to coax her into the cage, but when all was settled, and Ebenezer's finger bathed and dressed, the latter said, "I think we'd best be going, Jack."

"Sure you don't need the money?" Jack asked for the second time. Letty had been so positive that John had wanted the money safely back.

Both were quite sure.

"Oh, John—a minute," said Jack, awkwardly, on the mat. John and the rest, including Mrs. Weydale, evidently thought it was to have a little private chat about the money.

John Stone took his brother-in-law into the "drawing-room," so splendid a place that Jack felt uncomfortable in it, until he bethought himself of what he intended to say. It was not quite so easy to say, after accepting a cigar from John.

John, meanwhile, was thinking how little resemblance there was between Elizabeth and her brother.

"What's up wi' my sister?" queried Jack.

He frowned at John, over the big cigar, the laddish, open countenance with its oddly childlike look, which in Mrs. Peel had been ignorant credulity, and in Elizabeth was refined simplicity, clouded by a menacingly questioning look. His affection for his sister suddenly flashed out in him, like angry lightning, and illuminated him, making John see things in him he had never suspected.

"What doesta mean, Peel?" queried John.

He dropped into the vernacular always with Jack.

"That what I—said," and Jack actually scowled now, like a big schoolboy but a rather splendidly indignant schoolboy.

In the other room they could hear Elizabeth telling Ebenezer his finger would be all right, she thought, in a few days. Mrs. Weydale was shovelling up coals in the cellar.

"She looks iller nor ever I've sin her in my life," said Jack, shortly. "More nor ill. She looks as moithered as a wet hen."

A short silence.

"She's noan happy," accused Jack, "an' any chap as makes my sister miserable—has to reckon wi' me," he finished, angrily.

231

He got up from his chair and tossed the fat cigar into the fire, as though fearing he had been bribed by it, or that John might think so.

"We've neither of us been very happy yet," said John Stone.

He spoke seriously, but could not help a humorous inward smile.

Jack Peel started at the candid confession.

"She's ne'er given me a fair chance, Jack," said John, coolly, "but happen tha can help me. I'd like to know just where I stand. Has Elizabeth ever cared for any body—to thy knowledge?"

"Oh—oh!" thought Jack.

So Letty had not been wrong on that point.

And, as his brother-in-law looked at him in that searching way, Jack began to wonder if John really had "all his chairs at home".

"My sister ne'er cared for any other chap to my knowledge," said Jack, the anger gone from his tone. Then he added, slowly, "Unless it were t' old chap. When he died, she didn't say much—but it nearly broke her heart."

John Stone started.

Could it be that Elizabeth's reference to the grief that had turned the World into ashes or her, for a long time, had been a reference to her grief for her father? The little picture came back to him— himself by the window, and Elizabeth telling him she had felt even as he did, and wrestled as he was wrestling.

"Jack, lad," said John, "I believe—I believe— I've bin bein' jealous o' thy father."

"He must be a bit barmy," thought Jack.

For to him, it was ridiculous that a man, only six months married to a woman of his sister's character, could have even a jealous thought.

But he took John's offer of another cigar.

"Yon mon in yonder, now?" queried John.

Jack smiled.

"She ne'er wanted him," he said. "Don't be a fool, Stone. Patch up your differences. We all have 'em, tha knows."

John wanted to smile, but did not. Jack spoke with such ancient wisdom for a man married so few weeks.

They chatted as they smoked, and John threw Jack off guard, when Jack tried to find out more of the matter. It would be disastrous to let the story of their domestic life get all over Dimpleton, via Letty, for John saw that Letty could not keep a secret.

He had got to know all he wanted to know. The amazing truth was dawning upon him. Elizabeth had never cared for any other man. He had been jealous of her love for her father, and he knew now that her blush that day by the window had been a sudden half-shame at having bared her heart to anyone. He knew it, just as he knew that his memory of that moment, his keen sense of how the trees were swaying, of the way her accents had lingered ever since, in his memory, were tokens—of the love in him for this big woman, so hard and yet so soft, so narrow in her creeds and so wide in her human faith.

He felt almost drunk with joy as he stared across the room at Jack, who had thus made all things plain.

"Thanks, old lad," he said.

Jack, as he afterwards expressed himself, felt rather in a "fog," but he mumbled something about hoping John would trust his sister more in the future, and though he murmured refusals, pocketed the cigars John thrust on him, this time without the qualm that there was bribery in it.

"Come on here, Stone, let's be having thee," called Ebenezer, impatiently.

"He's comin'," said Jack.

They re-entered the room they had left. Mrs. Weydale was sitting darning John's socks. In the chair on the opposite side of the hearthstone, sat

Elizabeth, with Ebenezer's chair quite close to hers, whilst she looked into his face, as she spoke, in the frank way she had when speaking to anyone but— John. But John was not jealous now, nor afraid of any man. He was noticing the way she had of holding her head a little on one side, as her father did in his photograph. He had read somewhere it was a sign of a lovable nature.

"Yes. Tell your mother that's how I make salad-dressing," said Elizabeth. "And tell her Jane Wild is doing splendidly."

For Ebenezer's mother had been foster parent to Jane.

John came and stood behind Elizabeth's chair.

He saw by the stiffening of her back, the atmosphere of discomfort that suddenly netted her around, that she knew he was there.

He purposely placed his hand on her shoulder, in a half-loverly attitude, and—Elizabeth jumped up on the excuse that she wanted to find Ebenezer his overcoat.

Which did not delude John in the least now. It seemed to him that a mote had been plucked from his eye. Elizabeth Peel cared for him—and before a month was over he was going to make her say so, proud as she was, though just how he would do it he could not see at present. But John had made up his mind.

He took their two guests to the door five minutes later. The stars were out now, showing through the network of the giant lilac by the gate. Ebenezer was still growling about his finger.

John Stone walked close to his brother-in-law.

"Don't worry about us, Jack, he said, in a low voice, "we shall be all right soon—and—not a word to Letty."

Jack mumbled a promise.

He was beginning to realise himself that Letty was not a very reliable person, without loving her any less, though it made him love himself a little more.

Then Elizabeth came down the garden-path.

She also had something to say to her brother, a message to Letty, maybe. But whatever it was, it went clean out of her mind as she leaned over the gate ready to say it.

Jack Peel had touched his sister's hand in the darkness. He could see the ghostly whiteness of the white wrap she had thrown upon head and shoulders.

"An'—I think I'd not be so proud wi' John," said Jack, awkwardly. "I'd humour him a bit, Cis. After all, tha took him for better or worse, an' if it's worse— tha mun make th' best on it. He's studyin' too hard. I never did believe in it, an'—-I think he's a screw loose. These inventors often have. For mysel'—I find a game at 'Snakes an' Ladders' does me a lot o' good— summat on th' leet side. Anyhow—Letty wouldn't shy her nose up at presents, if I bought' her any, which I wish—"

Then he saw John looming up black again.

Jack's tones had revealed muddled, dog-like anxiety.

Elizabeth drew her hand from his, like one stung.

So John Stone had been complaining, actually complaining of her to—outsiders. By which it may be guessed the deep feelings she had for John, when she thought of her brother as an "outsider."

"Mind thy own business, Jack," she said, in a tone Jack had never heard from her before. Then, before he could attempt to appease her anger—John came down to the gate also.

"If tha doesn't be comin', Peel—" yelled Ebenezer, some twenty yards away, in a voice that told how he must once have sung in the "Messiah."

John followed Elizabeth back into the house closely. He scarcely knew why he followed her so closely— unless it was because there was the dimness of the passage to be traversed—and his courage before

Elizabeth was greater when he did not meet the calm, quiet beauty of her eye. He caught up with her midway in the passage. A ray of light from the chandelier made a round disc of gold fall on the centre of her forehead, as she turned on hearing his murmured "Elizabeth." She was a dim figure, with a white cloud on her head, and a round golden star on her brow, it seemed to the now trembling John. For he was suddenly afraid of Elizabeth, even though they stood in the darkness, and he could not see her eyes.

He realised too, that she had paused on the mat, to his murmur of her name, to prove to him that she was not afraid of being alone with him.

"I'll have my supper early, Elizabeth," said John, firmly.

He had meant to say something quite different.

But somehow—it had seemed that Elizabeth's soul, or what the parsons would call her soul, stood near him in the dimness of the passage, and she had seemed less of a woman than a presence, her courage challenging him.

Mrs. Weydale complained of headache, when Elizabeth pushed open the door of the kitchen.

"Well, you need not stay up," said Elizabeth for all the world like a real wife.

John could not but admire the genius of her acting for Mrs. Weydale's benefit, whilst the knowledge that she had it in her to play one part, gave him hope that he was right that she had been playing one with him.

As for Elizabeth, she was quivering already with remorse for having spoken as she had done to Jack. It was the first time she had ever crossed swords with her brother, and there was a bitter thought that it had been through John Stone, the man who had only missed, by pure luck, telling all Little Hareton that he had asked her to marry him and had—rued.

There was an embarrassed silence after Mrs. Weydale had gone upstairs with her refined and gentle 'Good-night, Mrs. Stone. Good-night, Mr. Stone."

Elizabeth broke the silence by getting out a cup and saucer.

"Where's yours, Elizabeth?" queried John.

Elizabeth did not want supper.

John was thinking of words to approach the subject he had in mind.

Elizabeth stood his cup upright on the saucer, and surveyed him across the table with the light of battle in her eyes.

"Why have you closed your account at the Manchester and Liverpool?" she asked.

"Just my fancy," said John, coolly.

He was blockading Elizabeth—endeavouring to starve her pride, by giving it nothing to feed on. She had not been able to pay her weekly dole into the bank for food and lodgings.

She turned pale.

He could see the heaving of her bosom under the black dress she wore for her mother. Elizabeth's anger was not shrewish, however.

"What do you take me for, John Stone?" she asked.

She was again seeking calmness in physical moving, setting the sugar-basin in her methodical way.

"What do you take me for, John Stone?" repeated Elizabeth.

She was setting the cream-jug.

"My wife," said John, lazily eyeing her, leaning his head back against the chair cushion. "My loyal, loving, lion-hearted, generous, comely wife."

He muttered the words over slowly, meaningly, maliciously—watching Elizabeth turn red and white, half-open her lips to retort, then grow dumb with dignity, and express quiet scorn by moving a spoon that really did not deserve it.

"That man, Elizabeth," said John, "him you cared for, before me—I mean."

Elizabeth started.

The terror he had hitherto put down to some other cause he now attributed to its right one. Elizabeth was afraid—that he was guessing she cared for him.

"Was he married?" asked John, casually.

Elizabeth moved a plate into position beside his cup and saucer.

"He was a married man," she admitted. "Will you have that cheese and onions warmed up for supper, John?"

Evidently she thought that ought to settle John.

"With children?" queried John.

"With a wife and children," said Elizabeth, believing she looked most wicked. "I suppose the cheese and onions—"

"I will guess his name, and in three times, say 'peas' twice," said John.

"I am very tired," said Elizabeth, "and, after all, it is nothing to do with you."

She did indeed look worn.

But John knew that he must have no mercy.

"The man you mentioned—that day—by the window," said John, "was your father. All this time I thought it was someone else, and then—anyhow, I know you love me now."

His face was less confident than his tone.

"None but a madman would think so," said Elizabeth.

John wished he had taken her more off her guard.

"I am mad," said John.

He smiled again.

"You know you care for me, Elizabeth," he said, rising from his chair and standing with his back to the fire.

Elizabeth did not speak.

Her attitude expressed a fineness of scorn before which John would have quailed, had he not made up his mind to win Elizabeth in one month.

She did not deny it, but went on setting the table.

"Anyhow," said John, dropping his attacking method all at once, "I care for you—more than I have ever cared for any living being, Elizabeth." There was a little silence.

"Why do you hold out?" he asked, in the same breath. "There is really no barrier—but your pride —because—because Mary asked us to marry each other, and—anyhow, we are both in the same boat. We both fell into the same trap. You are playing to an audience of one, Elizabeth. All Little Hareton thinks we are married. Why should you be proud with me, with me, whom you like? And I know you do like me." He used the colder word, meaning the warmer one, in northern style.

He advanced towards her, in appeal.

Involuntarily, as he moved towards her round one side of the table, Elizabeth moved further away. He saw with a comical sort of misery that he was going to be chasing Elizabeth round and round the table, and wondered half-humorously if they both moved round long enough and often enough, and supposing they gathered speed, if they might not eventually drop down in dizzy fits, like canaries! There was something terribly sane in his affection for Elizabeth, a sanity altogether lacking in that he had held for Mary—even though he had wanted to kill Ebenezer, a few weeks ago.

He stopped when they had completed a half-circle of the table.

"Tell me you don't care for me, 'Lizabeth," he said, "and look me square in the eyes, and—I'll believe you."

Elizabeth was very white now.

239

She stared at him across the supper table, where she was trying to cut a loaf of bread straight—and managing superbly, all things considered.

The little dropping of the "E" from her name moved her strangely to softer feelings. On the other hand, in the panic of her heart, she turned at bay facing John, Stone, who was telling her that she loved him, daring her to deny it.

"I don't love you—John;" she fold him, cutting a thin slice perfectly, and then she faced out the lie.

"You have perjured your immortal soul, Elizabeth," smiled John Stone.

Her eyes stared his out.

And he knew, without the slightest changing of his opinion, that it was going to be a tough fight.

She left him eating his cheese and onions—and going upstairs, sat down. That night she had spoken hastily to her brother, for the first time in her life. And she had lied—lied deliberately and without the excuse she had had before—of covering Mary Stone's fault. She had lied from excess of—pride. She sat quite a long time, quite miserable, then getting out pen and paper, wrote to Jack, apologising with real humility. Indeed, a tear dropped from her eye so that she re-wrote that sheet. The big heart was wounded to think she had hurt her brother, whom she had taught his letters. As for the lie—her feelings were mixed. She prayed, however, quite a long time. And when she got up, dragged softly from under the bed—a box—within another box, presumably a hat-box. Then she took out of it 'little things", the things that John's mother had made, buying the stuff with difficulty, week by week, a whole history of love in every one. One by one, she laid them on the dressing-table until she came to the last garment, took that out—and then came to her nightly torment and joy.

She looked at it, and pressed it to her heart. It was a faded photograph of an infant child, with curly hair and serious eyes, and underneath the picture was written in Mrs. Stone's writing, which was like bad imitation print :—

Owr Jon Aged 1 yere and 6 mons.

Whilst she thrust the man from her, she could love the child, John, like this, every night.

For Elizabeth was now far out of her depths.

She only knew that John Stone was on her track, seeking to discover whether or not she cared for him— and that her whole nature rose up in arms against his discovery, that she would lie, and lie, rather than acknowledge the fact. It was all in vain that she tried to analyze the stubbornness of her own will. Elizabeth was not clever in self-analysis. She told herself that John Stone would not win her— though that opened up, at times, visions of stone walls closing around her, realisations that they could not go on much longer like this—realisations that to go away meant—confessing to all Little Hareton not that she had not married at all, but that, at the age of thirty she had married badly. She was stranded now between two prides—the pride she had to keep up before John, and the bigger communal pride which had to deceive Little Hareton.

It was as she closed the box with the little garments, the photograph snugly tucked away underneath them, that Elizabeth fancied she heard a sound outside her door. She opened it softly. But all was quiet along the passage, where the arc-lamp cast soft light on the new carpet. The door of Mrs. Weydale's room, however, stood ajar. For the second time the suspicion crossed Elizabeth's mind. Then she sighed, believing her nature to be getting warped—from fear—from fear of being "found out" and having to tell John that he was the man.

241

When she got inside her room she stood by the window, looking out on the garden. The moon seemed to be swinging amongst the boughs of the trees, now. Yet it looked cold and desolate, the outside world.

Little Mary stirred in her cot that stood by Elizabeth's bed.

"Choc chocs!" she murmured.

She also was dreaming of heaven, and for her, no human pride barred the chocolate gate.

Elizabeth stood looking at the child—the child that was becoming something of a torment to her, a reminder always of joys she had not known.

She stood for a moment, looking—then, undressed rapidly, and got into bed.

For a long time she lay awake in the dark, hearing John come up. The sound of his door closing was like a challenge.

"I will go and see Ebenezer's mother," she told herself, "and—act on her advice."

For Elizabeth, self-contained as she was, was getting to the point when confession was becoming imperative, and his mother was so old, and so very deaf, and even if she talked, no one would take seriously what she said.

Mrs. Weydale said in the morning, at breakfast table, that her headache was better.

"Going to church?" queried John of Elizabeth.

She nodded.

"So am I," said John.

Elizabeth could not change her mind. It would look suspicious to Mrs. Weydale, she thought. A saturnine humour shot through her for a moment.

"Do, dear," she said, in true mockery of wifely affection.

Even John was surprised.

He wondered if this also was a heritage of the deceased James Peel's character.

"Put on your new dress," said John.

"It's a beautiful dress," said Mrs, Weydale, in her refined and humbly impartial way.

Elizabeth went upstairs, and came down in the velvet dress.

"Where is Mrs. Weydale?" she asked.

"Down the cellar. I'll fasten you up," said John.

"I can wait—" said Elizabeth.

She looked at him with dignity.

"There are a great many buttons on that frock—" said John meditatively.

"Just thirty," said Elizabeth.

She was backing away from him, and he recalled reading that people had to walk out of the room backwards before royalty—the incongruous thought having its foundation in the royal look of Elizabeth.

"Just thirty—you are thirty, are you not?" said John.

He meant to fasten those buttons.

"I often did it for Mary," he told Elizabeth.

When Mrs. Weydale came up with the roast she found John fastening up Elizabeth—Elizabeth was very pale, John was red.

Mrs. Weydale passed on through the room, and into the little one with the gas-oven.

"I'm sorry, Elizabeth. I couldn't help it!" said John.

He had kissed the back of the plump, beautiful neck.

They went to church.

But Elizabeth did not take Communion. John mentioned the fact.

"I felt—too wicked," she confessed.

"A sign of health," said John.

It had been snowing again. Elizabeth in her black velvet dress which he had buttoned—the wind in the bare boughs against the cold blue-green of the sky—the sun making the snow sparkle. The robin that followed them down behind the hedge, the old, old man whom they did not know, who stopped to talk to them without introduction, and made rambling remarks, staring into their faces, and finally leaving them abruptly, saying, "I had a wife—once," it was all part of a picture-poem to John.

He helped Elizabeth over a stile.

It was broad noontide.

The world lay wide and awake under the great sun. Before them lay white clouds piled up like mountains. He remembered that he had always felt most loving towards Mary under the light of the moon.

"Elizabeth—" he said.

She turned and looked up at him, as he descended the stile.

"Why won't you give in?" he asked. "Can't you see—I am weary for you? The world—is made up of giving and taking. Why don't you give in?"

He strode by her side now; looking into her face like an impassioned lad—a lad with a man's understanding.

"I don't care for you in that way, John," she said. But for a moment her pride had reeled.

She was glad she had not taken Communion.

"I don't believe it," said John emphatically.

"Men are conceited," quoth Elizabeth calmly.

"They are persistent," said John meaningly.

"Persistence is a savage virtue, and I've got it. Look out, Elizabeth."

Which was a warning not applying merely to the gate she had almost walked into.

Elizabeth set her gloved hand to the gate.

As she passed through it, she half-turned. There was a smile on her face.

"Don't drive me too far, John," she said.

"Well?" queried John.

"There are other men in need of housekeepers," said Elizabeth, "and you have done me out of my job."

"I have offered you a new vocation," said John.

"I do not care for it," said Elizabeth.

When they got home she was careful to get Mrs. Weydale to unbutton the dress before they had dinner. Mrs. Weydale always went out Sunday afternoons. John still kept up his foundry-formed habit of having a snooze on Sunday afternoons.

When he got up at tea-time he passed into the drawing-room, where Elizabeth had lately been sitting. Her handkerchief was on the chair. He took it up and smelt at it, and was sure it was hers. Parma violet was her only perfume—her only unprimitive luxury. He pushed it into his vest pocket, that handkerchief. John was getting desperate, too—since touching her neck with his lips, though passion was a very small facet of the love he had for Elizabeth.

A book was open on the table, just as she had laid it down, and beside the chair where she had been sitting was little Mary's sock. He looked at the book— Thomas-a-Kempis's *Imitation of Christ*, a humble book for so proud a woman to read.

"Tea is ready," called Elizabeth, from the other room.

He went in to tea, and tried not to feel like a most guilty but triumphant thief, with Elizabeth's handkerchief in his pocket, as she gave him tea—calm, and contained as ever, her morals unshattered. Whilst he could not guess that Elizabeth went to church that evening, to try and forget the kiss on the back her neck, and that whilst they sang of erring and straying like lost sheep, she was thinking of John in the light of a lesser Satan, tempting her. It had been the same when she prayed in the quiet, echoing church at Dimpleton, for her prayer had been to be saved from the sin of idolatry, from the human weakness of allowing her love for John to blot out everything else. Elizabeth was afraid—afraid not only of John discovering her love for him, but of her love itself.

245

Perhaps, after all, she had been well on the way towards old maid-hood, when Mary Stone caught her in that ironic position, for old maid-hood way only means a hardening of the bones of pride.

Chapter XVI

Elizabeth and Mrs. Weydale surprise each other

Elizabeth went over to Dimpleton to see Mrs. Hardacre after she and Mrs. Weydale had washed, two days after making up her mind to do so. She did not take little Mary with her, though Mrs. Weydale showed that she would have been glad had she done so. Elizabeth wanted to think. John Stone had barricaded her fast in her fortress of pride—leaving her no loophole of escape. He was eating his bread and salt—and stayed from giving service in return.

It was a windy morning when she tramped over the moors to Dimpleton. Half the moors were bare of snow, but in some places the drifts took her up to her knees. She went through recklessly. The singing of the wind in the rushes and the gorse-bushes that stuck up through the snow, had a wild note of rebellion in full accord with her mood. Had she not been so practical, it is possible that Elizabeth might have been a poet.

Snow had got in through the lace-holes of her boots, when she dipped down into Dimpleton. She was very tired, yet knew that she would not sleep again to-night.

"What, passing the door?" queried little Jane Wild, reproachfully, coming out on the introspective Elizabeth like a figure in a weather-clock.

"I was just goin' to see Mrs. Hardacre," said Elizabeth.

"Eh—have you heard, then?" asked Jane.

"Heard?" said Elizabeth in surprise.

"She had a stroke two days sin'," said Jane. "Eh—I said you'd be sorry?"

Thus was closed the door of Elizabeth's confessional box, with a sad sound.

"I'll go up to see her?' said Elizabeth, after having satisfied Jane by sitting for twenty minutes in the shop, and hearing of the prosperity it had spelt.

She went up to Bullgate Farm.

Ebenezer came to the door in answer to her knock. He was in his shirt-sleeves, and his face was drawn with sleeplessness and grief.

"She is very old," Elizabeth reminded him gently.

"Ay! But—it's strange, whenever it comes," he said. For it was only a question of time, Elizabeth learnt.

Two neighbours were in.

Elizabeth found that they had all the help they needed. Had it been otherwise, she could not have stayed. She had come to see Mrs. Hardacre—to ask an old, old woman's advice, more as a safety valve for her feelings than anything—and her Granny Confessor lay, with mouth pulled to one side, making strange noises, and all that was poured into her mouth trickled out again. It was a house of trouble, as one of the neighbours, a genial woman in a bodice with huge flowered pattern, remarked very cheerfully.

An hour later Elizabeth left Bullgate Farm. At the end of the stony lane she paused irresolutely. The sensible course was to go back to Little Hareton, and to John Stone's house. But Elizabeth was not sensible to-day. She felt capable of foolish things. And outside—under the sky, away from John's house, she had a homeless, free feeling that she had never felt in her life before, she, who had always thought of a home as a shelter. A flock of wild duck went screaming across the sky—and she stood, staring up into it, her eye following them out of sight.

"Why should I go back any more?" she thought, standing by a quiet pond, lower down the fields.

Elizabeth winced.

Not to go back—meant—never a child of her own.

"He married me for convenience," said Elizabeth's pride. "No—I will die first."

She walked on thinking, seeing the countryside as in a dream. There, outside, she had no part to play. She was letting herself go. Though she knew that when her father had begun to let himself go, which was rare, he had used to make an utter fool of himself. Elizabeth did not care. The crisis was approaching. She did not care.

She noticed a woman holding up a baby to look through the window at her, as she passed along—and recognised the way she went as familiar. But it was not until she actually reached the third stile away from the upland fields that began the acreage of Hilltop Farm that she realised she was coming—towards John's mother's house.

"As well here as anywhere else," thought Elizabeth, with a certain devilry that had used to be a forerunner of her father's fun follies.

"Eh—our John's wife," called Mrs. Stone. Then, "What's brought thee?" she queried, opening the door. "Naught's the matter, is it?"

Elizabeth shook her head, reassuringly.

"Sit down an' get thy wind," said Mrs. Stone, and shook up a cushion.

The climb had made Elizabeth's heart palpitate in an unusual manner.

"Tha looks ill," said Mrs. Stone in concern.

Elizabeth was taking off her coat.

"I don't sleep very well," she admitted. Even that admission was a relief to her.

"Try a cup o' hot milk or a boiled onion," said Mrs. Stone, the curtain of her cap wagging. "I'll back either o' them two things to bring sleep—unless tha's an ill conscience."

Elizabeth smiled in answer to her smile.

But she wondered if it were really conscience that was making her unable to sleep.

"An' how's our John?" asked Mrs. Stone.

John was quite well, said Elizabeth, whilst her humour was irresistibly tickled by the thought of how John's mother would stare, and what she would think, if she knew of the "goings on" in her son's household. Then she told Mrs. Stone that John's patent was going on very well.

"He allus had a lot o' perseverance," said Mrs. Stone, proudly. "If he set his mind on a thing, he'd get it."

Elizabeth nodded.

"Oh—will he?" she thought, grimly.

She was going to help Mrs. Stone get dinner ready for Charlie and Ned coming in, but Mrs. Stone refused.

"Sit thee quiet, lass. Tha looks right ill," she said. "I reckon there's a lot to do in yon big house. Rest thee whilst tha's chance."

Elizabeth did not protest.

She was almost uncannily weary. The homeless joy that had touched her, as she watched the wild ducks, was gone. She watched Mrs. Stone thumping away at a piece of tough beef with the rolling pin, at the fire flickering in the black, shining grate, and then away at the window where the thin trees swayed in the restless wind. She had a dreamy, grotesque sense that nothing was real. It seemed a long, long time since she had heard the gate of John's house close behind her—and little Mary crying after her, whilst she had hardened her heart.

"Mrs. Crane—her as were here before when thee and John come, is comin' again this afternoon," said John's mother. "She'll stare when she sees thee."

Elizabeth realised that Mrs. Stone was wondering at this visit of hers—that she was suspicious.

It was as she sat the frying-pan on the fire that John's mother put the direct question.

"Thee an' our John hasn't bin havin' any bother?" she asked, anxiously.

Elizabeth laughed.

"He had ways of his own, at hoam," said Mrs. Stone, "But—he were a good lad."

She prodded the meat.

Elizabeth re-assured Mrs. Stone.

As the old woman surveyed her, the crazy desire to tell the truth, the whole truth, and nothing but the truth, flickered out of Elizabeth's heart, leaving cold, hopeless despair. She had noticed for the first time how like Mrs. Stone's eyes were to her son's, though they were deeper set, and of colder colour. It was a look that was in them.

In the afternoon, after the bustle of dinner for the men who had been out since five that morning, and after Elizabeth had been greeted with surprise by the wives of Charlie and Ned, coming in from the dairy, Mrs. Crane arrived, muffled up to the eyes, and wearing stocking-tops over her clogs, though the village streets were run quite clean of snow.

"If I slipped at my age," said she, laughing, "I should be ill to put together again, Bella. An' it's like Scripture says, we're queer put together."

"It's allus as weel to be careful," said Bella Stone.

Elizabeth was very kindly disposed towards the idiosyncracies of old folk. But just now she was only struck by the cocksureness of them both. And in her present mood, she was deeply conscious of the uncertainty of everything, the absolutely one sure thing being—that anything could happen.

Her two sisters-in-law were evidently out of patience with the chin-wagging of the two old dames.

251

They went out to take tea, leaving Elizabeth to bear the racket of the conversation.

"I think I'll be going," said Elizabeth, as the clock struck three. After two hours she felt weary.

She could hear Ned shouting at the horse to "come over" in the stable, which came against the wall just behind her chair. Both the old dames were busy knitting. Everybody appeared to have a place in the world, but herself.

"Eh—what's thy hurry?" quoth Mrs. Stone.

"Nay—I'll get back," said Elizabeth.

"See—Jerry Young, as I'm a living woman!" exclaimed Bella Stone, jumping up from her chair.

She stared through the window at the figure of the old man, crossing the farm yard.

"An' drunk as a fiddler—at his age, too!" she exclaimed, between laughter and horror.

"Enough to kill him," said Mrs. Crane.

Both old women had crossed over to the window. Elizabeth could see the old man's head between them by bobbing to one side.

Mrs. Crane went to open the door for him. "What's ta bin doin', Jerry?" she asked.

"Christmassing," explained Jerry, stumbling in with his fiddle. Drunk as he was, he was very careful of it.

"Why, it takes weeks an' weeks to Christmas," laughed Mrs. Crane, catching the word despite her deafness.

She led him in and almost literally sat him down in the chair Elizabeth vacated for him.

Jerry would keep singing, and across the singing Mrs. Stone and Mrs. Crane were talking at him and to him.

"His feet's wet," said Mrs. Crane. "It'll not do—at his age."

So, acting under orders, Elizabeth took them off, whilst Jerry sang of geese getting fat, occasionally reminding all and sundry that he was creeping on towards a hundred, and not out yet.

When Elizabeth looked out of the window, snowflakes were coming down.

"Tha'rt going for to stop, Elizabeth," quoth Mrs. Stone. "Tha allers brings snow wi' thee?"

She laughed.

Then she added, "Our John'll manage by hissel' for a neet."

But Elizabeth was not convinced that John could; at least, that was the impression she gave to Mrs. Stone. Another mood was seizing her now. John could certainly manage by himself. He had a housekeeper. But restlessness made her feel cooped and out of harmony with these jolly, cocksure old folk, with their talk of old times, and old friends, their stringing of old and fragrant memories. She caught herself wishing that she was old, quite old, and reviewing the past with calmness, rather than viewing the future with this restless inactivity.

Despite all protests, she went out into the snow half-an-hour later, Mrs. Stone shouting out directions of the best way to take, until Elizabeth disappeared from sight. Elizabeth chose the moor way. When she reached the edge of it, those places that had been bare were speckled where the bilberry beds still resisted the snow covering, and those spots already covered had little winds blowing the snow up by fits, like imitation smoke. Indeed, smoke appeared to be puffing out of the whitening face of the moor.

Elizabeth knew the direction in which she must strike for Little Hareton. She did not particularly want to go to Little Hareton, but went towards it by force of habit. Sometimes she had to bend her head to stop the snow from blowing into her eyes. She had, however, no difficulty in finding her way, and reached the path leading down through the ghostly, snow-powdered bracken, and out upon the road to Little Hareton, just before the red sun disappeared. It reminded Elizabeth of Humpty Dumpty on the wall, that big, round, red sun—and she watched him apparently topple off the cloud-wall into nowhere, with a childish humour in the scene. But when once she came in sight of the houses, the childish outlook that was upon her vanished. She was going back to John Stone's house. She did not go round to the front entrance, and ring the bell, out of consideration for Mrs. Weydale's legs, but passed in, along the dim passage where John had meant to say things, and had not said them, and into the fire-lit kitchen. All was rosy, tea-time quiet. Little Mary was asleep in the baby chair, still grasping in a fat hand a dilapidated animal meant originally to be a rabbit—one of Mrs. Peel's gifts. The kettle sang on the hob. John's slippers were warming inside the fender. He was certainly taking no harm, he nor his house, nor his child, nor all that was in it, thought Elizabeth, surveying the whole. She could go away—and all would go on just like this.

Then—she heard someone moving in the drawing-room.

She passed out of the kitchen lightly, so as not to awaken the child.

"It's only me, Mrs. Weydale," she was about to say on the threshold of the drawing-room, when she saw that which checked the words.

Mrs. Weydale, a dim figure, had John's desk open—the desk of which John kept the key.

She was bent over it—and she was dressed for going out.

There was only one meaning to it.

Elizabeth held her breath, until she heard the crackle of bank notes, then she could play eavesdropper no longer.

"What are you doing, Mrs. Weydale?" she inquired.

Mrs. Weydale's exclamation in itself was absolute acknowledgment of guilt.

The two women faced each other in the dim room. Then Mrs. Weydale spoke.

"If you tell about me, Mrs. Stone, I'll tell about you—all Little Hareton shall know that you and Mr. Stone aren't married."

Had a bombshell dropped at Elizabeth's feet, she could have been no more surprised.

"Let me see what you have in your hand," she commanded, calmly.

Mrs. Weydale handed the notes over angrily.

"So silly, too," said Elizabeth. "You were bound to be found out."

"I shall tell how you don't sleep with him," shrilled Mrs. Weydale, suddenly.

Elizabeth could not forbear a shudder at Little Hareton being told that.

"Better class people do not sleep with each other," she condescended to say. "It shows no scarcity of beds. Anyhow, don't think I care whatever you say. But what do you mean by my not being married to my husband?"

Her dignity angered Mrs. Weydale.

"Give me your key, Mrs. Weydale," said Elizabeth.

She received it.

Then she made a light.

It was a skeleton key.

"I suppose your box was packed ready," said Elizabeth.

Mrs. Weydale started at the excellent guess.

"Very well, then, you shall go," said Elizabeth. Mrs. Weydale burst into tears.

Going with notes, and without, was a vastly different matter.

"You might as well cry to John," said Elizabeth.

"Are you going to hand me over to the police?" queried Mrs. Weydale. "If you do, I shall tell everyone in court, too, how you were not married—"

Three minutes later Elizabeth showed her the marriage lines.

"I heard you say you weren't his wife," said the surprised Mrs. Weydale. "Anyhow, if you'll give me twenty pounds, I won't tell anyone you didn't sleep—"

"Not a farthing," said Elizabeth, firmly, Mrs. Weydale grew desperate.

"Nor that you've some baby things hidden in a box. I could tell Mr. Stone that—how much?" asked she, triumphantly.

"Do you think it possible?" queried Elizabeth, with a smile, "that you could blackmail me?"

Mrs. Weydale gave up in despair. She did not, could not think she could. Elizabeth was one too many for her.

Elizabeth helped her down with her box, noticing the label.

To the last Mrs. Weydale preserved her bold front.

As she went out of the gate she turned and faced Elizabeth. There was utter viciousness in her voice and look.

"In the morning—all Little Hareton will know you couldn't sleep with the poor man," she said.

Elizabeth watched her vanish, lugging her box through the snow.

"Where is Mrs. Weydale?" quoth John, when he came in.

"I've sacked her," said Elizabeth. "She was just about to waltz off with twenty pounds of yours."

"Oh!" gasped John.

Elizabeth was so indignant, it made him want to laugh.

"She is going to tell all the world about us," said Elizabeth. "And—she appears to have been in every room in the house and to know every word we have said. So—be prepared."

"Good Lord!" said John. "You should have stopped her. Couldn't you have—"

"No," said Elizabeth, calmly. "Let her tell."

But he knew all it meant to her.

Elizabeth would suffer all Little Hareton to know before—be blackmailed.

They had a week of perfect misery—then found that Little Hareton was in ignorant bliss about their farcical position.

"She would have told before this," said Elizabeth, with decision. Which was true.

Three days later Mrs. Weydale, unable to find employment, down in the depths, received a registered letter, which said merely, "Do not think I send this because I am afraid."

It was a cheque for five pounds.

Mrs. Weydale was more astonished than she had ever been in her life, and there had been some astounding things in Mrs. Weydale's life.

She certainly did not think the cheque was sent for fear. She had recognised Elizabeth's calibre on that day when they had surprised each other.

It was on the night after Elizabeth's cheque had reached Mrs. Weydale that John suggested that they go up to the house of his boss. It was a little party in honour of the success of his patent.

"Put on the velvet frock," he said.

Elizabeth put it on.

In some mysterious manner she managed to fasten it up the back herself to John's surprise. He had got little Mary ready.

She would have to have it unfastened, he thought, maliciously.

It was late when they returned.

Little Mary was cross.

Elizabeth looked very tired.

John made supper whilst she took the child to bed.

After supper John said gently, "I'll help you undo the frock, Elizabeth."

It was the most humble plea, as his eyes met hers, with that look in them.

"Thanks, John, I can undo it myself," said Elizabeth. She went to bed.

After fighting to get round to the back of her bodice for ten minutes, Elizabeth got in a rage.

Taking a pair of scissors from the table drawer, she cut the dress down from top to bottom.

And creeping under the bedclothes, after a look at little Mary's placid face, sobbed herself to sleep, amazed at the wickedness of her own heart.

Chapter XVII

The experiment

John Stone came home on the following night, thinking triumphantly that Elizabeth was being hounded out from her lair of pride, only to find a very old adage true—"that pride goeth before destruction, and a haughty spirit before a fall." Unfortunately for him, it was his own pride that had a fall.

The key was under the round stone set in the shade of the lilac-bush.

He unlocked the door thinking she had gone out on an errand. The table was set for one. The light was turned low. He lifted his plate and found a note of telegrammatic brevity, in which Elizabeth stated that she had gone away, that she would never come back, and that she had paid the milkman. It was the last item made John despair, for surely no woman ever left a man in colder blood than one who could tell him that she had paid the milk bill.

Little Mary was quite obviously "pinched" by Elizabeth. The parrot-dish was filled up with food, as a last good-bye, and the household keys were on the table. Every door was unlocked, excepting Elizabeth's door, as John found, on investigation.

He sat down, trying to smoke a pipe, and think—how to act now, pondering on the likeliest places to which Elizabeth had fled—from him, John Stone, her pursuer. Therein lay John's hope. She must have got afraid of him.

It was already dark by the time he finished his pipe. He went to the door and looked out. There were no stars shining through the boughs of the lilac tree. He heard the rain drip-drip from the branches in the darkness.

He turned, went inside, put on his coat—and began his search, going by train to Dimpleton.

He surprised Letty and Jack on the point of making up their first quarrel.

Elizabeth was not there.

He did not ask if she was there, or give himself away in any way, but sat and chaffed Letty out of a sulky fit.

"Our Elizabeth all right?" quoth Jack.

John said she was all right.

He left them, and called in at Jane Wild's, to her great surprise. No Elizabeth. He walked along to Bullgate Farm, and knocked boldly on the door. Some lingering remnant of jealousy may have been the cause of his going there, or the recollection that Elizabeth had promised to go there, to see Mrs. Hardacre.

"Come in," said Ebenezer.

John went in.

"Just gone," said Ebenezer, heavily, nodding towards the curtained bed.

"Who?" asked John dazedly.

Ebenezer did not notice John's manner.

"The old woman," he said. "They've just laid her out."

There were tears in his eyes.

"Eighty this Christmas," he said, "but somehow—you never think on it. You expect they'll go on being there, like they've allus bin—"

He tried to light an empty pipe.

John handed him some tobacco.

"Tell Elizabeth. She'll be sorry," said Ebenezer.

John said he would.

He went out into the rain, and on towards the lights of Dimpleton. In the waiting-room he remembered that his mother lived in Dimpleton, and that mothers died—like Ebenezer's, but he was getting into agony now about Elizabeth.

Reaching home, the house presented a dreary, dead-house appearance.

"It's Ma-a-ary!" screeched the parrot, as he sat, brooding.

He hurled the tea-cosy at the cage in irritation.

He got off work next day.

In the rain that set in, as though determined to depress him more than ever, he set out on the pilgrimage he recalled to the end of his days. He went round to visit Elizabeth's scattered relations. How scattered they were he discovered on the traunch. And during his progress of disgrace he called on Uncle Ned, in a feeble hope that she might be there.

It was like seeking for a stud he had once lost— when he had looked inside the kettle, though he knew quite well it could not be in there.

Elizabeth was not at Uncle Ned's.

He had tea and buttered pikelets with Uncle Ned and his wife, then trudged along in the grey rain again.

This was on the third day.

He religiously made himself shave then, and he explained to the charwoman that Elizabeth had gone on her holidays, which the charwoman said was going to be a very wet one.

It was on the night of the third day that John began to be obsessed by that closed bedroom door of Elizabeth's. He knew it was impossible that she could be inside that room—but it was the old case of the stud all over again.

At length he burst open the door.

The room, as his common-sense had told him, was empty. He sat down on the edge of the bed, drumming with his heels, and staring at the mirror where Elizabeth had looked at herself as she did her hair.

There was the same feeling of being in a church or some holy place which he had experienced once before in Elizabeth's bedroom.

He got up and opened the wardrobe door, on the half-crazy thought that she could be in there. Not content, he lifted the lid of a hat-box, possibly to see how much headgear she had taken with her. A copybook of the old school-days style stared up at him. It was called "The Monster Wonder"—sixty pages for one penny. John took it out, and opened it.

He sat down on the bed again, and began to turn the pages.

Twice he stopped, and rubbed his eyes.. Once he felt at the dressing-table to persuade himself that he was not really dreaming. But the dressing-table was solid.

Elizabeth had written poetry to him. John did not know much about poetry, but this was not a question of rhyme or metre so much as a recitation that Elizabeth did really care for him, much more than he deserved. He placed the copy-book back into the hat-box very reverently, and his neck was quite red with his blushes. Then, a sudden thought struck him. If Elizabeth had not gone where he could not find her, would she have left such things behind her?

He set out now investigating the bedroom.

He found the box with his own clothes and photograph as an infant.

His mother must have given them to Elizabeth.

"She has gone to your mother," something told him.

But so absurd was the idea that a woman would run from the son to the mother, he decided to go to bed.

Carefully replacing everything, he pulled the door to and locked up the house, trying to make himself sleep.

But the best part of the night was spent in his chair downstairs.

Quite early in the morning he set out for Dimpleton, before the first train ran.

"Fancy any woman treating a man like that—and caring," mused John.

Then he recalled Mary marrying him, and allowing him to kiss her every morning for two years, passing as his wife, but married really to Dick Burnham's ghost.

It was a change, certainly.

He knew what he must do before he reached the village. Elizabeth must never know that he had broken open the door of her room until he was thoroughly compromised.

"Our John," said Mrs. Stone. "I thought he'd be comin' after thee."

For Elizabeth had gone there.

But—the fit of folly was over, and Elizabeth knew that she could never leave John Stone, and—she had kept her secret.

It was after breakfast that John got his chance to speak to Elizabeth alone.

Mrs. Stone had taken them into the pig-stye to let Mary see the pigs, as she did every morning.

"Get ready and come home with me, Elizabeth," said John.

"Pig-ee!" cried little Mary.

"Get ready," said John.

There was silence.

"I worship you, Elizabeth," said John.

"Grunt, grunt," said the pig.

"I will go to get my things," said Elizabeth. "I have left several things at your house, John."

John knew it.

They went by the noon train.

"Does anyone know?" queried Elizabeth, as they approached the house gate.

"Nobody," said John.

He knew that she referred to her having gone away.

They entered the house with its dead fire. John Stone played his trump card.

"There was no need to go away," he said. "I have got my pass for America—going on business, of course. It is there on the dresser. The boat sails Saturday."

This was Thursday.

Elizabeth was trembling.

Then, she made up her mind.

"Don't—don't go—John," she said almost inaudibly.

John went calmly on, raking the fire,

"Do you know—how I may take that—?" he asked.

Elizabeth sat down.

She was paler than ever he had seen her.

She only nodded her head.

"I am—to take it—that way?" queried John.

Elizabeth nodded.

John Stone got slowly up from the fender. He had yet his hat on his head. He took it off, and said merely, "Then I'm hangin' my hat up, 'Lizabeth."

He suited the action to the word.

Then—he tossed the fictitious "pass" to America from the top of the dresser.

She opened it, her limbs shaking yet.

She was standing in a whirl, with her forts of pride about her ears.

It was an advertisement—of Beecham's Pills!

"Oh, John!" said Elizabeth.

She hovered for a moment between tears and laughter—then laughter won. John laughed also— and little Mary laughed, too, in the imitative way of a child.

"What did you pray about—that morning in church?" quoth John, later.

"To be saved—from idolatory," confessed Elizabeth, smiling.

As they took little Mary to bed, John carrying the candle, Elizabeth paused aghast—seeing the door of her own room slightly ajar.

"I went inside—to look in the wardrobe for you," said John.

Elizabeth gave him a look.

"Did you look anywhere else?" she queried.

John shook his head.

Elizabeth looked at him very fixedly.

John lied—lied with his look of absolute honesty.

Elizabeth never knew that he had read those poems, and John found they disappeared entirely.

"Would you believe, it," said John once, as he and Elizabeth and the baby came home, after a day's outing, "that we had both been such fools, Elizabeth, as to go on as we did?"

Elizabeth shook her head smiling.

They passed into the house that was now a home and closed the door gladly on the outer world.

THE END.